The Four Givings

Unlock the Miracles Within

Jeffrey A. Gillespie

Copyright © 2008 by Jeffrey A. Gillespie

To find out more about Jeff Gillespie,
The Four Givings, or additional projects:
You can go to www.4givings.com
Or contact:

Boyer Publishing Company
P.O. Box 121
Temperance, MI 48182-0121
734-625-2044
sales@boyerpublishing.com

All rights reserved. No part of this publication may be reproduced, stored in a retrieval system or transmitted, in any form, or by any means, electronic, mechanical, recorded, photocopied, or otherwise, without the prior permission of the copyright owner, except by a reviewer who may quote brief passages in a review.

Library of Congress Control Number: 2007903221
ISBN: 9780979603082

Printed in the United States of America

Acknowledgements

I would like to extend my appreciation and gratitude to Jo-Ann Langseth, my editor, for the advice and support. Also, thanks to Dawn and Diane for your time, input, and all your hard work. A special thanks to my family for the years of learning and inspiration.

Ten percent of all net earnings the author receives from this publication will be donated to the American Red Cross.

All main characters in this story are fictional except for Buddy Guy. He is real and awesome.

Can you decrypt the hidden message in the book?
The clues are in the poem below.

As is found in the Book of Luke,
A message hidden in the story
There is no need to refute
For the message will bring you glory.
Seven reads of a little finch in a passage,
The vision of bright color is illuminating.
Following phrase, first word, fills the message.
Adding them will leave you joyfully contemplating.
Decrypt the fifth key for it will bring a new birth,
With the Fifth Giving, we'll see peace on earth.

_____ _____

_____ _____ _____

_____ _____

Chapter 1

THE BEDROOM WAS DARK when he opened his eyes. All blinds were closed so that not even the glow of the moon could shine in. A ringing alarm had interrupted his sleep. Keith Kerrigan slammed his hand against the clock radio but the ringing continued as he lay there. The fog cleared and he realized it was the phone. He glanced at the clock — 6:24 a.m. Who would be calling this early? Maybe it was his wife, he thought. She was out of town, staying with her parents in Phoenix, Arizona, for an extended Labor Day holiday. Desperate to stop the annoying sound, he groped for the handset. The familiar pain stabbed him in his stomach. An ulcer, he thought, surely from the stress of everything. He hoped it was only acid reflux. He was much too busy to see a doctor. So he continued to live with it. On the third attempt he found the cradle but the handset was missing. He shot up in bed as the ringing continued. "Where in the hell is that damn thing?" The next ring identified the living room as its probable location. Darting out of the bedroom, he tripped over a basketful of clean clothes in the hallway. His body fell hard onto the carpet as the answering machine picked up from the base station on the nightstand. He ran to the coffee table. The handset was sitting on the newspaper. He quickly picked it up and hit the "Talk" button.

"Hello?"

The clock radio's alarm was triggered by the next digit of time. It was set to play music. Keith returned to the bedroom to turn off the alarm. He sat back down on the bed and pulled the covers over him.

"Daddy, it's me."

It was his daughter, Linda. "You woke me up. Are you all right?"

The testiness in his voice barely registered, for Linda was in an urgent situation. She knew her dad was the only person who could help her through this. She felt his support was close to divine. He'd never failed her before.

"No, Dad, I'm not all right. Something's wrong! I'm scared! I'm at work and there was a huge explosion and…"

"Where are you?"

"I'm at work. There was an explosion and someone said there was a plane that crashed into our building, into one of the twin towers. The office is getting filled with smoke and people are screaming…"

Keith and Jillian's daughter, Linda, had moved to the city two years ago. Fresh out of college, she'd been offered the opportunity of a lifetime to intern at one of the major companies in the World Trade Center. It was a move that he was against. He felt that New York was not the place for his daughter and that she should stay on the West Coast, but he'd never said a word to her.

Helpless, he could hear her crying and then hyperventilating. She began gasping for air. His daughter was trying to breathe! Logically, he reviewed the facts. A large plane had crashed into one of the tallest buildings in the world. Linda worked on an upper floor. He remembered when they helped her move there and seeing the large towers erected into the sky. The hairs on his neck raised in alarm. He knew his daughter was in grave danger.

"Linda. Linda! Listen to me. You have to stop crying and listen. Get out of that building! Go down the stairs. Now! Do not wait for an elevator. Go now!"

"I'm scared! It's getting hot! I don't know what to do!"

Trying to sound calm, yet forceful, Keith directed his daughter. "Listen to me, Linda. Grab a towel or a coat. Then go to the door that leads to the stairs. Use that coat, or towel, or whatever you can get, to open the stairwell door. Open the door slowly. See if the stairs are safe then take them all the way down and get out of the building. Did you hear me? "

An unidentifiable scramble of sounds, mixed with loud human voices, filled his ear. Finally, she spoke. "Yes, I hear you. Is the building on fire? I don't want to move. I'm so scared!"

"Grab a coat or towel," he repeated. "Use that to open the door. Don't touch the railing. Just quickly go down the stairs — but you need to leave now!"

"Daddy, I love you. I don't want to die."

"Linda, I am not going to let you die. You are not going to die. Now listen. Run to the stairs now, Linda. Now! Move now!"

Keith could only hear air howling in his daughter's cell phone. He remembered when he bought that phone. She'd picked it out when she arrived in New York, but the bill was in his name. He thought how he'd cursed the bill every month, but now, every dollar paid was worth it.

"I'm at the door."

"Open it slowly and keep your face away from the door."

Linda opened the door to the stairwell. A gust of wind blew up the stairs from the air evacuation system that forces up fresh, outside air into the stairwell. It was clear of fire but she could smell smoke. She expected to see smoke but instead there was a breeze in the stairwell. She could hear people yelling, and the trample of a herd of footsteps. People from upper floors began to quickly pass by her. A man she knew came through the same door she just passed. Enraged, he told her to get out of the way. She started her descent. It seemed like a thousand voices were echoing off the walls.

"I'm going down the stairs!" She yelled. "There are a lot of people!"

Two firemen passed her as they continued up the stairs in the opposite direction.

"Linda, you're about to lose your signal. Do not stop until you are out of that building. Call me soon as you get out! You are going to be all right, but keep moving! Do not stop for anyone. I love you!"

Static began breaking up the call. Keith could hear yelling in the background as Linda sobbed into the receiver. Never had he felt so helpless. He wrapped his arms around his knees, hugging his chest. The word echoed through the stairwell and into the telephone, "Terrorists!"

Faintly, he could hear her again saying, "Daddy, I love you. I don't want to die! I want to..."

Dead silence overcame the earpiece. In one New York second, the voice was gone, and his heart sank. Keith pushed back the covers and rose to his knees. He reached for the lamp switch.

"Linda! Linda! For God's sake, Linda!"

He yanked the handset away from his ear and looked into the earpiece, as if seeking her there. His scream filled the house.

"LIN-DAAAH!"

His voice shook the receiver, but that was the only sound. He paused, hoping the signal might resynchronize. It never did. Falling back onto the bed, he raised his hands to his face, his torso curling like a baby in the womb.

"I love you. . . I love you, my little girl," he crooned. "My baby girl. I love you. I love you. Oh, my God! What have I done?"

He broke down and sobbed. It was the first time he'd cried since his father's death, one year earlier. It occurred to him that he must stay alert and in control, listening for the phone to ring. He stared at the ceiling, his arm across his forehead, waiting. "God, please let it ring." A thought came to him: The television! A fire at the World Trade Center would be on the news! Keith grabbed the remote, pausing for a moment as he pointed it toward the dresser. Horrible possibilities flashed through his mind as he clicked the power button. The answer stared him in the face. Footage of a commercial airliner crashing into the World Trade Center appeared on the screen. "Tell me what's going on!" screamed in his head. He changed the channel. The same footage appeared. As in a bad dream, from which one cannot escape, each channel showed the horrific black cloud of smoke billowing above one of the towers. I should call Jillian, he thought, but immediately thinking that it is better not to tie up the phone lines. . .

This had to be a dream! Keith closed his eyes and said a prayer. He wasn't a religious man, but it was the only thread of hope that he had. He prayed for twenty minutes, begging for the telephone to ring. When he opened his eyes, the television showed an anchorwoman, stating that a second plane had crashed into the other tower. All hope vanished. His prayer was never answered. The phone call never came. Later, he was to find out that his precious daughter's body could not be found.

James came home a little early from work on September 11th. There was not much productivity that day with everyone glued to the television set. James, an independent consultant in the field of automotive production management, decided not to bill the customer that day. It didn't seem right to bill for his time when nothing was getting done. James left work at 4:00 p.m. but his commute was an hour and a half. He worked in the northern suburbs of Detroit but his house was seventy miles south, just above the Michigan and Ohio state line, in a rural area outside of Toledo. He drove to the consulting engagement every day, passing through the depressed part of the city. At the end of the day, his lonely drive left him feeling stressed and tired.

Pulling into his quarter-mile driveway, James's only thought was to get a hold of his brother, Keith, to make sure his niece, Linda was out of harm's way. He'd called again and again, but there was no answer. He noticed that the sun was starting to set over the trees a little earlier, which is always one of the first signs that summer is over. He was anxious to get back to a TV set. Something new must have developed since the last time he'd watched, two hours before.

James entered the breezeway between his garage and kitchen. The breezeway, lined with four large sets of windows on either side, was a light-green-painted room with green tile and a pool table in the middle. He unlocked the kitchen door, then turned back and threw his keys onto the pool table. Stepping into the kitchen, James caught sight of his stepson Michael, lumbering up the stairs from the basement, a stack of dirty plates in hand. It looked like Michael had just crawled out of bed. James hadn't heard him coming in the night before, so he figured it was another late night. Michael, at the age of twenty-one and still not working, routinely kept late nights, and sleeping past noon was common. He was wearing a pair of blue sweat pants and a grey T-shirt that said, "This Whole Town Must Be High. Aspen, Colorado," They could pass for father and son. Both were over six feet tall, weighed about the same, a good two-thirty, and their eyes were green.

On that infamous day, as most parents rushed home to find their children and hug them with all their love, James's heart felt heavy with something close to hatred. How could this kid sleep all day when thousands of people have died?

"Did you look for a job today?"

Michael ignored the comment as he brushed past his stepfather and put his plates in the sink. James turned as if to catch a response, knowing he would not receive one. Understanding this boy should have been easy for him: at twenty-one, he'd done the exact same things, staying up late, drinking, and getting high. Of course, he would deny it if Michael ever asked. Their lives in high school and their early twenties were actually very similar. If they weren't twenty years apart, they could have been twins.

"Did you know that terrorists crashed planes into the World Trade Center and the Pentagon, killing maybe thousands of people at work?" he asked his stepson in an almost accusatory tone.

"Yeah, I heard it on the radio."

"I should call Keith and make sure that Linda is okay. You know she works at the World Trade Center, don't you?"

"Huh? She does? I thought she was still in college."

James shot his stepson an icy glare. "No. After finishing college, Linda moved forward in her life, unlike some people we know."

On this day, like many days previous, James was looking for a fight. But this time, he wanted some relief beyond verbal sparring.

"What do you mean by that?" Michael asked, trying to sound bored.

"I don't know — you tell me! You never look for a job, you sleep all day, and you party all night. I would think you'd be tired of living like a mole in our basement, that maybe you'd want to move on. Isn't it about time for you to move forward in your life?"

"Hey! Maybe I'm just tired of you on my ass all the time."

"Move the hell out if you don't like it!"

Michael looked incredulous, almost amused. "Why can't you ever be nice?"

All of the frustration and anger that had built up in James over the years suddenly exploded. With closed fist, he struck Michael squarely on the cheekbone. Pain shot from his hand through his body as Michael's head snapped backward. Stumbling back against the refrigerator, James's victim directed the momentum of all his body weight toward James, pushing with a crowbar-like forearm against his stepfather's throat. James retreated back against the kitchen counter. He felt the wetness of the droplets adhering to the sink as Michael kept pushing against him. Seeing the cocked arm and tight fist, he braced for impact. But then – nothing. Michael could not throw the punch. Michael actually loved and respected his stepfather, even though he was verbally mistreated by him. The sight of the fist, still poised in midair, opened a path for James to blast two more punches against the side of Michael's head. Michael screamed "I hate you!" "I feel the same about you." grunted James, side- stepping Michael and grabbing at the young man's throat. James continued to throw punches with his right hand while squeezing Michael's throat with his left. Michael let go of James's shirt and stepped back. He grabbed his head in agony. Michael didn't feel anger. He felt embarrassed and ashamed. Why this man that he looked up to hated him so much was beyond him. Again James advanced with his fists clenched. Like a viper, he lashed out and grabbed Michael's throat again.

"What the hell are you doing?" shrilled a female voice.

Karen had just walked into the kitchen with two bags full of groceries. She quickly set them down and ran between the two. Her husband was beyond yielding. With all of her strength and a quick downward thrust, she pulled James's hand off her son's throat. Still in a rage, James began punching with both hands, striking at his stepson over his wife's head. Michael deflected one of the punches but the force of the blow continued downward, knuckles scraping across Karen's skull. James realized that, for the first time in their marriage, he had struck his wife. She screamed and shoved him with both hands. He raised his hands in a gesture of truce and fell back against the sink. His chest heaved heavily with each breath. Suddenly James knew that, considering the shape he was in, Michael could have taken him. Michael really hadn't fought back. He'd only protected himself.

And yet he taunted, "Are you scared to fight me?"

"No," he replied sadly.

She looked at the tears welling in his eyes and knew they were not from pain. It was the same expression she'd seen since childhood. Even before James was in the picture. Michael's tears were tears of disappointment and sorrow. Karen turned to her husband. He was still leaning against the sink, his nostrils flaring with each breath. His fists were up in the air, in a boxer's pose. The ugliness of the scene overcame her and she began to cry. Seeing his mother's anguish, Michael ran to the telephone. It didn't matter what this madman did to him, but he would never again make his mother cry. No, never again!

"I am calling the police. He hit you. You bastard! I hate you. You're disgusting."

Karen looked at her son but did not stop him. James looked at his wife, wanting to say he was sorry, but the words never came.

"You better go," she instructed. "I don't want you here anymore."

He'd never heard those words before. They were wounding words, words that slashed like a razor across his heart. He stared at her, wanting to say something.

"Go. You need to go."

"Yes, I want to report that my step dad is beating up my mother," Michael began.

James watched Michael speaking in the hall with the cordless handset. He looked at his wife in disbelief. What he saw there was not anger, but torment. Michael repeated the address of the house twice, and then looked at his mother to make sure that the monster was leaving.

"I will always love you, but I will never love him!"

James picked up his keys from the pool table and walked out the door. He didn't look back. Everything that he loved was slipping away. The agonizing finality of what just happened began to set in. Tears poured down his cheeks as he slammed the breezeway door, jumped into his car, and peeled out of the driveway.

For both brothers, Keith and James, years passed before healing could begin.

Chapter 2

"Look again at that dot (the Earth). That's here. That's home. That's us. On it, everyone you love, everyone you know, everyone you've ever heard of, every human being who ever was, lived out their lives. The aggregate of our joy and suffering, thousands of confident religions, ideologies, and economic doctrines, every hunter and forager, every hero and coward, every creator and destroyer of civilizations, every king and peasant, every young couple in love, every mother and father, hopeful child, inventor and explorer, every teacher of morals, every corrupt politician, every 'superstar,' every 'supreme leader,' every saint and sinner in the history of our species lived there - on a mote of dust suspended in a sunbeam."

— Carl Sagan, 1935 - 1996

Keith awoke from his dream and saw icicles hanging from the gutter outside his window. The gray sky began to wake up, lighting the sheer white curtain. The wind blew against the window, rattling the pane. He shuddered under the covers, feeling the cold outside. His teeth were sore from grinding, and his stomach ached. For the past years, it was a morning tradition.

Keith had just arrived in Toledo, Ohio. He'd flown in from San Jose, California, and spent the day visiting his mother and stepfather. That evening he went to a Mexican restaurant with his sister, Diane, and some old high school friends. Keith had left Toledo over twenty years ago. He now lived in Pleasanton, California, and worked as an executive vice president for a large software firm. Having been a Californian for so long, he wasn't used to the snow in Ohio. The buzz around town was that "TomKat" Tom Cruise and his fiancée Katie Holmes had just bought a house in the rich suburb of Toledo called Ottawa Hills in anticipation of their baby. A Toledo native, Katie now joined the roster of other famous Toledo Hollywood actors such as Danny Thomas, Jamie Farr, and Joe E. Brown. Danny and Jamie were both Lebanese and grew up in the same neighborhood. It was rumored that Danny gave Jamie his big break. Joe E. Brown's most famous role was in "Some like It Hot," playing the clown-faced man who was smitten with Jack Lemon, dressed as a woman. The three actors had a city park named after them. Keith wondered if someday, there might be a park named "TomKat."

Staring at his arms resting on the bedding, he noticed that his skin was as white as the sheets. For someone living in California, you sure wouldn't know it from these arms, he observed idly. Keith looked around the spare bedroom in his sister's house. She had purchased the elegant 1940s-era house that year. He glanced down at the hardwood floors with approval.

He could hear Diane getting ready for work in the bathroom, the next room over. Shakespeare, her Old English sheepdog, had broken the seal of the unlatched door and joined the strange man in his room. Panting with excitement, the dog jumped into bed with him. Keith propped himself up on the pillows and petted the man of the house. A few minutes later, Diane came in singing to her brother, and handed him a cup of coffee.

"Is it Starbucks?" he asked hopefully.

"No. It isn't Starbucks. This isn't California. There's not a Starbucks on every corner. It's Folgers."

"Thanks."

She regarded her brother with mock disapproval. "You need to run a comb through that hair."

Keith's hair was blond and receding, and his eyes were green. For his age, he definitely was in shape, and didn't look like a forty-eight-year-old. Both brother and sister were very tall. Diane too, did not look her age. Though Diane is six years older than Keith, she looked at least ten years younger than her age, with a clear and smooth complexion and a shock of healthy brown hair.

"How do you feel this morning?"

"Fair to partly cloudy."

"You had a lot more to drink than I did and I feel like hell."

Keith coughed to clear his morning throat and reached up to grab the coffee. He still tasted the tequila and lime from the margaritas of the night before. Shakespeare rose and spun around on the bed, repositioning his furry hundred-pound body in response to Keith's movement. Streams of the jiggled coffee ran down Keith's hand. He steadied his grip and licked his hand. Diane returned to the bathroom, leaving her brother to lick his wounds.

After taking a few sips to get the coffee down to a manageable level, he gingerly got up, trying not to disturb Shakespeare. The last thing he wanted was his sister's dog jumping up and biting this relatively strange man in the rump. But as feared, Keith barely had one leg over the massive animal when it sprang into action. Shakespeare jumped off the bed, barking manically. A moment later, in an abrupt change of mood, his tail wagged, narrowly missing Keith's coffee cup. Giving up, he set the dripping cup on a nearby table and began to dress. A T-shirt with an unknown Napa Valley winery logo and a pair of blue jeans was his choice for the day. He walked out into the hall. Diane was still in the bathroom, with the door open, finishing the final curls in her hair.

"Hey beautiful, how much longer are you going to be?"

"I'm about done. Are you going to call Critter?"

Critter was her childhood nickname for her youngest brother, James, who was eight years Keith's junior. Growing up, they'd never really hung out together, but this weekend Keith and James had planned a trip. Keith promised his brother that he would treat. He liked to live large and could afford it. Knowing that his brother was having a hard time financially, and was rather frugal, Keith offered to pay for the hotel, meals, and the transportation. To describe James's cheapness as "frugality" was an understatement. The man would waste more in gas than he would save, driving around to different stores just to save a dollar on a product. He was penny smart and pound foolish.

It would be the first time that they did something together since they were kids. In fact, the main reason for Keith's visit was for him and his brother to take a weekend road trip from Toledo to Chicago. James was a big Buddy Guy fan, considering him the best blues guitarist on the planet. Knowing his brother was a fan; Keith had gotten tickets for the last Saturday concert that Buddy was giving at the blues club Legends, before starting his yearly tour. It was the first day in February. James had talked Keith into the trip a few months back. At the time, Keith thought it was a good idea because he really didn't know his younger brother that well. It would be good for him to spend some time and get to know James. They barely spoke on the telephone — a couple of times a year, max.

"I'll call Critter after I shower. I thought I would let him sleep a little longer."

"Okay," said Diane, looking distracted. "I'm running late for work so I need to get out of here. I'm finished in the bathroom and there's more coffee downstairs, but it's not Starbucks. "

"Thanks. I'm good. I'll stop and get a Starbucks before picking up James."

"You're addicted to that stuff!" she gently chided.

"Starbucks and Jim Beam. Because of me, their stocks have done well."

"Well, it's definitely the drug of choice in the new millennium." She smiled warmly.

"Hey, I have to go. Give me a hug. Watch out for Critter. He likes to party a lot. I'll have the front door locked. All you have to do is walk out and it will stay locked. I'll see you Sunday when you get back."

They embraced, kissing each other on the cheek. Keith moved into the bathroom as Diane said her goodbyes to Shakespeare. "Bye, I love you, Sis," he reminded her easily.

"Love you too," Diane called out as she ran down the stairs.

Keith showered and redressed in the same clean underwear, T-shirt, and jeans. He threw a wool sweater over the T-shirt and grabbed his shaving kit. Then he took half of his clothes from the suitcase and dumped them into an overnight bag. He was about ready. A quick shave and a quick brush later, he looked into the mirror and saw that he passed inspection. Keith threw his shaving kit into the bag and zipped it.

In the kitchen, Keith noticed Diane's vitamins out on the counter. He selected a few bottles and removed one capsule from each. He looked for bottled water in the refrigerator but couldn't find any. Diane also had multigrain bread and the toaster out. With the vitamins melting in his hand, Keith put two pieces in the toaster and found peanut butter in the fridge. He thought: Why does she keep this in the refrigerator? Snow fluttered by the kitchen window. The words "We don't" rang in his head. Standing in the kitchen he realized how alone he really was. Not alone in his sister's house. Not alone in the sense that he was in an unfamiliar town, which had changed dramatically since he left. He was alone without his daughter, Linda. Since her death he had isolated himself, away from his friends and even from his wife Jillian. It occurred to him that he had actually become a hermit. The only thing that mattered was his career. At times, he would feel furious at Jillian because it seemed that she was moving on with her life without their daughter. One time, when he came home and found his wife repainting Linda's bedroom, he'd thrown an open gallon of paint at her in a screaming rage. After the incident, they had to repaint the room and replace the bedspread and carpeting. Over the past couple of years, they had definitely grown apart. Ever since their daughter's death on that dark September day, they'd been living with two different agendas. On the positive side, Keith still had the golden touch that had made his career so successful. Financially secure, he estimated his net assets over the million-dollar mark. His business was thriving, the best ever. He was in great financial and physical shape. Two years prior, Keith had a five-bedroom house built in the hills of California. The empty rooms now underscored the fact that his life was empty, and Linda was gone.

    Keith opened several of the unfamiliar kitchen cabinets until he found the glasses. He grabbed an old jelly jar bearing the image of Fred Flintstone. Fred's face had almost worn off from age. Just then, a golden finch landed on the brick ledge outside of the window, and the little bird looked up at Keith, moving its head back and forth. "Do not cry," he said to himself, as tears welled up in his eyes. He leaned over for a closer look. For a brief moment he saw the reflection of his own face in the windowpane. But who was that other person directly behind him? The other reflection looked just like his dad! He quickly turned around but nothing was there. His quest was interrupted by the ringing of the cell phone in his pocket.

"Hello, this is Keith."

"Hi, it's me." It was Jillian.

"Hey, babe, how are you?"

"I just wanted to call before you headed out on your trip. Did you have a good flight?"

"Yeah, the flight was good. How are things at home?"

"I am lonely without you, but good." Her tone darkened. "On the news they said that they are getting close to finding Osama Bin Laden in Afghanistan."

"Well, it's about time they find the person responsible for my daughter's murder," he said tightly.

He took a deep breath and sighed. His blood was beginning to boil. He thought, "I am losing control."

"I'm going to ignore that comment," his wife shot back.

"Yeah, sure! Go ahead and act like it never happened. Keep your head in the sand."

"You think I forgot? I wish you could understand what I'm going through."

"What you are going through? Try to think what it's put me through. I was on the phone when she died and I couldn't do a damn thing about it."

A long silence passed. Only breathing could be heard. Jillian thought of another tender subject that needed to be discussed, but had been mutually avoided.

"So what did the doctor say?"

"What doctor?" Keith drew a blank.

"Your doctor's appointment before you went to the airport. What did the doctor say?"

"Not much. The test results aren't back yet. He gave me some pills to take for my stomach. That's about it."

"Oh? I'm surprised it's taking so long." She sounded suspicious. "So, when do you know the results?"

"I do not know! I'm supposed to call back. Do you understand? I just don't know!"

"Look, I love you, Keith. And I know that you love me, but you don't live life anymore. You walk around here like a zombie. Most nights you don't even say a word. What do you want me to do?"

"I have to go. Bye." Keith pressed the END button before she could even answer. He looked outside. The bird launched into flight, scared off by the moving reflection. He watched the bird flap its wings as it rose into the sky and out of sight. Keith felt envy. He was alone. Deep down, he knew it was his fault. He thought back to that fateful day in September. He could still hear his daughter's panicked voice. He wanted to punch something. He looked around his sister's kitchen but there was nothing to hit. Keith was usually a peaceful man, but there were moments like this when he wanted to kill the people responsible. He could feel his heart fluttering. The acid in his stomach burned.

Like an alarm clock, the burn reminded him that he needed to take the medicine that his doctor had recently prescribed. He reached into his pocket and pulled out the bottle, then filled the jar with tap water and threw the pills and vitamins in the back of his mouth. He gulped it all down and refilled the glass.

His gaze fell on the window shelf above the kitchen sink. There was an ornament, still left out from Christmas. It was a ceramic figurine of Santa Claus sitting in a rocking chair as he studied a list of boys' and girls' names. At his feet was a small, round bowl. In the bowl were a well-used S.O.S. pad and a small piece of soap. Keith thought back to when he was a boy and pictured the Santa Claus that used to visit him. He remembered that Santa had the most beautiful ice-blue eyes, just like his dad. Standing alone in his sister's kitchen he reflected on the realization that Santa Claus was his father. He missed his dad. He'd passed away in the summer of 2000. When he wasn't sure what to do, he would always call his dad for advice. "Dad, where did I go wrong?" he spoke to the still room. He paused, but the answer never came. Keith broke his trance by downing the rest of the water and picking up Diane's telephone. It was time to call his brother. It was time to go to Chicago.

Chapter 3

THE FROST WAS ON the window as the sun started to peek over the snow. James Kerrigan rolled in his bed to other side where his wife had lain earlier that morning. She had already gone to work and he was still asleep. He pulled the covers up and realized, as the warm air from under the blanket escaped, that he was sweating. He looked up at the ceiling, then over to Karen's side. James was temporarily out of work. Or, shall we say, he didn't work. James was an over-paid consultant in the automotive industry. He project-managed large assembly reconstruction projects. When he was working, James made more than six figures. Now, for the first time, he was bringing in no income and felt that his career was at a dead-end, just like the Detroit auto giants. He really wanted to get out of the industry but didn't know what he could do. Even though it was good money, he'd been very careful about how he spent it, knowing that the gravy train could stop any day. It finally did.

Sunlight illuminated the ice on the window. Under the covers was comfortably warm, and he was certain the house was going to be cold when he got out of bed. He lay there, dreading his existence.

Ring.... Ring...RING....

"Hello? Yeah, I'm up. Yeah, I'm up. Okay, I'll see you in a bit.

James's feet hit the floor as he stretched his arms forward, "Ahhhrrrrruhrrhhh." He stood up and shook from the tingling cold air. He wrapped his robe around him, then marched into the kitchen and opened up a cupboard door. The coffee grounds smelled good. He filled up the coffee pot with water and sprinkled a pile of coffee into the filter. The daily coffee process was started. What an accomplishment. He pressed the ON button for the remote control of the small television on the kitchen counter, and then reached into the cabinet for his prescription bottle. Counting out enough pills for the trip, he swallowed one and threw the remaining pills into a plastic sandwich bag. The prescription was for high blood pressure and high cholesterol. James had recently visited his doctor because of shortness of breath and heart palpitations. The tests came back and James's party was pronounced finito. He was instructed to start an exercise regimen and eliminate the junk food.

Once the television warmed up and The Morning Show appeared on the screen, James took off his robe and headed for the bathroom. He stood in his underwear, balefully inspecting his belly in the mirror. He felt old. He was an inch taller than his older brother, but was more overweight. The big belly hung over, causing his underwear band to fold in half. His blonde hair was receding, and combed to the left. In his younger years, James had been in great shape. But over the past couple of years, because of his work schedule and improper eating habits, the weight poured on. He liked to think that it was more because he was comfortable. He loved his wife Karen, even though he had had rough times with his stepson; they patched everything up after the fight between James and Michael.

Anxiety washed over him as he realized that it was Friday, a workday, and the first time that he didn't have to let anyone know that he was taking the day off. It was the first time that he felt scared about his career. Even though his resume showed quite an impressive history, he wasn't sure if his technical skills were current. He knew that it could take up to two years to get another contract that would pay as well. If he went to work for a company, he would make a lot less. James's ego was wounded. He loved showing off to his friends and now he didn't know where to go. He felt that unlike his friends, who were always afraid to take risks, he, James, was quite daring, and the risks had paid off. But now he felt like a failure. Success that used to come so easily was now eluding him. For the past few months he'd diligently looked for work, but with no luck. For the first time in his life, James felt unworthy. "What a farce!" he spat at his reflection. He cursed the trip to Chicago, now seeing it as a waste of money. Even though his brother was picking up the hotel tab, James knew there would be additional costs that he just couldn't afford. He really didn't want to go at all, but it was a long time since he had seen his brother. He thought of various excuses to get out of going as he sipped his coffee. He thought some more as he took his shower. Too late – none of the ideas would work.

With only a towel wrapped around his waist, and hanging onto the two ends, James walked into the breezeway. The blinds were all open, letting the sunlight stream in, and a great view awaited anyone who happened to pull into the driveway. He tapped the ON button of the stereo amplifier and tuner and music instantly blared through the speakers

James wondered whether he should talk about the job situation, or the lack thereof, with his brother. He decided not to. It was just too embarrassing. He'd always looked up to and compared himself to his older sibling. Yes, he'd definitely fallen short of his brother's expectations. Conversations they'd had over the phone usually revolved around the subject of what makes someone successful, how to make tons more money, and how they were both conquering the world. His brother seemed to have hit the mark, but James felt he could barely conquer getting dressed. The last couple of years he'd been reading about spirituality and metaphysics. Always searching for "the answer," he'd never had the patience to reflect on anything long enough to derive any insight.

As he drank his second cup, he walked back to the bedroom and let the towel drop onto the floor. Grabbing a leather backpack from the closet, he threw in socks, underwear, and two T-shirts, one with Buddy Guy on the front. Two sweaters; two pair of jeans; and a black, button-down shirt featuring bright red Rolling Stones lips, which will work for casual wear. A pair of Dockers and a gold-and-black, tweed blazer would probably do for more formal events. His weekend wardrobe was complete. Now into his third coffee, he listened to the national morning show. The story was about restitution for the enslavement of blacks: should we compensate black Americans for the subjugation and dehumanization of their ancestors? James thought: how can that be? I shouldn't have to pay! I didn't live in the South hundreds of years ago. I am not the heir of a plantation owner. That's crazy. Why should I apologize? I listen to black music. I listen to the blues. He grabbed the remote control just as the announcer concluded that yes, restitution should definitely be made.

"I'm not prejudiced! So why should I owe them anything?" he sputtered between sips.

The next story was about casualties in the Iraq war. The anchorwoman was detailing a road bomb incident that killed three Marines in Iraq.

"There are young men and women, innocent children, dying because of a lie! When are we going to learn?"

He turned off the TV. James thought back to a time when he was about nine years old. It was his first exposure to racism. His mother and sister had taken him to a shopping center. He asked if he could go by himself to the hobby store, three storefronts down from the large department store where his mother and sister were going. In those days, abduction was never a concern. He was allowed to go for ten minutes, but instructed to get right back after that. They agreed on a location in the store where he could find them. Inside the hobby store, two black boys around his age were playing with an older teenaged boy. James proceeded to buy what he needed — a pack of rocket engines and some spray paint for the newly constructed rocket he'd built at home. As James exited the store, one of the younger boys came up to him very confrontationally, two inches from his face, and asked him, "What did you call me?" James replied, "Nothing." The boy shot back, "Yeah you did! You called me nigger!" It was the first time that James had heard the N word from a black person. In those days it was common to hear it from friends' fathers, though he couldn't recall any time that his own father had used the word. To his father, it was an epithet that none of his children should use. James was afraid of his father, so he'd automatically obeyed. He knew for a fact that he had not so much as whispered the word. With no further ado, the boy landed a right hook across James's jaw. Then he shoved him hard on the chest with both hands. James fell to the sidewalk. He quickly got up and ran away as his attacker returned to his older brother, laughing triumphantly. This was just a couple of years after the Detroit riots, when Toledo, the next closest city, had its own conflict. Angry and humiliated, James wanted to cry. He held back the tears as he went into the department store. His mother and sister never noticed, or never mentioned, the swollen redness on his cheek. And James never shared the incident with anyone. He could still feel the pain in his jaw, and the bewildering shamefulness of it. He could never understand the hatred that the boy felt toward him. For James, who could barely say "Boo!" — Let alone utter such a degrading name, especially the one word his father had commanded him to never say — the memory was an incomprehensible nightmare.

James snapped back to the present. The painful recollection reminded him that he needed to get back in tune. His latest spiritual adventure was meditation. He grabbed his yoga mat and blue foam block and lowered his heavy frame onto the mat. James had started studying yoga a few months before. Karen had suggested it to relieve his stress. Sometimes he suspected that he might be an anal-retentive, type-A, ass; yoga, he hoped, would be the antidote. Though usually upbeat and positive, he could also be easily swayed to the dark side of anger and hatred. James loved to argue. He thought that he should have been a lawyer because he could match wits with anyone.

"Oohhhmmmm," he intoned, taking a deep breath.

"OOOOOOOOOOHHHHHHHHHHMMMMMMM-MMMMMMM." The inhalation filled his abdomen to the bursting point. "Ah, that crap doesn't work," he gasped, taking note of his discomfort. James continued to breathe. He tried to focus on nothing but his breath. Yoga teaches that by clearing the mind, one may reach a state of perfect harmony between body, mind, and spirit, which can lead to self-realization. James wasn't there yet. In fact, he was far from the level of a Buddha. His mind stayed busy on his current situation. Nothing could break the uneasiness in his mind. He decided to launch some affirmations.

"Namaste, I see the God in you."
"I am powerful!"
"I am the presence of strength and power!"
"I am abundant!"
"I am prosperous!"
"I am rich!"
"Namaste."
"I…ah hell, I'm out of coffee."

He'd read books on spirituality, studied mind-power, and tried practicing Eastern religions, all to no avail. That was the extent of James's journey to enlightenment. The last cup of coffee was darker from sitting in the pot most of the morning. He didn't take the time to add milk. He brushed his teeth and took his vitamins, then donned a pair of jeans and a Jimmy Page and Robert Plant T-shirt. He slipped a U.S. Open sweatshirt over the T-shirt. James was ready. Keith would be showing up any minute. They'd been planning this trip ever since their father died.

He strode into the living room to look outside. He knew what he would see and that the sight would increase his self-induced irritation. James drew open the drapes and saw a snowmobile in the front yard, atop a mound of snow. Michael had been riding the snowmobile the day before while James was away for the day. He'd left the sled in the front yard. Michael would ride around James's five-acre property as long as James was gone. Although the house was set back from the road and no neighbors could see the snow machine, this infuriated James. He thought: Michael is still leaving crap all over. He makes my house look like a pigsty all the time!" Trembling with rage, he marched down the stairs to Michael's bedroom door. Opening it, he yelped, "Get that piece of crap..." The bed was made. Michael must have stayed out all night. He peeked into the bathroom just to make sure, but the room was empty. James noticed that the room was clean. He looked back into the bedroom. It was the same. The bedroom was clean! James figured Karen must have cleaned it. But where the hell was he now? He ran back upstairs, frustration festering inside of him. James was always looking for excuses for getting mad at Michael. Everything was Michael's fault. He picked up the telephone and called his wife to vent, which was a weekly ritual.

"What are you doing?" he curtly began.

"Well, I'm in the midst of an issue. I have a network down at one of our plants."

Like his brother Keith, Karen was in the Information Technologies field, or better known as IT. She was in charge of over a hundred computer networks at different plant locations for a large manufacturer.

"Well, I just called to ask you to tell Michael to get his piece of crap out of my front yard. I'm sick of him trashing the place. I went down to his bedroom but he must have never come home."

"He got up with me and is already out working. I'll call him when I get a minute," she said wearily.

"No, that's not good enough. This is bullshit. It always seems that we're picking up after him. When is he going to find a real job? I'm tired of you wiping his ass all the time," he thundered.

Karen waited for James to run out of complaints before responding. This strategy was developed over the years. Just let him vent, she thought.

"Okay, James. I will drop everything that I'm doing and call him."

"Also, tell him he needs to be paying rent," he put in sourly.

"Why don't you call him and tell him? I'm busy."

"I don't want to call him. I will just go off on him. You handle it, all right?

In James's mind, keeping the peace meant not confronting Michael face to face. It was easier to bitch at Karen and let her deal with him. She always had to play the mediator.

"Let me ask you again — why is it that you're always looking for something to bitch about when it comes to my son? As far as his job is concerned, he has been working and saving his money, so you should be proud of him. All he wants, you know, is for you to be proud of him. He's looking into some technical schools and some two-year colleges. He could use your support. Why don't you worry about that instead of worrying about a dumb snowmobile in the yard? All he wants is your approval. But all you do is criticize and try to make him feel guilty."

"If history is any indication, you know that he will fail at that and we'll end up throwing money away, trying to make it work for him, just as we always do."

"He isn't asking for money. He wants to do it himself. All he's looking for is your advice. I don't know why you're always condemning him when he so much looks up to you." She took a deep breath to make her final appeal. "Yes! After all you've put him through, he actually looks up to you! Why? I don't know, but he does. You aren't working. This will be a good time to help him."

James laughed humorlessly. "Sure! The only help he's looking for is money. You'll throw money at him and he'll waste it. I'm too busy to help."

"Whatever you think, James. You've always been too busy since he was eight. Well, I have to go. I have a plant down. Go to Chicago. I hope you have a good time. I hope you'll think about how you've been treating me and Michael. I feel like I'm always walking on egg shells around you. I don't need it. You need to take a look at yourself and figure out how to make you happy. I love you. I have to go."

"Bye," he said forlornly.

He thought about his love for Karen, but it was times like this that he wished it was just him and her. No kids. He studied the picture on the dresser of Karen, Michael, and himself standing in front of a Christmas tree. This pre-made family deal was a giant rip-off! The picture was the first Christmas that Karen and Michael met his family. He remembered when Karen and Michael met his dad, and how Michael thought he looked like Santa Claus because of his balding head and whitish beard. Then James remembered another ghost of Christmas past. It was the following year, and his mother and stepfather were visiting them at the new house they had just moved into. Karen was making dinner for them. That year James, Karen, and Michael picked out a freshly cut Christmas tree from a nearby lot. The tree was having a hard time standing that Christmas. It had fallen several times, and each time James would try to prop it back up. He would position the tree differently, thinking it was more secure. Michael was around nine years old. He'd helped his mom hang the lights and ornaments, and wanted to show them off to his step-grandparents. James didn't bother to help. He was always too busy. That evening, in front of James's parents, Michael crawled under the tree to plug in the lights and the tree came crashing down on top of him. The scene in his head made James very uncomfortable. He remembered how he chastised Michael in front of Karen and his parents. James replayed the event with clarity. The yelling had become screaming. He witnessed it all as it played in his head. He hadn't checked to see if Michael was all right. He felt like Scrooge, being taken around to different Christmases of his past. The hurt on Michael's face made James feel for him. It was the first time in a long time that he felt sorry. How ashamed and frightened Michael must have felt at that moment! James began to cry. He wondered if he was crying because he missed his dad or because of his frustration at not finding work. The tears poured down James crinkled face just as the tears had flowed down Michael's young face that day the tree fell. Through his crying bubble of spit, James whispered, "I'm sorry."

Chapter 4

KEITH AND JAMES HAD grown up eight years apart. Their parents, Ron and Susan Kerrigan, first separated when Keith was fifteen and James was seven. Their parents tried to make it work when Ron's restaurant business went bankrupt, but the strain proved too great. The boys could remember when their Uncle Bob came over to see their dad. Ron was penniless, sleeping on the couch. He broke down before his brother. It was the first time Keith and James had seen their father cry. Soon after, he suffered a nervous breakdown. Once he was emotionally better, Ron and Susan divorced. This scenario became the boys' drive for success, vowing to never go through what their father did.

Keith and James had loved their dad very much. He was not a faithful husband, nor was he a sharp businessman. What he was to them, and to anyone their father met, was an inspiration. Ron had a way of seeing the best in people. It was as if he was seeing beyond the frame and skin, through the eyes, and into the true spirit of his fellow humans. Years after the divorce, he had expressed the one lesson that still rang in their ears: "Never let the love of family to be broken; it is the core of your life. If it unravels, everything else will fall apart."

Being eight years older, Keith had already moved out and was doing his own thing while James made his way through high school. But Keith was a major influence on his little brother. In high school, Keith bought James books. The books were mostly inspirational or motivational in nature.. If it weren't for those self-help books, James would have probably ended up in jail, or strung out on heroin, or crack. He'd grown up around drugs and did his share of experimenting. After graduating from school in 1985, James moved to Denver and lived out west for six years before moving back to his hometown with Karen and Michael. Two things saved James's life — the books, and Karen. James fully acknowledged that. Before moving to Colorado, he and his friends were heavy into drugs. He left Toledo to escape his environment. His best friend eventually became a heroin addict. It could just as easily have been him.

Over the years, the brothers had become avid readers of motivational and inspirational authors. They'd invested in just about every "get rich quick" book and tape. During phone conversations, the two would debate authors' views, contrasting them with their own philosophies. That was the only thing they had in common. Both were searching for that pot of gold. It had become their common ground.

James took a sip of the remaining shot of coffee. It was cold, but most of the sugar was at the bottom, so the final sip tasted sweet on his tongue. Now eager for his brother's arrival, he watched as tentative snowflakes fell to the ground.

One of his favorite songs by The Talking Heads came on the CD player.

Everyone is trying to get to the bar.
The name of the bar, the bar is called Heaven.
The band in Heaven, they play my favorite song.
Play it one more time, play it all night long.

Oh, Heaven...
Heaven is a place...

A place where nothing...
Nothing ever happens...
...when this kiss is over, it will start again.
It will not be any different;
it will be exactly the same.
It's hard to imagine, that nothing at all,
could be so exciting, could be so much fun.
Oh, Heaven...
Heaven is a place...
A place where nothing...
Nothing ever happens...

James remembered what Keith had gone through when his daughter died in the World Trade Center. Like most people, he remembered exactly where he was and what he was doing when he heard the news. It was just hours before that terrible fistfight he'd had with Michael. He'd been at work when Karen called him with the news. It occurred to him now that despite the fight, it had actually been the horrific events of 9/11 that started the healing between him and Karen, eventually bringing them back together. Somehow, that episode had quickly faded from memory and she'd forgiven them both. After the fight, James had spent the night in a hotel and returned the very next day.

Keith pulled into the driveway in a dark blue Ford Explorer — obviously rented, James thought. Keith stepped out of the vehicle and stretched his arms in the air while holding a coffee mug. He'd forgotten how cold it could be. He thought about back home, in California, where the weather was so much milder. He noticed that he was standing on ice. The coldest day I ever knew was a summer day in San Francisco, he thought. He ran it through his mind again. Is that right? He was trying to quote a line from a scene in the movie, 48 Hours. He pictured Nick Nolte with a red scarf around his neck. He tried to remember the phrase. It was something like: The coldest day I ever knew was a day in July in San Francisco." But who was the girl who starred in that movie, Nick Nolte's girlfriend in the movie? Keith searched his memory in vain.

James grabbed his overnight bag and turned off the stereo. Keith was standing outside the driver's side door, waiting to greet his brother. He raised his Starbucks mug in greeting.

As his brother drew near, Keith opened his arms. James walked up and dropped his bag on the ground. "Namaste. How's it going?" James said, warmly embracing him. If a stranger saw them on the street, he would be able to tell that Keith and James were brothers. Keith was a little thinner but you could definitely tell they were brothers. Both were blond, with receding hairlines, green eyes, and above-average height.

James opened the back door and threw his bag in, then jumped into the passenger seat. Keith already had his seatbelt fastened. The car backed up enough to pull around the circular driveway, and then headed for the highway.

"It's about two hundred and fifty miles to downtown Chicago. I hope we don't run into bad weather on the way," Keith said ominously, getting the conversational ball rolling.

"Don't worry about the mule going blind — just load the wagon!" expressed James.

"What?" James's joke had definitely not computed.

"It's just a saying. You know, don't worry — just drive, and we'll get there eventually."

James reached back, leaning over the armrest. He unzipped his pack and pulled out a black nylon case. Keith looked over to see what his brother had retrieved. It was a CD holder. James flipped through the selections until he found a local favorite, and then slid the CD into the slot. Keith lifted a Starbucks coffee from the safety of the cup holders and handed it to his brother.

"Oh, thanks. Take the next right," James directed. "I'll tell you how to get onto US-23. That will take us close to the I-80/90 turnpike."

Keith turned to look at his brother. "So, how have you been? You look good."

The crowd on the CD began to roar as the music started. It was Bob Seger playing an Ike and Tina Turner song.

> *There's a church house, gin house,*
>   *Schoolhouse, outhouse*
> *On U.S. 19,*
> *Hey, the people keep the city clean…*

James groaned. "I am fat as hell, I have no job, and my life is miserable. Besides that, everything is fine. So, how are you?"

Keith jumped right in. "Jesus said, 'By words ye are justified and by your words ye are condemned.' Joking about being fat or poor becomes your reality. The subconscious mind doesn't know the difference between a joking comment and reality. You can joke yourself into unhappy experiences, did you know that, Bro? Proverbs 18:21 tells us that 'Death and life are in the power of the tongue.'"

"Great! I get a Sermon on the Mount all the way to the Illinois line. How are you doing, Keith?"

"Work is going great. I've been running a bit and watching what I eat. Doctor's orders, you know."

"Are you seeing a doctor? Is there something wrong?" James probed.

"Aw, it's really nothing," Keith said calmly. "Who is this on the CD?"

"Bob Seger and the Silver Bullet Band, Live Bullet." On the CD, Bob yelled over the cheering crowd.

"... As I told everyone last night, I was reading *Rolling Stone* where they said, 'Detroit audiences are the greatest rock-'n'-roll audiences in the world.' I thought to myself, shit, I've known that for ten years!"

"Bob Seger is the best!" James enthused. "He recently got inducted into the hall of fame. You don't mind if I play D.J. on the trip, do you? I brought a bunch of CDs.

"No, that's fine," Keith said cheerfully.

They continued their introductions, and small talk. James occasionally would tell Keith to turn here or there by pointing to the left or right.

"So, how is work for you?" Keith asked.

"I still haven't found any work." James replied.

"Something will come up."

"Well, I have been thinking about opening up a cat house."

"Are you talking prostitution?"

"Yes, and you can help. While I am out finding the girls, you can stay back at the shop and do everything by hand."

James cracked a smile and tapped on the dash to make a short drum roll sound. It was his way of dealing with issues. Make a joke out of it. Keith looked over, paused a second, then shook his head, "Two hundred comedians out of work and you are looking for a job."

James sipped on his coffee, "I'm here all week. I got a million of them."

"How are Karen and Michael?" Keith inquired.

"Karen is fine. She's been really busy at work." He paused, sighing. "To be perfectly frank, though, Michael drives me crazy. He has all these big ideas."

"Sounds like you!" Keith shot back.

"At least my ideas are attainable. So how's Jillian?"

"She is good." With both hands on the wheel, Keith bobbed his head up and down, confirming his answer. James put his feet up on the dash, sporting a big grin. He lifted the cup of coffee and removed the lid to take a big gulp. Keith, forgetting about the winter landmines in the cold Midwest, drove the vehicle into a six inch deep pot hole. The passenger tire slammed down into the crater then bounced out without a bruise. The steaming coffee erupted over James right hand, streaming down to his pants.

"Damn it!"

Keith turned the steering wheel to head down the US-23 entrance ramp. He looked over at his still shaken brother.

"Are you all right?"

"Oh hell, it hurt! But I'll be OK." He rubbed his scalded hand.

"It looks like it really hurts badly!" Keith said, seeing the red hand. "I think there's a towel in my black bag back there."

"Thanks," James said, reaching back and grabbing something blue that appeared to be a towel.

"No, not that. That's my Notre Dame sweater." He hoped that James hadn't begun to use it.

James opened the blue sweater and saw the words "Notre Dame" and the little Fighting Irish mascot scripted in gold below its left shoulder. He made a feeble attempt to fold the sweater but then gave up and threw it back. He reached farther behind the driver's seat and grabbed the towel, quickly wiping his face and hands, then gingerly dabbing at his crotch area. From US 23, they exited and drove another mile before the car turned into the entrance for I-80/90, the Ohio Turnpike. The car was quiet except for the yearning strains of The Moody Blues.

I'm looking for someone to change my life
I'm looking for a miracle in my life
And if you could see, what it's done to me
To lose the love I knew

Could safely lead me to
The land that I once knew
To learn as we grow old
The secrets of our soul.

Keith drove west across the Ohio plains. As they drove down the expressway, the houses disappeared and only a few farmhouses could be seen in the distance. The sun gleamed over the snowy, white blanket that covered the farmers' fields. The road, like a black ribbon, split the blanket of snow in half. It was a beautiful day even though the temperature was a balmy twenty-three degrees. The sun shined brightly. The leafless trees stood motionless in the distance, their ice-covered branches making them look like they were made of glass. James stared out the window. There was a red barn in the distance, its rooftop laden with snow. Horses munched at their hay on the mucky ground. James slipped on his Gargoyle sunglasses which wrapped tightly around his eyes. He looked like a cross between Tom Hanks and Dan Aykroyd. It didn't take long for the boredom to set in. Keith thought of things he could ask his brother. Keith tried to put a new spin on his question. "I know I just asked, but how are Karen and Michael doing? I mean, what are they up to?"

"Like I said, Karen's fine. Michael drives me nuts." He shook his head and raised his eyebrows, trying to convey his distress.

"Okay. Have you gotten any leads on a consulting job?" Keith asked gently.

"No. Not one. I'm thinking about becoming a bartender."

"That's inspiring. Or should I say, aspiring?" A little levity might downplay James's difficulties, he figured.

James stared back out the window. Keith thought about what his brother said. James could see his reflection in the window as his head rested on it. Twenty minutes passed as quickly as the white stripes zipping by on the highway. James didn't know what to say to his brother. The last time he saw him was at Linda's funeral. James hesitated, trying to find the right words.

"Are you and Jillian doing okay since, you know, Linda's death? I mean, if you don't want to talk…"

"No, it's okay. I guess we're functioning. Lately, we don't talk about what happened because every time we do, we start crying to the point where we can't stop. So we don't say anything."

James studied his brother's face. Keith continued to drive with both hands on the wheel. His face was scrunched, trying to fight the glare from the snow and the thoughts coming into and out of his head.

"I think of her, Linda, every day. But sometimes I feel guilty that maybe I don't think of her enough, or that I haven't done anything to avenge her death." His lips pressed together in an angry hard line.

"What do you mean?" James hadn't understood one word.

"I feel I should never have let her go to New York. I feel that I should kill or hurt someone who was responsible for it to make up for it. I just want the pain to go away."

James could hardly believe his ears. "Wow, that doesn't sound like you at all! So you think that by hurting or killing someone that will help?"

"Yes, of course!" Keith shot back. "If I can avenge her death, then I am not letting her down. You don't know what it's like. I never hated like I do now. I hate those people. I want them to die. I want the terrorists to pay by an agonizing death. I hate them or anyone like them… I mean —"

"No, you're right!" James cut in. "I don't know how you feel. I can't imagine."

"No, you can't. It's hell. It's a living hell."

"So you hate all those people being Muslims?"
"All of them," Keith said with stony emphasis.
James looked thoughtful. "You're probably right. I'm sure they hate us just as much, considering we slaughtered half their population during the Crusades."
"What? Are you defending them? Are you saying revenge is why my daughter is dead? What the hell do you mean by that? That we deserve this? Damn it. You know what? Screw you."
James didn't know what to say next so he fell silent. He escaped the confrontation by staring back out the window across the snowy fields. Keith's stomach burned once again. He paid no heed to Bob Dylan's wisdom, which had started up almost on cue.

How many roads must a man walk down
Before you call him a man?
Yes, 'n' how many seas must a white dove sail
Before she sleeps in the sand?
Yes, 'n' how many times must the cannon balls fly
Before they're forever banned?
The answer, my friend, is blowin' in the wind;
The answer is blowin' in the wind.

How many times must a man look up
Before he can see the sky?
Yes, 'n' how many ears must one man have
Before he can hear people cry?
Yes, 'n' how many deaths will it take till he knows
That too many people have died?
The answer, my friend, is blowin' in the wind;
The answer is blowin' in the wind.

Chapter 5

"So tell me," Keith began, changing the subject, "why is there so much conflict between you and Michael?"

James snorted and shifted in his seat. "I don't want to waste your time."

"You're not wasting my time. I care. So what is it between you two?" Keith persisted.

"He is always an embarrassment ... getting into trouble..."

"He was in trouble with the law?" Keith couldn't imagine Michael as a law-breaker.

"No. He was just in trouble around the house."

"In other words, you are yelling at him all the time, right?" Keith glanced at his brother to see if he'd stepped over the line. James looked comfortable enough, so he went on. "So how is he an embarrassment to you?"

"It's just that I'm always worried about what people think of us letting him still live at home. They must think we're fools."

"I remember when I used to push Linda to the limit, just to show my friends what a great parent I was. But then I lost my daughter and realized that what others think doesn't matter. What matters is what our kids think."

Keith could see that he and James were in entirely different places. He remembered what it was like to always be putting on a show. Perhaps now he could help his brother.

"But aren't you enabling them to be dependent on you, and lazy?" James blurted.

Keith sighed. "I would rather have my kids dependent on me than hating me. Wouldn't you?"

"I just want him out of the house."

Keith decided to be direct. This is no time for diplomacy, he mused. "Look, if I were you, I wouldn't expect the bad all the time. I bet if you showed Michael some interest, something genuine and personal, he'd get motivated. Kids are scared to face their futures. If you constantly beat them down, they won't have the courage to step forward. I guarantee that if you showed him support and quit worrying about what the family or your friends are thinking, he'd move on. It just takes some kids longer than others."

James looked out the window in silence. The sunlight shined off the mounds of snow and glittered from the icy branches. Time rolled by with small talk about friends from school and stories about kids in the neighborhood. As they drove up to the last toll booth along the Indiana Turnpike, they could see the smokestacks of the steel mills of Gary, Indiana.

"Didn't Gary beat out Detroit for being the murder capital of the world?" Keith wondered out loud.

"No," said James, who was up on such statistics. "I think this year it's Washington, D.C., or Baltimore. I think Gary was the winner last year. Remember, don't worry about the mule going blind — just load up the wagon."

"Whatever that means."

They rode along in silence as they stared at the mile long factories and smoke stacks. He popped a CD into the player. Buddy Guy – perfect.

I got a job at a steel mill, I'm shucking steel just like a slave
Five long years, every Friday y'all I went straight home yeah,

I went straight home with all my pay
Yes, I've been mistreated.
Then you got to, you got to know just what I'm talking about.
Lord, I work five long years for one woman,
and she had the nerve to kick me out.

Chapter 6

THE SILENCE WAS BROKEN once they'd crossed the state line into Illinois. Keith noticed that the fifty-cent tolls lay straight ahead. He reached into his pockets, feeling for quarters. James glanced at his brother reaching for change and then looked forward. The yellow barriers were coming up in front of them. Traffic began to slow down. In Chicago, it seems that every few miles you have to pull up to a toll booth and throw two quarters into a bucket to lift the gate. All the cars scrambled for the best lane position.

"Do you need some quarters? James asked.

"I'll take them if you have any."

James pulled out a pack of Juicy Fruit gum, then reached back down and found a couple of quarters. Keith started to slow down as James removed the gum wrapper. Keith scrunched his forehead and squinted, trying to assess the situation. Together, they scrounged a couple dollars' worth of quarters.

James dropped his quarters into Keith's hand. "Gum?" he offered.

"No thanks. That should be enough quarters to get us through."

"Look!" James called excitedly. "You can see the skyline of downtown Chicago. Wow that is huge!"

The buildings shot straight up out of the ground like a dark blue wall, slicing the gray sky. Bands of expressway poured into the city from all directions.

"What's the exit?" asked the driver.

"Congress Parkway. It's up quite a way. I'll tell you when you need to get over to the right." James felt suddenly bored. "It's time to change our music to electrified Chicago blues! It's the one, the only, Muddy!"

The gypsy woman told my mother before I was born,
"You got a boy child's comin', goin' be a son of a gun."
He gonna make pretty womans jump and shout,
Then the world gonna know, what's it all about. I'm him...

James continued, "Muddy Waters started rock n' roll, not Elvis. Most rockers of the sixties and seventies, listened to Muddy Waters, Robert Johnson, and Howlin' Wolf, the great Chicago bluesmen, than they listened to Elvis or Sinatra. The greatest blues players, definitely is Buddy Guy, Albert King, and Luther Allison. Greatest rock n' roll band of all time is 'The Who'. And the greatest 80's dance tune was 'Safety Dance'.

Keith looked down at the fuel gauge. "Remind me to get gas before we leave on Sunday."

"Okay."

They drove for about another twenty minutes until James saw the sign for the Congress Parkway exit. Once on the parkway, they drove through the tunnel under the post office building, and then through another tunnel under the Chicago Mercantile Exchange Building. The car crossed Wabash Avenue, and passed under the elevated train tracks.

James swiveled around, tapping against the passenger window. "Buddy Guy's Legends blues club is right down the street," he added excitedly, thinking about the concert they were about to see that night.

They passed the Congress Hotel and moved into the left-turn lane. A park appeared to the right, across from the hotel, and straight in front of them was a bridge with a large stone statue of an Indian on a horse. Keith turned left, then preceded around a bend until he came to a stop light. He turned right onto Michigan Avenue, "The Miraculous Mile." James rolled down the window and threw out his gum in front of the art museum. Festive green and yellow banners hung between the marble columns. Passing the stone steps of the museum, James looked up and saw a black man in a yellow parka. The man was singing the words, "Wake up and live, wake up and live!"

"Wake up and live," James repeated dreamily. Arching an eyebrow he smiled and turned to his brother. He pointed back with his thumb extended.

"Marley," he said in the same dreamy voice.

"What do you mean?"

"The guy was singing Bob Marley," James explained.

The brothers pulled up in front of their destination, The Peninsula Hotel on Superior Avenue. There was a light dusting of snow on the road. In front of the hotel, the pavement was stamped to form square tiles. There were three revolving brass doors and two large, oriental lion statues in front. It was a very posh place. Large snowflakes fell upon the doorman's black rabbit fur hat, and the padded red shoulders of his long coat. It looked like dandruff. The doorman opened Keith's door and asked him if he needed help with the luggage. Their music was now blaring into the street.

> *Oh, when I leave I'm goin' back south*
> *People, where the weather, you know,*
>   *they suit my clothes.*

You know I think I move back south
You know where the weather,
You know that good weather sure suits my clothes.
You know I've been here in Chicago so long
But in the last two winters, man,
  you know I've almost froze.

They had one bag each, so Keith declined the offer as he stepped onto the snowy pavement of Superior Avenue. He gave the bellman five dollars, who passed it on to the valet standing next to him, ready to drive the car to the hotel's parking garage. Both men walked to the back of the SUV and Keith lifted the hatch door. The strains of Buddy Guy's lament got much louder as the speakers were exposed.

You know it snowed in Chicago
'Till I could hardly see myself,
Oh, you know it snowed in Chicago
'Till I can walk down the streets, you know,
And I couldn't see myself.
Well you know I was tryin' to find my baby
You know, she was right over, right over
Snowin' with somebody else.

The valet was already sitting in the driver's seat, bobbing his head to the music, waiting to exit once the men were finished. James slammed the hatch door and the SUV sped away. Its tires instantly melted the flakes, leaving black tracks in the soft white blanket of snow.

James watched the retreating vehicle with real suspicion. "That didn't take him long. I hope that guy works for the hotel."

The doorman waited as Keith passed through the revolving doors.

"Have a nice day, gentlemen."

Keith leaned into the glass partition in front of him to try to get the door moving. The doorman grabbed the next panel, helping him to rotate the heavy contraption. James stepped into the next section and glided through using Keith's momentum. The lobby featured black-and-white marble floors and rich-looking cherry panels. Both noticed that the room was decorated in Art Deco — well, maybe Art Nuevo design. The lobby appeared rather small for a hotel lobby. A desk clerk greeted them – "Welcome to The Peninsula!" — and pointed to a hallway to the left. "Take the elevator up to the hotel lobby. Have a nice day."

A little confused, the two weary men obeyed, following her pointing finger to a set of elevators. The interior of the elevator was also ornate, with red-stained wood panels. The grain of the wood was different from most. It reminded Keith of a jewelry box he bought for Jillian at the San Francisco Box Company. He pushed the L button for lobby. A few floors shot by and the doors opened. A long hallway stretched in front of them, with bright golden wallpaper and Persian gold travertine marble-tiled floors that reflected the light like mirrors. Against the walls, on each side of the hallway, were fancy display cases. The ceilings were painted white with decorative millwork. The cases displayed expensive merchandise that could be purchased, including jewelry from Tiffany's and Hastang beds. They continued down the hall taking in all the elaborate décor. In one of the cases was a painting.

"I think that is a real Marc Chagall," Keith observed.

"I thought it was painted by Alfred E. Newman."

"Who is Alfred E. Newman?"

"Exactly, thank you."

Keith spun around, looking bewildered. "Damn! I left my sweater in the backseat of the car."

"Well, I hope you brought more than what you're wearing."

"What's wrong with what I'm wearing?" Keith challenged good-naturedly.

"Oh there is nothing wrong. I just think that you're going to freeze to death."

"I'll buy another sweater while I'm here," Keith said casually.

At the end of the hall was a large mural. In front of the wall was the concierge's desk, made of walnut. Just ahead they could see the dining area, with its elegant furniture, wooden floors, and windows that rose to the ceiling, showing the Chicago skyline. The front desk was in yet another room, to their left. As they approached the three smartly dressed clerks stationed behind the counter, Keith noticed that his brother's face, shirt, and pants still bore traces of coffee stain. James looked a mess. Keith was chuckling as he set his bag down.

"I have reservations for two rooms for two nights under Kerrigan, first name Keith."

James stood behind his brother as he checked in. A clerk looked up, asking, "May I help you, sir?"

"Oh, no thanks, I'm with him," James said, pointing gauchely to his brother. It was embarrassing to James to have his brother paying for his room. The attendant who'd spoken was the elder of the three, in her fifties. The other two appeared to be in their late twenties. One was a tall black man who was helping Keith. The other was a young white woman who was reading her computer screen. James fidgeted with the change in his pocket. After checking them in, Keith made a beeline for the gift shop to find a sweater. James took the elevator up to his room.

Chapter 7

THEIR FIVE-STAR HOTEL OFFERED all the latest in electronic gadgetry. Next to the bed was a touch panel to control the mood lighting, temperature, television, and radio. James was astonished to note that even the marble bathroom had a television and the same controls. The rooms were decorated elegantly, with gilt wallpaper and inlaid wooden furniture. The bed seemed comfortable and had a cream-colored bedspread with golden tassel-prints on the pillow cases. The financially strapped James had been leaning toward the Holiday Inn outside of the downtown loop, but now he was glad he'd taken up his brother's offer to bask in luxury.

Keith finished unpacking and booted up his laptop. Just as he'd logged onto his e-mail application there was a knock at the door. He opened the door and James walked in, wearing a large grin. Keith continued looking at his e-mails.

"Did you find a sweatshirt or anything?" James could only imagine how "wickedly expensive" – as Michael would say – that gift shop was.

"Yes, I found a red wool sweater," Keith said, unaware of his brother's preoccupation with money.

"Good. Are you ready to rock and roll? I'm getting hungry."

"All right. Where do you want to eat?"

"I don't know. Hey, what are you watching?"

James sat on the bed as Keith tapped on his keyboard. James instantly recognized the TV show, "Oprah," which happened to be filmed in Chicago.

"I'm watching Oprah. She has Julia Roberts on," Keith said.

"Oh."

"Did you catch the show where she goes to South Africa for Christmas, to give gifts to the children? She and her volunteers actually went to South Africa to bring joy to 50,000 schoolchildren and orphans devastated by the AIDS epidemic."

"Yeah, I heard about it."

"She wanted them to know that somebody remembered them, somebody cared. It's called the Angels Network and it's on her website." Keith stopped typing and looked respectfully at Oprah.

"That's cool, but I'm always worried that the money won't go to the children."

"Oh, you are right! As if Oprah really has a big scam going. What are you — nuts? Why would Oprah rip people off? You dumb ass! She's richer than Solomon."

James knew his brother was just ribbing him. "That's true. She's pretty cool. You know, she lives somewhere in Chicago."

"Yes, she lives in one of the high-rises downtown. So where do you want to eat before going to Buddy Guy's Legends?"

James didn't answer because he was mesmerized by the television. Keith resumed typing what James assumed was e-mail for work. His brother always seemed to be working. Keith paused from typing once again, and unlocked and opened up the mini bar, grabbing a couple of Molson beers from the door.

"You want a beer or a cocktail?"

James heard him that time. He reached for the Molson beer.

"Yeah, Oprah goes back every Christmas," Keith said between clicks. "Kids from all over South Africa come from miles around and she hands out presents under a big Christmas tree."

A long-ago memory was starting to surface in James. Suddenly he looked pained. "I remember one Christmas we had this real Christmas tree. We couldn't keep it standing. It was lopsided and top-heavy."

"How can a tree be top-heavy?"

"We put it in upside down... I don't know! Just stay with me. I'm spilling my guts here. Anyway, Mom and Pop, Pop being our stepfather, were over for dinner. They were admiring our tree. So Michael crawled under the tree to plug in the lights. As you can guess, the tree started to fall and all its ornaments went flying. I proceeded to verbally chastise Michael in front of Karen and our parents."

James swallowed hard as he pictured Michael's face, red and ashamed.

"I want to tell him that I'm sorry. Sorry for the way I treated him sometimes. I'm just..."

"Scared. I know. I've been there too. With Michael, I think you need to start by changing how you think and feel toward him."

"What do you mean?"

"I would just try to think about how phenomenal children are and how they're all on their own spiritual path. It's just amazing how all those positive thoughts turn into reality."

"Sometimes I actually love Michael like he is my own son. But other times he drives me nuts!" James shook his head, as if trying to shake out memories. "I expect so much more out of him, but he just goes at his own pace. He could do well if he would just bust his butt. Everything is at his own pokey speed."

Keith nodded to show his understanding. He'd been down that road himself. "We always want them to do well, or to attend some impressive school and then go out and set the world on fire. Part of that desire was fueled by my concerns about: What are the neighbors going to think? What is our family going to think? What are our friends going to think? If we just show them that we love and support them, and we take care not to push them, they are going to feel that accepting energy and do better. Isn't that what we really want for them — happiness?"

"You're right." James couldn't think of anything more to add.

"And you can't make Michael be like you. My daughter was never going to be like me."

"But we really don't want another you!" James teased.

"No. Of course not! That would be scary. But seriously, what parents should want for their children is for them to be the best at whatever they want to do. And you know you get frustrated, because you want the best for your children and you see their potential, but they have to go through their own learning process. You're actually harming them when you're worrying and projecting negative outcomes onto them, rather than seeing them as they really are which is as beings with limitless potential! I hope I'm not getting too philosophical for you, little bro!"

He was. James's mind was fixed on physical realities. "Easy for you to say," he shot back. Keith could see that James wasn't about to walk a mile in his moccasins. Better that we go eat, he thought. "How about we resume this conversation at another time?" he suggested. "Come on. I'll buy you a Chicago pizza. One of the best pizza places is practically next door."

Keith and James exited the hotel through the same uncooperative revolving door they'd come in through. The forceful wind blasted against their bodies as the door opened to the outside. The air was freezing cold. They could see their breath as they turned toward Rush Street, known for its many restaurants. Night was starting to fall as all the businesspeople made their way home. The stores were lit up and cars crawled bumper to bumper. Right across the street from the hotel was one of Chicago's most famous pizza places, Giordano's. They crossed Rush Street, passing the white statue of a naked man, and then passed through the revolving doors of the pizzeria. The name "Giordano's" was lit up in neon script.

It looked like the restaurant hadn't changed in fifty years. Little white floor tiles, and some strategically placed black tiles — an old design seen in many old bathrooms and Italian restaurants – gave the place a cozy old-time feel. One could picture the place packed with mobsters in wool-vested suits. The two men waited at the bar for about forty-five minutes before their name was called. Keith again took the tab.. After a brief negotiation, they decided on a large pepperoni-and-mushroom pizza, which arrived steaming hot. Keith had also ordered two new beers, even though James's first beer was barely touched. Keith placed his napkin on his lap and picked up his knife and fork. Forgoing such niceties, his brother quickly grabbed a slice and rammed about half of it into his mouth. The noise level was high from conversations at the surrounding tables. Between bites, the two engaged in more small talk. James found his thoughts wandering to his long-awaited evening with Buddy Guy . . . and to the ritzy hotel . . . the relaxed conversation with his brother . . . the pizza . . . and now, soon, his favorite performer! He'd all but forgotten his problems.

It was getting close to show time. The brothers hurriedly finished their dinner and went outside to hail a cab. "Can you take us to Eighth and Wabash? Buddy Guy's Legends," Keith directed. The passengers sat quietly in back, taking in the sights. The cab crossed the bridge by the Wrigley Building and the Chicago Tribune, then turned right onto a darkened street and left onto Wabash Avenue.

"Boy, how many times have you seen this in a movie? It reminds me of the Blues Brothers," said Keith as they passed beneath the "L's" viaduct.

"We are on a mission from God!" cried James, quoting the movie.

The cab pulled up to Buddy Guy's Legends. James opened the door and stepped into the wet street. Waiting on the curb and watching his brother paying the cabby, he again felt the slight sting of being a moocher. The bouncer held the glass door open with his massive frame and took their tickets. Keith could tell that his brother, smiling broadly like a child at Christmas, was very excited, But why was he heading for the cashier? Keith wondered. Mystery solved: behind her was an array of Buddy Guy paraphernalia, including T-shirts and coffee mugs. To her side was a glass display case. James showed Keith Buddy's Grammy Award inside the case.

"I believe that Buddy has won five Grammy's thus far," James informed his brother.

Keith bought a bourbon and coke for himself and a beer for his brother. The two walked around the half-filled bar looking at memorabilia, including pictures of Muddy Waters, Eric Clapton, Lightning Hopkins, Howlin' Wolf, Junior Wells, Jimmy Reed, Otis Rush, Little Walter, and Stevie Ray Vaughan.

Two more drinks later and the place was packed with a sold-out crowd. The band took the stage and started to warm up by playing little riffs. Once all tuned up, the band started to play an upbeat melody. After some time of playing, the bass player stepped up to the microphone and introduced "The one, the only, Buddy Guy!" Buddy came on stage, flashed a huge smile to the crowd, and immediately wailed into a lead guitar solo on the very first note. James leaned over and screamed above the music.

"Buddy's on fire! He's smoking!"

Keith looked over at his brother, who was playing air guitar and bobbing his head up and down like a teenager. Buddy slid right into the next song without saying a word to the audience.

Damn right I got the blues,
From my head down to my shoes.
Damn right I got the blues,
From my head down to my shoes.
You know I can't win, people,
'Cause I don't have a damn thing to lose...

Still playing his guitar, Buddy started walking through the crowd, a stagehand following close behind with a flashlight. He came over by Keith and James, who were standing next to the bar. James's hero was now just a few feet away, playing another solo. After that, Buddy paused, put his arm around a spectator, and had a young lady in the audience strum his guitar as he made the chords with his other hand. He wore a glittering, bright gold blazer and a fedora with a gold band. James noticed that his guitar idol didn't have his hair anymore. Buddy used to wear his curly hair long in the back. Now it appeared that he shaved his head totally bald. His Stratocaster was red, with white polka-dots. Buddy then kicked the men's bathroom door open and headed in. With his wireless guitar, you could still hear him playing after the door closed.

"Isn't he the best?" screamed James.

Keith shook his head up and down but could not understand a word. Moments later, Buddy emerged from the men's room and headed straight for the ladies' room. As before, he kicked open the door and went in. The crowd went nuts. Jamming out of sight for several minutes, Buddy was clearly living it up in the ladies' room! Just as James started to worry that he'd spend all evening in there, the door suddenly burst open and out he came, still playing. A shot was sitting at the bar with his name on it. Without missing a beat, Buddy downed the shot in a second, his other hand continuing to pick the strings from the neck so that the rhythm wouldn't stop. Everyone cleared a path as he walked. Buddy passed the cashier's station and stepped outside into the cold night. Everyone could still hear him through the amps on the stage, belting out the tune. Some fans ran outside to see him. A few minutes later he reentered through a side door and stepped back up onto the stage. He finished his song with some heavy turnaround.

"Thank you! Thank you, Chicago! Excuse me while I take my medication."

Buddy took a sip from a cup that was sitting on one of the guitar amps.

"Can you believe that he's almost seventy years old?" marveled James.

Buddy continued to take a long sip of his drink as a stagehand spoke to him in his ear. He started to tell a story but the crowd was too loud. He tried to continue, but people were yelling above him. Buddy paused patiently until the crowd settled down enough to hear what he was trying to say. He leaned over into the microphone. The noise was now at a manageable level — except for one idiot in the back, by the bar.

"Yeahhhh! Buddy!" James screamed.

"Shut the hell up," said Buddy, looking straight at him.

"See, Keith? I told you he would recognize me! I've seen him four times!"

Buddy finished the story in his soothing voice. When he finished, he swung right into James's favorite song.

Down here the river meets the sea.
And in the sticky heat, I feel ya open up to me.
Love comes out of nowhere, baby, just like a hurricane.
And it feels like rain.
And it feels like rain.
Lying here, underneath the stars, right next to you.
And I am wondering who you are, and how do you do?
The clouds roll in across the moon
And the wind howls out your name
And it feels like rain.
And it feels like rain.

Buddy continued ripping through the metal strings, whipping up the crowd.

After playing for almost two hours, Buddy finished his concert, as he always did when playing in his own club, by sitting down at the end of his bar in the very front. He abruptly played the last chord and it was over. It was one of Buddy's more strategic moves: this way, he could sign autographs as people bought memorabilia and he could still get a drink at the bar.

Knowing Buddy's tactics, James had already bought what he needed and then walked briskly to the bar, beating everybody else to the front of the autograph line. It seemed that everybody in the room wanted a chance to meet the guitar legend. He had Buddy sign his autograph on the poster. James paid his respects by telling Buddy how great he was and by reverently addressing him as "Mr. Guy."

Elated and slightly dazed, the brothers weaved their way through the crowd and stepped outside to find a cab. Steam was rising from the sewer as they started down Wabash, heading for a cab parked right under the track for the 'L' train. By the time they got there, the cab had pulled away, loaded with passengers. The two men looked at each other, dumbfounded Thirty seconds later another cab drove by, ignoring their plight. James noticed that the air was now warmer and that it was snowing lightly. He paused for a moment under a streetlight, taking in the sight and the feeling. His adrenaline was flowing! He could feel sweat rolling down his stomach. He unzipped his coat. Keith headed back to the corner, hoping for better luck at finding a cab as James continued to watch the snow fall. He picked the highest snowflake he could focus on and watched it fall in the light beam. It was too hard to follow one individual flake so he focused on the space in between the flakes. For the first time in quite a while, he felt alive. The winter wasn't an issue at that moment.

Keith was busy hailing the two cabs that were heading their way. James excitedly jumped off the curb and took a few steps into the street. He quickly unrolled the poster and held it up to get their attention. The cabs flew by, one of them splashing a chuckhole's worth of muddy water all over James's freshly signed autograph. The signature ran down the soaking wet poster. In disbelief, James turned and watched the cab's red taillights as it slowed down to pick up a concert goers standing on the corner.

"Son of a . . ." Taking a deep breath, he looked back up at the falling snow, and then beyond to the starry heavens. The stars looked brighter to James than they usually did, and the snowflakes glittered and danced under the streetlight. It was beautiful. The same cab stopped at the corner to pick up his brother. James looked back up into the sky and spread out his arms like a bird.

"Oh, Father. In Christ's name, help me find the answer. I feel lost. Help me, Lord. Help me find the answer to life. Help me get back on track. Help me to be a better husband

and father, to be more patient. Father, be with my brother. His heart is hurting so. Help him to find his way. Teach us this weekend. Lead us, Lord. Place angels around us…"

"You ready?" Keith yelled. "C'mon, man!"

Keith waved his hand to tell James to come now. James looked at his dripping poster and laughed. Oh well, it was still a good night. He ran up the street, back to the corner, where Buddy Guy's bar stood. There was a garbage can outside the club. James slammed the poster into the can and jumped into the taxi next to his brother. He was all wet.

Keith looked at his wet and panting brother. "What happened?"

"Oh it's nothing. It doesn't matter."

James realized that the fault was his, not the driver's. He smiled, laughing inside at himself. Once again, James's pants were soaked. When they got back to the hotel, James paid and tipped the driver.

Chapter 8

KEITH WAS LYING ON the hotel bed, writing on a legal pad when the phone rang. It was Saturday morning. He felt good, considering the late night and his one too many drinks. His stomach seemed to be taking a vacation from its usual pain.

"Hello?"

"Good morning, sunshine," rasped the caller. "Are you sleeping?"

"No. I'm up. I have been up for a while." Keith sounded eager to start the day.

"I just woke up. How about we meet in an hour down in the lobby?" James suggested.

"Okay. See you in the lobby."

Both men took their time grooming in the luxurious bathroom. James even drew a bath and luxuriated in its soothingly hot water, instead of taking his usual quick shower. Keith called Jillian but there was no answer. He took his morning pills, hoping he wouldn't have any stomach pains that day. The pizza was probably a bad decision. How hard it was for him to break old eating habits! In the room next door, his brother was also taking his daily doses. Once in the lobby, Keith settled into a leather chair and opened The Chicago Sun-Times. He was wearing his new red sweater, blue Dockers, a pair of black loafers, and a blue fleece jacket. James got off the elevator and walked into the lobby wearing a black knit cap, a bomber jacket with fleece collar and trim, gloves, and boots. Keith looked at his brother and was reminded of a character from "Hogan's Heroes."

"Hey Hogan. Are you ready?"

James quickly looked his brother up and down to find a dress-code violation, so he could respond with a witty retort. He zeroed in on Keith's fleece jacket.

"Is that all you brought, you left-coast pretty boy?"

"Left coast?" sputtered Keith. "You are way more left than I am. At least I don't look like I'm ready for a WWII prison break-out."

They walked passing the long hallway with the display cases of expensive merchandise. It was unanimously decided that they'd head for the nearest Starbucks, which was about five blocks away. The brothers walked along Michigan Avenue, looking in the storefronts of the high-end shopping district known as "The Miraculous Mile." Starbucks was a welcome sight, especially for Keith, who started every day with a cup. James ordered a double shot espresso; Keith succumbed to habit and went for his usual latte. Both men added half-n-half and sprinkles of cinnamon and nutmeg to their drinks. After throwing away their swizzle sticks they stepped outside. The warm, aromatic cup felt good in their hands as they strolled together, sipping their coffee in the sunshine. It seemed a little warmer than the day before and the sun felt good, especially to James, who was used to long, sunless Midwestern winters. A cab stand was up ahead, with several cabs available to take them to their first destination of the day, the John Hancock Building and Water Tower Place. The buildings were sentimental favorites of both men. The John Hancock building is an unusual black structure that gets narrower at each ascending floor.

Keith purchased two tickets to ride the elevator to the top of the Hancock building. The view was spectacular. You could see Lake Michigan on one side and the whole downtown skyline on the other.

After returning to the ground floor, they walked next door to Water Tower Place to get some lunch. The building is a very tall, and, like all the other buildings along the "Miraculous Mile," it has shops at the lower levels. On the floors above the stores are the Ritz-Carlton hotel and high-end condominiums. Across the street was the old stone water tower and adjacent pumping station. The limestone bricks reminded them of material that might be used to build a castle. It was a small Gothic-looking building with a tower in the middle. Keith reminded James that this historic tower was the only building to survive the Chicago Fire. After admiring the stone water tower across the street, the two brothers entered the glass doors of the Water Tower Place.

At the food court, James ordered a spinach salad and a mixture of wheat grass, ginseng, carrot, beet, apple, and parsley. Keith ordered a cheeseburger, fries, and a Diet Coke. There were people scattered randomly at the tables, with shopping bags filling up empty seats. They sat down at a white table that looked like it was lawn furniture from Marshall Fields. James looked over at Keith's orange plastic tray and Styrofoam plates.

"I don't get it. How can you eat that crap?" James asked enviously. "You work out. You run. You're in better shape than I. But you eat like hell! How can you eat that?"

James waited for an answer but Keith did not respond to his brother.

They fell silent in deep thought, people-watching, and listening to snippets of passers-by conversation. Eventually James looked at his brother's face. He appeared to be upset. It was obvious that something was weighing heavily on his mind,

James thought. Keith felt the stare. To distract James from asking any questions, Keith focused on his brother.

"What are you thinking about, James?"

"Oh, I was thinking of Karen," James responded, instantly forgetting about his brother. "I got into a fight with her on the phone before we left. I guess I'm feeling bad about it."

"Hey I know what you can do. After we eat, we can go shopping for her. You know, get her something nice, a gift or something."

"I don't know."

"You know what our sister Diane told me that all women love?"

"What?"

"Anything wrapped in a Tiffany's box."

"Who is Tiffany?"

"The store called Tiffany's. I bought a bracelet, years ago, for Linda when I was on a business trip. She loved it!" Keith continued to watch his brother's face, hoping for signs of encouragement.

"I don't know," James said doubtfully. "What am I supposed to do — buy something from 7-Eleven?"

"No! We'll go to Tiffany's!" exclaimed Keith.

"Tiffany's the jewelry store? Isn't that a little on the expensive side?"

"Yes, of course. Tiffany's! And no, it's not expensive if you don't mind spending around a hundred and fifty dollars."

"What do you mean 'Just a hundred and fifty bucks'?" James sounded defeated. "But I'm not working."

"Ah come on, James! Don't tell me you didn't save any money. I know you. You're a tightwad. You can get a small heart bracelet and they'll wrap it in a little blue box that says Tiffany's on it. Women love to get things that are from Tiffany's!"

"What the hell? Who told you this?" James could hardly believe his ears.

"Diane, our sister, you know her."

"Do you think I'm married to — Katharine Hepburn?"

"Audrey Hepburn, in Breakfast at Tiffany's, do you remember? Believe me, it works. Take my word for it."

James was taken aback. He stared at Keith, dumbfounded.

"Well, whoever it was! It scares me that you even know all this crap. What are you some kind of fruitcake?"

"Whatever happened to your Namaste, one-love bit? Do you want to make it up to her or not? Come on. Trust me."

They crossed back over Michigan Avenue, and, "just for fun," started heading in the direction of Tiffany's. James looked around for other alternatives. He spied a Saks Fifth Avenue and immediately dismissed it. But then he found his saving grace. There was a Pottery Barn right next door.

"What about there?" he said, pointing. "I can get something in there."

With a disappointed look, Keith opened the door to Tiffany's and waved his hand, motioning for his brother to go ahead in front of him. Just two steps into the store and James was already feeling inferior. Set against the poised clientele and glittering décor, he felt like a fish out of water. Above James's head was a magnificent chandelier that, James figured, must be worth more than he'd earned in a lifetime.

"Blue box, huh?" James whispered sarcastically.

"Yes."

A saleslady asked James if she could help him. He replied, "Sorry, just looking," and walked around her. Set against all the grandeur and delicate treasures, James felt like a clumsy rube.

"Follow me," said Keith kindly. "Over here are the less expensive items where I bought the heart bracelets."

They walked over to the display case and Keith pointed down over the counter. James studied all the items in the case. Everything looked tremendously expensive. Just then a sweet fragrance caught his attention and he looked up. It was the same salesperson, a pretty older lady, dressed very smartly.

"May I help you?" she asked extra-courteously. She had followed them to the display case, perhaps wondering if a heist was in progress.

"Yes, can you tell me where your chainsaw department is?" James asked innocently.

"Yes, of course," said the polished lady, not missing a beat. "It is right next to the garden hoses, adjacent to the auto parts department."

"Ah, funny," James blurted. "I like that! You have a sense of humor. Good! Uh, can I see that bracelet?"

Following James's eyes, the saleslady looked to the left side of the case. He tapped the glass top with his fingernail, showing her where it was located.

"Yes, right there."

She took out a sterling silver bracelet with a gold heart at the top that also acted as a clasp.

"How much is it?" James asked, suddenly embarrassed.

"This item is three hundred dollars," she said quietly.

"Hell, I could buy a new chain saw for that much!" he roared, suddenly emboldened.

"I don't know him." said Keith, trying not to laugh. "He was just asking for directions."

"Oh, he's fine. There is an inscription on the inside." she said, unruffled.

James admired the silver piece in his hand. It was much more than what he wanted to spend, but he was too embarrassed not to buy anything. He thought back to the conversation he had with his wife. He wanted to make it up to her.

"I guess I'll take it," he said, trying to sound casual.

"Would you like it gift wrapped?"

"Yes. Is it wrapped in a little blue box?"

"Yes it is," she said, sensing the situation. "And it says Tiffany's on the box."

"Whew, how exciting!" said James, sounding sarcastically.

Keith lifted his eyebrows as the saleslady opened a drawer behind the counter and brought out a light blue box and matching ribbon.

"Hey Keith, look at that box! I thought you said it was going to be blue, not light powder-gay blue. How am I going to cart that around?"

"Blue is blue. No one's going to care. I'll tell ya, for a guy who's so in touch with his inner being, you are very self-conscious."

The lady finished wrapping the little box, and then gently put the gift into a matching light-blue bag with white string handles and the insignia, "Tiffany & Co." on the side.

"Well, isn't that beautiful!" James announced. "I just love it. Thank you." He handed over his credit card, then signed the slip to complete the transaction.

Keith wore a big grin. He acknowledged the saleslady with a nod of his head. She smiled back.

"Are you ready, smart-ass?" James inquired.

"You look so sweet!" Keith lisped, playing on his brother's fears.

"I'm just going to stuff it in my pocket," James decided.

He started to jam the light blue bag with its delicate white strings into the pocket of his bomber jacket.

"Hey, don't do that!" Keith warned. "You're going to squash it."

"No, I'm not. Besides, my dignity is worth something, isn't it?"

"Ah, that's just great. I can't wait for you to hand Karen a Tiffany & Company bag all crinkled up like a discarded hamburger wrapper. Then she'll pull the box out of the bag and that will be all smashed up too. Nice! You're nothing but class."

"Thanks, man. I knew you would appreciate it."

They resumed their walk down Michigan Avenue. The wind was whistling through the tall buildings and right into their faces. Pedestrians struggled against the blasts as they passed with hands clenching their shopping bags. Others hugged themselves inside their coat pockets.

"Hey," suggested Keith. "Let's go this way to get another Starbucks."

"You've got to be kidding me. How many of those do you have to have in a day? I'm surprised your stomach doesn't hurt."

"I got to make sure my stock goes up. Come on," Keith urged.

"No. I think I'm going to meet you back at the hotel. I'm getting cold, and I wouldn't mind popping into a few more stores just to look around. I want to see how the other half lives."

"Remember, don't think that way! You've got to think abundance and prosperity. Remember that your thoughts create matter."

"Yeah sure," quipped James. "And 'Tidings of comfort and joy.' I'll meet you back at the hotel."

James turned against the wind as a tear ran sideways across his face. He lowered his head and slightly closed his eyes for a hint of relief.

"Go spend a little money," Keith said cheerfully. "Keep the faith, baby!"

"I will, you little freak show."

Keith walked quickly through the crowd, dodging people as if they were pylon cones. As he walked, he looked at the other pedestrians; their eyes would meet briefly, then the person would disappear forever. Keith was feeling the cold. He had his hands in the pockets of his fleece jacket. The wind blew through his Dockers making the hairs on his legs stand at attention. It felt as if he were being swept away by the wind, wherever it wanted to take him. Man, I hate winter, he thought. It was hard to think of anything else as the cold blew through him. Keith could see the Starbucks sign a half a block away. He thought about the delicious drink awaiting him, and how warm the store would be. It was an oasis in a block-and-mortar desert. Keith moved closer to the buildings where there was less wind. He could see a line of people stretching out past its front glass doors. At the end of the line he could see a street person, holding a Maxwell House Coffee can and leaning against a window ledge of the tall granite building. The man was dressed warmly, but as Keith looked at his face, he realized the man's cheeks were blue under his snowy beard. His face was wrinkled and weather-beaten. His beard was scraggly with bare patches exposing sunken jaws. Keith figured that the man was probably around his own age. He pulled out his wallet and grabbed a dollar. He noticed that the man was shaking and his hands were chapped and grayish in color as they wrapped around the blue can filled with change. This vision hit Keith in the heart. He put the dollar back and grabbed a twenty.

"Here you go, man."

Keith stuffed the bill in the can. The man looked up at Keith with his ice-blue eyes.

"God bless you. God bless you, sir. Thank you."

Keith continued to wait his turn at the door. He thought about the man and how he seemed to be so grateful for the money. He wondered if the bum — if that's what he was — was going to waste it on booze or drugs. Keith justified his action by concluding that he did it for himself, not for the street person. He opened the glass door and stepped into the warm café where he was greeted by a Tracy Chapman song.

Here I am, I'm waiting for a better day,
A second chance
A little luck to come my way.
A hope to dream, a hope that I can sleep again
And wake in the world with a clear conscience
    and clean hands
'Cause all that you have is your soul.

Don't be tempted by the shiny apple,
Don't you eat of a bitter fruit.
Hunger only for a taste of justice,
Hunger only for a world of truth
'Cause all that you have is your soul.

Oh my mama told me
'Cause she say she learned the hard way,
Say she wanna spare the children.
She say don't give or sell your soul away
'Cause all that you have is your soul.

All that you have
All that you have
All that you have
Is your soul.

    At first he'd felt anxiety, and a little frustrated that the line was so long. Then he realized he wasn't on any schedule and it felt good just to be in a warm place. He looked back and saw the man's back leaning against the large glass window. Keith was in a warm room with a good smell, beautiful people, and the warm colors of the décor. He thought about the man outside. When his turn finally came, he looked up at the colorful menu on the back wall. There were so many choices for him. "I'll take a café latte and a café mocha."

Keith put cream and one packet of Equal into the latte. He glanced at the café mocha, thought for a second, and then figured it was probably sweet enough but that he'd let the man decide. He replaced the lid on his latte and grabbed a couple of packets of sugar. He started to walk off but took a quick step back and also grabbed another pack of Equal. He used his back to open the windblown door as he held the two coffees. The man hadn't moved from his spot. "Here you go, sir."

Keith held out the steaming drink and the packs of sweeteners. The beggar set down his can of money, then reached up slowly with both hands as if he were being offered the Holy Grail. He wrapped his hands around it and looked up at Keith with one thousand more times the gratitude than before. The man's concave jaws opened and a soft moan escaped from his lips. A blue hand was extended in friendship. Keith looked down as the man's hand turned upward and opened. He grasped his new friend's hand deeply. It felt like ice compared to the latte in his other hand. The man shook Keith's hand slowly. Their eyes met and locked. Keith brought his cup against the back of the man's hand to warm the tendons.

"That was the nicest thing that anyone has done for me in a… since I can remember. Thank you. Thank you, sir."

The man let go first. Keith felt sad. It was time to move on. The man stood up.

"Can I ask you your name?"

"Keith."

"Keith. Keith. Bless you, Keith."

"Thank you. God bless you too."

Keith took a step backwards, continuing to keep eye contact with the man for as long as he could. Then the waves of people obscured the vision of a man holding a steaming cup. The man, still standing, raised his open hand, gesturing good-bye. Keith waved back. The man's face stayed fixed in Keith's mind for the next block. He felt emptiness. He felt scared and alone. He wanted to help but he didn't know how. The image finally left when he heard singing from another street person wearing a yellow parka. It was the man they'd seen the day before when they came into town.

One love, one heart.
Let's get together and feel all right...
As it was in the beginning...
"Give thanks and praise to the Lord
  and I will feel all right."

Keith knew those lyrics well. "Marley. What a trip."
He kept walking. A smile returned to his heart.
"I shot the sheriff," he sang, his mental synapses firing wildly. "But I did not shoot the deputy. Ooh. Ooh. Ooh!"

En route back to the hotel, James had jumped into a specialty store for just for a moment to get warm. Remembering his conversation with his brother, he looked at the young lady behind the counter and said, "Namaste." She frowned at him, looked away and started whispering to the other clerk. James realized he'd actually mouthed the words. She nodded in his direction as she talked. Scared and embarrassed, he quickly headed for the door.

Waiting at the crosswalk for the Walk light to come on, James noticed that everyone around him, and the pedestrians across the street, looked in all directions to prevent eye contact with anyone. Again he mouthed "Namaste," and its translation, "I see the God in you." This time he kept the words in his mind. He looked at each passerby and repeated the phrase. The light turned green and everyone started across the middle of the street. He looked right at two young guys with black leather jackets.

"Namaste!" he said aloud, without meaning to.

One of them froze in his tracks. "Screw you, you fag!" he sneered.

James walked faster and hopped up onto the curb. He looked back to respond, but the two teenagers had disappeared into the crowd.

"I am such a jackass," he said, wondering if it was true.

Continuing down the sidewalk, James suddenly realized that he'd made a full circle, for there was Superior Street, and the hotel on the corner. The doorman stood in front with his black fur cap and red coat. James could see the man's breath, and it reminded him of the witch's guardsmen in The Wizard of Oz.

"Oye ye yo! Awhoa oh. Oye ye yo! Awhoa oh," he intoned for his own amusement.

He wasn't ready to go back to the hotel and figured Keith would be awhile. Resuming his walk, he crossed Chicago Avenue. James felt excited and warm. He wondered if it was just from the positive vibration he was giving out or if those vibes were also in the air. Seeing that there were a lot of people around the old limestone water tower, he headed in that direction, all the while holding positive thoughts about everyone he passed. He decided to say other things besides Namaste. Meanwhile, though, he'd keep his jaws clamped, lest some other embarrassing salutation pop out.

What might he say? God bless you? May health be bestowed upon you? No, that wouldn't do. How are you? No, that wouldn't work, either. How about I love you? Yeah, that was it. You could never go wrong with love.

"I love you!" he called out into the frigid afternoon air. "I love you too."

"Aaaahhhhhh!" James responded. "What was that?" Was someone addressing him?

"It was me. AAAAaaaaaaaaaahhhhhh is the sound of creation."

And yet – no one was speaking. The reply had come into James's head. He stopped in his tracks and looked up, then around, then down. Finally, he spun completely around. Nothing. Okay, James thought. I can live with a little ambiguity. He was now standing right in front of the historic water tower. In front of the water tower was a small park area with one-person wooden benches. Cold and still, a horse-drawn carriage waited for customers alongside the curb. James watched as the draft horse roused itself from its apparent torpor long enough to drink from the fountain. His whiskers were coated in ice. As cold as it was, there were still many people in the little park, shoppers carrying bags, clusters of jumpy teens, and older people, sitting like still-life models on the wooden seats. As James began to read a plaque that explained the historic significance of the water tower, his eye was caught by the sight of an unusual-looking man seated on the steps just left of the plaque. It was a street person. James stopped reading and strolled over to him. Behind the transient's back were large wooden cream-colored doors, carved with ancient geometrical shapes that reminded James of clover leaves. The man smiled up at James and, in a soft, Jamaican-accented voice said, "It was I who answered you." James was, for once, speechless. On closer inspection, this dark-colored man, although strange, did not look like a street person at all. Were he not slouching on the steps, he would've come off as an ordinary guy. He was wearing a blue goose-down vest and a bright red wool sweater. Carhartt pants, leather hiking boots, and a red wool hat completed his ensemble. Next to his feet was a tattered paperback: Ask and Given: Learning to Manifest Your Desires (The Teachings of Abraham) by Esther and Jerry Hicks. He was strumming an old Guild guitar. His hair was in long black dreads hanging from the wool hat and dangling over his guitar. A black cat with a half-white face sat next to him.

The world is black, the world is white.
It turns by day, and then by night.
A child is black, a child is white. .
Together they grow to see the light, to see the light...

James watched the Rasta-blues man sing the song. He had a very deep, baritone voice. James also noticed that the man had a big space between his two front teeth – and one of the warmest smiles James had ever seen. The smile seemed to be resonating in his voice. James waited patiently for the song to end.

"The band, Three Dog Night." said James appreciatively.

"That's right, my friend. It is a beautiful song about unity. Yes indeed, we are 'all one.' I believe this is what you are trying to find through your affirmations of love," he added casually.

"H-h-how did you . . ." James tried to ask, his air supply failing him.

The man gave a big smile, again showing the gaps between his resin-stained teeth. He continued to pick at the acoustic guitar as he hummed the melody of the song. James caught a faint whiff of jasmine.

He tried again. "I mean, how did you…"

James's new friend laughed heartily. "How can me not?" he asked in an innocent, almost child-like tone. I could feel your vibration a block away! I feel everyone's vibration."

James looked around, blinked his eyes, and rummaged through his memories, but he couldn't quite get the meaning. He saw some boys skating on the sidewalk. Shoppers whisked by, swinging their shopping bags. Not a clue anywhere in sight.

"Don't look for it – it's not out there! Feel it!" prompted his new teacher. "Listen! AAaaaaaahhhhhhhhhh. Creation! Feel it!"

So saying, he closed his eyes, smiled, and took in the deepest breath that James had ever witnessed. Then he slowly exhaled. James followed suit by inhaling, then slowly exhaling, what must have been the deepest breath he'd ever taken. He watched his breath floating up to the sky.

"AAaaaaaahhhhhhhhhh," rejoiced the man. "Creation! Yes, the sound of creation!"

"What is the sound of creation?" James asked meekly.

Most religions have a name for the Almighty, and almost every one has the same 'aaaah' sound. For example, Allah, Buddha, Mohammad, God, Hashem, Jehovah, and, in Jamaica, Jah is the name they have for God. Feel the vibration with me. Try it once, will you?"

"Ah," said James.

"No, it's aaaahhhhhh!

James took a much deeper breath. "Aaaaahhhhhhh."

"Good!" exclaimed the happy man. Feels good to your body, yes? Your heart hums. Aaaaaaaaaaahhhhhhh."

"Aaaaaaahhhhh. Yeah, it does feel good. Is that from some ancient scripture?" James had never come across anything like this in the Bible or the Gita.

"Dyer."

"Is that the book after Exodus?" James asked, hoping he sounded intelligent.

"No, it's Dr. Wayne Dyer, the author. There's a Spiritual Solution to Every Problem, Your Erroneous Zones, The Power of Intention, Everyday Wisdom" — anything written by him will bring you to a new level of consciousness."

"Exodus, movement of the people. Bob Marley," mused James.

James proceeded to strum an air guitar, hoping to let the man know that he was hip to the Reggae movement.

"What is your name, sir?"

"Charlie."

James shook his head in acknowledgement. The man looked directly into James's eyes. James stopped his strumming, his attention riveted on the teacher.

"We are all waves in the ocean," the man said plainly. "We are all one, the Rasta vibration. Our suffering is caused by the mind, by a mind that insists on having preferences and will not allow others to be just as they are."

James was outwardly silent for a moment, planning his response.

"Yeah, I see what you mean," he put in excitedly. "It's like frequency. By being positive, your frequency is faster. So you –"

"Aaahhh!" the friend interrupted. "You are searching. You're searching for the answer! True joy and peace come to the person who lets their world flow from the pleadings of their soul."

"Well, what I'm personally doing is –"

"Everyone comes here to the big city looking for answers to the ages-old question, What is the answer to life? How to find never-ending abundance, prosperity, health, peace, joy, and love — but you know what? They never find it. And you won't find it either until you learn to shift from form to spirit. Know the will of the Father and fall back in the knowing." The Rasta-man's words came smoothly and plainly.

"Hey! What makes you think that I won't find –"

"Like everyone else, you are looking in the wrong places. You look here, there, over there, always seeking outside yourself. But you won't find it. You find it right here," he concluded, tapping his chest with the palm of his hand.

"Here," he repeated. "Here is where you will find the miracles including the greatest of all miracles."

"What do you mean by the miracles?"

The teacher ignored the question, "Yes, the miracles, the creation of all things that you desire, of all that everyone desires. Align yourself to your soul and listen to those inner promptings to be at ease and on purpose. It is in this mindset that real magic will become available to you. As it is written in The Game of Life and How to Play It by Florence Scovel Shinn, projection is the cause, perception is the effect. The world you live in, all that you visualize, and experience, is a reflection of your inward thought of it. If you believe the world is condemned by evil, you will experience condemnation and evil. If you believe the world is healed and holy, you will experience heaven on earth, through miracles in your life. When you desire something, it is on its way. When you believe something, it is on its way. When you fear something, it is on its way. The longer that you desire, or the stronger your belief is, the faster the energy moves toward it. The longer that you have been focusing on your fears, the faster the energy moves toward it."

James was perplexed. It all sounded so simple, yet somehow he couldn't accept it. No, the world is a complicated place, he thought nervously. This sounded way too pie-in-the-sky for a deep thinker like himself.

"I thought there hadn't been any miracles performed in thousands of years. In the world we live in today, any kind of miracle strikes me as implausible, if not impossible," he said, affecting what he believed was a subtle tone.

"As it says in A Course in Miracles, 'the Christ in you is very still.' The Christ looks on all things that He loves, knowing everything is a part of Him, just as He is a part of all things.

He knows that He is one with all. He knows He is one with his Father. Feel Him within as you did just a minute ago, and you will experience all miracles, including the greatest miracle of all," the Rasta-man said, winking.

"But don't my sins have to be forgiven by a priest or somebody?" said the altar boy still alive in James.

"For centuries we have searched for divinity from our elders and from the clergy. Too seldom have we looked within for truth, and made our own decisions."

James was starting to feel a little embarrassed, and almost ashamed. "You got it all wrong. You got me all wrong!" he declared with all the authority he could muster. "I don't even have a job. I'm not some peace-loving guru who sits on a mountaintop, forgiving the world's sins."

"Peace comes only from forgiveness; you don't need to confess to a confessor, do penance, and all that other rigmarole! The Christ sees only perfection. He is at peace because He sees no condemnation. You can be at peace too – it's a snap!" he said, snapping his fingers.

"Dude, I got to tell ya," James began, struggling for the right words. "You are kind of freaking me out, just like those nuns did in school!"

"Oh no, man. Nothing like that! No whacks with a ruler, no weird stuff! The Christ in you is simply love. That's who you are – pure love."

"I am pure . . . wah? Hey listen. Good talking with you but I got to go. I have to –"

"Sssshhh! Just listen to that small, still voice within. It's all there is to hear. Look within, and you'll see all there is to see. Bless all beings, and you will at last know the meaning of your beautiful word, Namaste, for the Christ in you indeed greets the Christ in me and in all others. It is good that you were doing so on this very street! It sure caught my attention!"

Questions were bubbling up faster than James could articulate. He wouldn't – couldn't – leave this man just yet. "But...but I don't get it! No offense, but I doubt that all the Christian religions are wrong and you are right."

"Haven't you been told that you are a child of God? Wouldn't that make you a son of God? All I'm saying is, just put your hand in His and let Him lead you on your journey. Do this, and you'll see what happens to your doubts!"

"How do you create these miracles again and what is this great miracle?" James asked, believing he was cutting to the chase.

Charlie gently tapped James on the chest with his index finger, "You. Miracles occur naturally when you let them. They are expressions of love. All miracles mean life, and God is the Giver of Life."

James wanted the formula, if there was one. "But I still don't understand. If it is an expression of love, how do I create miracles?"

"I will tell you this. There are only four ways to create miracles. There are only four keys to unlock."

"What keys to unlock? What great miracle?"

"Unlock your soul. All miracles come from your soul. Then you can see."

Ah-hah! I am getting closer, thought James, his mind racing. "How do I get these four keys?"

"You can never get them. You only can give them. That is why the keys are called The Four Givings. And in giving any of The Four Givings, you are in communion with God; you are accepting the body of Christ. In that moment, you are stating, 'I am that I am, and I am at peace with it.'"

"So in other words, by doing one of these Four Givings, I can have anything I want, money or anything?"

"When you desire something to come into your life, and you are happy and feeling good about it while envisioning the desired result, your thought vibration is in alignment with your desire. This means that the current from your Higher Source is flowing through you, toward your intended desire, with no resistance. When you desire something to come into your life, but you are sad, angry, or stressed, you are actually focusing on the opposite of your desire. Your Higher Source flow is restricted, so you will receive instead, the lack of the desired result. The Four Givings help you to realign with the Holy Spirit. The Four Givings help you realize that you are the miracle."

"But how will I know if it's working?"

"By how you feel, your feelings are your guides. They tell you to what extent you are connected to your Infinite Source, as well as to what extent you are in alignment with your desire. We all have desires because we want to fulfill them – and feel good! But let me tell you something — success in life has little or nothing to do with the stuff you accumulate! Success can only be gauged by the joy you feel. Remember what I said about the Son of God and how everyone is a son or daughter of God? Knowing this, being this – that's the miracle! Fear, worry, hate, jealousy, or anger, they all appear to break that connection, and you do not feel good – you feel terrible! We're all constantly transmitting waves of energy, either good or bad. We're receiving it too, in invisible waves, or in the form of physical matter. When emotions are strong, whether you feel good, or bad, your desire is strong. When emotions are weak, your desire is also weak. When your emotions make you feel good, whether they are strong or weak, you are allowing the fulfillment of your desire. When your emotions make you feel bad, whether they are strong or weak, you are restricting the fulfillment of your desire. You're always creating. That's why you must always pay attention to how you're feeling. In every moment, you must pay attention to your emotions. They'll tell you if you're letting the good in, or pushing it away. The Four Givings will align your will with God's will. Then miracles can happen."

"The Four Giving, huh?" James wanted to get to the bottom line — fast! – before this miraculous man was no longer available to him.

"Yes, The Four Givings."

Chapter 9

JAMES COULD HEAR MUSIC coming from behind him. He turned to look, and found the source of the music to be a nearby boom box. Someone had left it in the middle of a wooden seat all by itself. Standing on top of the boom box was a small finch with a bright yellow belly. Good Vibrations, a song by the Beach Boys just finished playing and the next song softly started. To James, everything felt like a dream. Here he was in the middle of a leafless tree-lined park, on a gray winter day, when suddenly appeared this luminescent bird rolling its head from side to side in time to the music. Kids with skateboards were lined up on the two-foot granite wall. One boy was standing in the middle of the flowerbed, leaning next to a tree. James quickly looked in the other direction, trying to find the owner of the boom box. No one seemed to be around that area of the park. The music was familiar. It was a song from the band 'Styx'.

> *Every night I say a prayer in the hope that there's a heaven*
> *And every day I'm more confused as the saints turn into sinners.*
> *All the heroes and legends I knew as a child*
>   *have fallen to idols of clay*
> *And I feel this empty place inside, so*
>   *afraid that I've lost my faith.*

Show me the way, show me the way.
Take me tonight to the river
And wash my illusions away.
Show me the way.

Charlie started picking his guitar to the melody of the song. When it ended, his fingers moved seamlessly into what sounded to be a classical piece of music. James tried to place the familiar piece, but could not recognize it. The song was Pachelbel's "Canon in D Major." The scent of jasmine filled James' nose.

"Now, tell me more about these forgiving? Tell me more about that! I can get rich off of it?"

His friend sighed patiently. "The Four Givings. And yes, you can prosper beyond the riches of Job. The Four Givings have been handed down from the beginning of time. Miraculous wonders appeared in the land of Ethiopia where its four keys were practiced in all nations. It is said that King Solomon built his empire based on these keys. The four keys unlock the secret whereby miracles are created."

"Do you mean like unexplainable things happening in our personal lives? Or do you mean miracles like Jesus performed of global magnitude?"

James's question hung in the air as his friend continued playing. "Is there a difference?" he finally asked.

James thought for a second but could not find an answer.

The Rasta-man tried to clarify. "With The Four Givings, fear and hate naturally subside to make way for creation and understanding. Appreciation and praise overcome envy and jealousy. Guilt and judgment give way to peace and acceptance. Covetousness and greed dissipate, bowing to Thy Self. Nothing and everything cannot coexist. To believe in one is to deny the other. Damnation is nothing and creation is everything. Where light enters darkness, the darkness is no more."

James let out a long whistle of appreciation. "Wow, dude you're deep! This is just like what I've been reading – that there are only two emotions, fear and love. And they say that one can't be there if the other one is. I keep coming across the idea that fear is the opposite of love, but doesn't fear have to be present for love to exist, to balance the world so it's in harmony? You know, just like they say, we need to love one another but also fear God."

James had grown tired of standing and now found himself seated one step lower than his new teacher. At the feet of the Master, he thought, in a mixture of wonderment and odd apprehension.

The man chuckled. "You have earnest intent, but you are misguided. A Course in Miracles tells us that God is not the author of fear. You are. The opposite of fear is not love. Faith and understanding are the opposites of fear. You fear something until you learn to understand it, but it doesn't mean you have to love it. Faith is the opposite of fear. But love is whole onto itself. There is no opposite of love. It is whole onto itself. It is harmony without opposite balance. It is all. Love is God's presence."

"I don't get what you mean." James scratched his head.

"God sees us only in grace, in service, in charity, in appreciation, in creation, in understanding, in acceptance, in peace, and in joy. Jesus asked when He was on the cross, 'Why, Father have you forsaken me?' thinking that God had turned His back. But God does not see sin or suffering, which is why He did not see Jesus on the cross. In the presence of God, there is no sin; there is no shame, no suffering…" the Rasta-man trailed off.

"Hey, but what about fearing God, Judgment Day, and all that stuff?"

"So, you believe that your God is a vengeful God, needing obedience? Do you believe that God continues to create us, knowing that the majority of us are already condemned to hell even before birth?"

That does sound kind of ridiculous, James thought. And yet, isn't that what all the priests, ministers, nuns, and Sunday school teachers had said? Even the Pope agreed! Who were they to think otherwise?

"Going back to what you said earlier, what did you mean when you said I am the author of fear?"

"When we know that God is present with us, we are at one with Him and the world. To be holy is to be indebted to the whole of humankind. As Lucifer fell from the kingdom of heaven, as Adam partook of the 'forbidden fruit,' your conscious mind was born. It is known as the ego. There are three parts of your mind — the subconscious, the conscious, and the Omni-conscious. The subconscious is powered and directed by either the conscious mind, meaning the ego, or the Omni-conscious mind, which is the Holy Spirit. The subconscious only does what it is directed to do, whether by the ego or the Holy Spirit. The conscious mind is the mortal, carnal mind, the ego. The Omni-conscious mind is the Holy Spirit. When your present mind is the Omni-conscious mind, the Holy Spirit is thinking, Christ enters the body, and you become aware once again that you are connected to God. In the marriage of the soul and the Holy Spirit, Christ embodied, God and you become one. At that point all ideas are of perfection, and you possess the power and dominion over all created things. At that point, miracles begin to manifest. Judgment Day and Hell were born of your conscious mind, or ego. We sit on our thrones of life, every day judging what is right, what is wrong. Don't you see —we condemn others, but mainly ourselves, to damnation! Hell is described as the burning, weeping, and gnashing of teeth of irredeemable sinners. Isn't that how we feel most of the time? Our heart burns, our stomach churns, we wake up with our teeth sore, we cry. That is our hell on earth, don't you think?"

"So you're saying that religion is wrong?" James asked, trying to gloss over his own burning belly and sore teeth.

"The words are usually right. But the interpretation is wrong. All religions hold that their God is the real and best God, and that anyone holding different beliefs is an infidel — that is, a person who lacks faith and, by extension, is an enemy."

"Huh ... So going back to the, what did you call them, The Four Givings, how can I get these four keys to create my own miracles, to have health, abundance, prosperity, all that?"

"Sure, you can create all of that for yourself. By the four keys, enlightenment is reached. The Four Givings are nothing more than Atonement. Through Atonement, fear, guilt, judgment, and greed are removed, like locks, and Nirvana is reached." For just a moment, the speaker looked as if he were already there.

"Huh? What about hate? Don't we need to remove that too?"

"Hate is actually nothing more than compressed fear, did you know that? The ego's emotion of fear is the basis for all other insane emotions, including greed, hatred, anger, worry, and guilt. Why do we hate others? Why do others hate us?"

"Because, we're afraid of them and because they're afraid of us?" James knew he had the right answer.

"Yes!"

James's critical faculty began to kick in. "But if these keys have been around for so long. why isn't everyone using them? Most people would do anything to get what they want!"

"That's a great question, my friend! You see, the bearer of the keys is held accountable! To create miracles for one, you must create for all. You must use the keys every single day, everywhere, and for all. The bearer becomes the debtor to all. Are you ready for that responsibility? Do you understand the responsibility?"

James sensed that this was the pivotal moment, but all he could honestly muster was an "Um…"

He looked around to see who was watching. The boys were still skateboarding, shoppers crisscrossed through the park, couples snuggled to keep warm. The wooden seat was empty. The boom box was gone.

"Well, I'm confident that –"

"Confidence is of the ego. As A Course in Miracles so wisely puts it, 'The ego tries to exploit all situations into forms of praise for itself in order to overcome its doubts.'"

"Say what? Come again? What was that?"

"'The ego tries to exploit all situations into forms of praise for itself in order to overcome its doubts.' But what you must raise is your awareness of the presence of God. Our goal is not to bring wealth to one, but to bring wealth to all. We want everyone to feel love, joy, and peace, all to have comfort, warmth, and security, all to have food, shelter, and abundance. For this to happen, we must accept and understand all. To accept everyone is to know love, joy, and peace. By removing your fear of others, you will remove fear from others. That is how to find heaven. And the way to remove fear from others is by serving them. Not by condemning them. Not by killing them. To end hunger is simple — feed the hungry. To end war is simple— serve your enemy with acceptance of their differences, their cultures, and their fears. We all crave peace. We all need love. But we are scared of each other. Follow your intuition. It is God talking! The object of life is to see clearly the good in all and remove all pictures and projections of evil. If you are afraid, you are giving in to the belief in two powers, good and evil, instead of abiding in the One Power. God is absolute. There can be no opposing power. Face an unpleasant event without fear, and it becomes a non-event, falling away of its own weight."

"But how can that be?" James wanted to know. It flashed through his mind that perhaps he'd never faced a challenge without fear.

"Through miracles created by unlocking your soul so that love may grow." The teacher made it sound simple.

On the surface, it appeared that James neither heard nor understood his new friend, whose name, he soon learned, was Charlie. But the words sunk deep into his soul. Charlie was not talking to James's mind; he was talking to James's heart. James glanced over and saw that the group of young boys was still skateboarding on the park sidewalk. One boy shoved the other off his skateboard, pushing him over the brick flowerbed and short iron railing into an island of dead flowers and grass. The kids were out there in the subzero temperature with just shirts on, as if they were on the beach. James began to shiver just looking at them. Charlie stopped playing his guitar and leaned forward over his instrument, edging his seat to the tip of the concrete step. His eyes focused with laser-like intensity.

"If you choose wisely, all abominations will cease. You choose. That's right. Not even the angels of heaven have the power to choose. But you do. You chose love when you were saying your Namaste to the people in the street, but as soon as you experienced ego, you chose that it would not work. Choose to believe and it will materialize. Solidifying thought into matter is a natural process, even though we believe sometimes that it's a miracle. Maybe you are not ready to accept the responsibility of The Four Givings."

"No, no, I'm ready. I'm ready. Tell me, please. I believe we can change the world if we try." James's awkward embarrassment had changed to a sincere resolve. He didn't understand everything, but he really wanted to act on what he did know.

"Good!" roared Charlie. "Then you are ready for the first test!"

"What test?"

"Yes, it's the first key, the first of The Four Givings. Listen from your soul and you will find your spirit. Music that is so powerful is that way not because of the notes but the gap of silence between the notes. Think of the most powerful song you know, one with a triumphal kind of ending. As the last note rings into space, the silence sets in. At that moment you feel the climax, the power, the awe, the beauty, the message, and the sensation. You feel the eternity. To live in harmony and balance is to live in the moment of the silence, the space, the clearing of the mind. How do we think today? We see our happiness, our salvation, as always being in the future. We owe our guilt and regrets to past failures. We spend hours on fearful fantasies of nonexistence. But we seem to overlook the most precious time of all. We forget about the moment we are in, the "right now." Right now doesn't depend on someone else. It doesn't depend on your spouse or that soul mate. Why do we think that we must wait for the riches of the kingdom, when the hand of God is reaching down and touching us right now? If you are willing to take a moment, I can teach you in a moment. All religions have their own particular belief about it. All spiritual pilgrims seek it. The Christians call it, " "being born again." They say that to be saved or born again, you must surrender your will to God by asking Christ to come into your heart and be your personal lord and savior. That is what they say will guarantee you salvation, your key to heaven."

James thought back to the time when he accepted Christ as his savior. He was eighteen years old and could still remember the feeling when, in that instant, the Christ entered his heart.

It seemed like enlightenment, Nirvana. He felt that all his cares had been washed away.

"I remember when I was saved," James said in a far-away tone, "when I confessed that I was a sinner and that Christ was my savior. The feeling was overwhelming. It was a feeling of Nirvana."

"Ah, Nirvana! The place of Miracles. Yes, to be saved and to feel heaven in an instant is to accept the Christ. It is your connection to God. The problem is, though, that even after we accept the Christ, are guaranteed heaven, and our guilt and sins are washed away. But we are also taught to fear God and to judge others. We misinterpret the message. Jesus said that we can do all things, and even more than He did, through Christ. Not through the man named Jesus, through by the living Christ that was in Jesus, and us all. 'I can do all things through Christ that strengthens Me.' He taught that to reach heaven and to live with God, one must live through the Christ. Have you noticed that sometimes Jesus is referred to as Jesus Christ, and other times only as Jesus? For example, in the story about Jesus becoming angry at the moneychangers in the Temple and throwing over tables of contraband, how is he referred to? He is referred to as Jesus. Not the Christ. Not Jesus Christ. God's will is for all of us to live in Christ at all times. To let the Holy Spirit guide us. It's the way to heaven, the way God communicates with us. God is not vengeful, and knows no judgment. The only judging god is our puny ego-god, as we decide each day whether to live in hell or heaven. Most of us judge and condemn all day long. But God's will is that we are to live our lives wholly in Christ. Notice "live" is the backwards spelling of 'evil.' And that backwards-living ego is what projects the evil, so-called, all around. There are times when the Christ cannot be perceived because the environment is so powerfully negative. Jesus knocked over the tables because he was angry."

To make his point, Charlie made a ferocious face and raised

his guitar over his head, as if he were about to bring it down on James.

"So Jesus wasn't Jesus Christ all of the time?" James wondered, smiling.

"Well, apparently the Christ was not in Him when He had to stand up for the oppressed, against the occupiers and Pharisees. You can search in the Bible and you will notice when he is not referred to as Jesus Christ or 'The Christ'. It's when he's confronting the scribes, or the Pharisees, or the moneychangers in the Temple — the evildoers, and it is always to defend the poor and oppressed. It is our godly duty to emulate Jesus by always standing up for what is right; Our problem is that we live without the Christ throughout most of our waking days. We condemn, sometimes in the most subtle of ways, everyone, including ourselves. And it's our own ego-fabricated guilt that's the root of our condemnation. When you meet others, you decide to be their judge or their savior. With Christ vision from within, you raise the other from their attachment to sin and guilt by seeing their True Self, lifting them into the light, and helping to restore their vision of The One."

"Shouldn't we fight our enemies? Is that so?" Charlie deadpanned. "If you think you must stand up to fight, so be it. But ask yourself: Is it God's will, or your own?"

"You should always follow Jesus by living your life in God's presence, through Christ."

James thought about the question but could not find an answer to justify his position. His thoughts were interrupted by a man walking by, yelling at the top of his lungs so that all could hear. "In five months, I will be coming for your soul. In five months, you will be mine!" James turned his head to see the man, but the self-proclaimed Lucifer could not be found in the crowd. The rhetoric faded as the man marched on.

"I am ready to accept the first key," said James with sincere reverence.

"Okay, "Charlie began sweetly. "If you think you are ready, than I shall tell you. The first key, the First Giving, is called the Giving of the Mind. You see, all attitudes are ego-based. By giving up the ego, you become aware of your connection to God, through your Holy Spirit, Christ in body. In that moment, all fear, guilt, and judgment cease to exist because the ego and spirit do not know each other."

"What? The Giving of the Mind — what does that really mean?"

"It means that you let the Holy Spirit think for you by letting go of the thoughts of the day. It is living in the moment, in Christ, with God. It is seeing beyond the physical appearance of others and acknowledging their Christ within."

"But how will I know when I have let go of my ego?" This isn't coming with an instruction manual, James wryly observed.

"The best way to describe it comes again from A Course in Miracles. It says that man's vision is fear while God's vision is love. The fear is our own invention; the love was given to us. When you meet someone and you see the God within them, then you are in spirit. See all brothers as sinless and Christ will rise in your vision of them."

"Namaste," James said for at least the tenth time that day.

"Namaste. Yes, I and I."

"So if I clear my mind and live in the moment, my ego, the devil, will be gone and Christ will enter?"

"Yes. One word activates the forces to create any condition in your life. God is waiting for you to take that first step. 'Draw nigh unto God and He will draw nigh unto you.' Inner silence lets you listen for God's voice. The Grace of God will fall upon you. Those who have lived in poverty and illness could have easily turned to faith, and received a perfect response to any need. In the Divine Mind, there is neither time nor space; therefore, the word instantly reaches its destination. Just one word of faith can turn sickness into harmony, meagerness to opulence — just one word."

James tensed, as if his lucky number were about to be drawn. "What is the word?"

"The word is Christ," Charlie said simply. "The Christ within brings comfort and surplus."

"Christ? I guess it does make you feel good."

"Remember, 'Whatever ye ask the Father, in Christ's name, it will be given unto you.' The Christ in each man is his own redemption. The Christ within, made in God's image, has never failed, and never known sickness or sorrow. It is the resurrection and the life of each man. All power is given to man, through right thinking, to establish his heaven on earth in the wink of an eye. 'Be ye transformed by the renewing of your mind.' Clear your mind. Everyone can choose the Holy Spirit in their mind, to fill their body with Christ and be connected to God. But everyone also has the devil – better known as the ego — in their mind, and that is where majority of us dwell. But if you can master this gift, you will raise yourself and help raise your brothers out of hell and into everlasting light, just by Christ's presence in you. It is what we all must do to save this world. Look beyond the body and the possessions of others to see the light within them, so they may be healed. Your vision of the Christ within them will raise their awareness of the light. The ego limits its vision of others to the body. And by limiting your vision to exteriors, you compete, and compare, based on appearances. The ego denies the gift that all other people have to offer you— their Holy Spirit, their Christ within. The Holy Spirit's vision of others draws forth the spirit within them, extending their rays, brighter than the sun, to God. All men in a holy moment can be God in manifestation. At that moment their vision of all others is divine, seeing their oneness with them. We are all one. You will only receive that which you give. Your thoughts, words, and acts boomerang back to you with pinpoint accuracy. The Christ within you is your Redeemer and Salvation from all inharmonious events. You can only be what you see yourself to be, and only attract what you see yourself attracting. You always get just what you desire. When you let go of your ego's will, you invite the Holy Spirit to work through you."

Charlie picked up his guitar and began to pick out yet another familiar piece. A security guard emerged from the cream-colored wooden doors. He took one look at Charlie on the steps, and then retreated back into the water tower fortress.

"Let's talk about now—right here, right now." The way Charlie said the word now charged the word with a meaning and a feeling that James had never before experienced. "You and I are experiencing the present moment — now! You are inviting the Holy Spirit into your consciousness, in communion with God, and accepting the body of Christ. In this moment you are grateful, you are forgiven, you are sinless, you see no sin, you see no past, you are joyously serving the universe — 'uni' meaning 'one,' and 'verse' meaning 'song.' There is but 'one song.' In this moment, you have the power to create, harmoniously. You can only create in the NOW. If you are not living in the moment, damnation is bred and ego is fed."

"How will I know if I am letting the Holy Spirit in, instead of my ego?" James pressed. "How will I know when I'm in communion with God, accepting the body of the Christ?"

"Feel your emotion. How do you feel? When you are feeling happy, joyous, and at peace, you are in communion with God. Any other feeling is demigod."

"That sounds too easy." It seemed to James that he himself, and just about everyone he knew, often felt very happy when they were doing something considered "sinful" and divorced from God. But then again, he thought, there are the hangovers, the excess pounds, the regrets... Pleasure isn't joy."

"Behold your role within the universe!" Charlie suddenly exhorted. James wondered how all these pearls of wisdom could roll off his tongue at the same moment that perfectly timed and modulated notes vibrated at his fingertips. "Let me quote once again from A Course in Miracles. 'To each one God has allowed the grace to be a savior to all the holy ones... When first you look upon a brother as he looks upon you, you see the mirror of yourself in him. In this single vision, you see the face of Christ and you understand that you look on everyone as you behold this one brother. For there is light where there was darkness before, and now the veil is lifted from his sight. The veil across the face of Christ, the fear of God, the love of guilt and death, are just different names for the same error.' It's saying that what appears to be a divide between you and your brother is kept there by your illusion of separation. The ego needs that separation to maintain its special ness. Ego always wants to rule – have you noticed that in your own life, James?"

"Uh...Yeah," James allowed, astounded that Charlie had not only read his mind but answered his question. Charlie started singing while James patiently waited in the cold for more instruction. He definitely recognized this tune; it was The Grateful Dead's "Ripple," one of his favorites.

> *Would you hear my voice come through the music,*
> *Would you hold it near as it were your own?*
>
> *It's a hand-me-down, the thoughts are broken,*
> *Perhaps they're better left unsung.*
> *I don't know, don't really care*
> *Let there be songs to fill the air.*

Ripple in still water,
When there is no pebble tossed,
Nor wind to blow.

Reach out your hand if your cup be empty,
If your cup is full may it be again.
Let it be known there is a fountain
That was not made by the hands of men.

There is a road, no simple highway,
Between the dawn and the dark of night,
And if you go no one may follow,
That path is for your steps alone.

Ripple in still water,
When there is no pebble tossed,
Nor wind to blow.

But if you fall you fall alone,
If you should stand then who's to guide you?
If I knew the way I would take you home.

After Charlie had sung the final verse, he continued to pick the melody until the last note faded in the wind. He then petted his cat and continued the lesson.

"I'll say it again, my friend. Just live in the moment, Christ within, fellowshipping with God. We think that to live in Christ, we must sacrifice. Why would God have you sacrifice to be with him? He sees you as perfect and without sin. You can live with God simply by surrendering your thoughts to Him. It takes but a moment. It's the moment, the moment of now. Why wait for death to be with God and receive from God? The moment of creation, in which man expresses his inner spirit by way of music, art, planting, singing, dancing – even just sincerely communicating with another human being, as we are here — that moment is his or her destiny. It's this wondrous event, when you invite God to see through your eyes, and you and He together feel, and are the creation. The idea is the birth of any creation. It is never a moment of struggle or labor. And in this holy moment you reach Wholeness, a perfect circle of Divine Love, resonating in peace and joy."

James noticed that his usual underlying tension was gone. He felt clear-headed, serene, and even happy. He needed to put it all into words that he could take away with him when they finally parted. Finding those words felt suddenly effortless, like the divine creation of which Charlie had spoken. "I think we all dream of how great life will be when we get that house, or car, or job, or vacation, or physique. We're always looking to some object or situation that we believe will make us happy in the future. But that thing or circumstance is available right now if we surrender to it, without giving up a thing."

James continued, "I think I am beginning to understand. This moment is where we are. We choose how we feel through our thoughts. We choose to either love it or hate it." James was happy with his words which were not, he knew, his own.

"And if you choose to love it all, just let go of your ego! Let go of any guilt, fear, or judgment. And in that moment, bask in God's love! To love and to be happy with whomever and however you are, and to love others unconditionally, just as you love yourself, — that is God! Pretty simple, eh?"

"Well, no! I have to admit, some days that's just about impossible for me to do!" An image of his stepson, lazing in James's leather recliner, beer in hand, flashed before his eyes. "Sometimes I start off having a good day but then some jerk seems to get in the way of that. For instance, there was this one time in particular when my stepson suddenly lit up in the car while I was riding with him. I was gagging on the smoke before he finally noticed and put it out. So what was I supposed to do – stick my head out the window like a dog and think 'Love, love?' "

"Your stepson was only acting on what he knows. It's all a matter of how you perceive the event. Right now, you can choose to be the angel, the judge, or the demon. Be careful of your motive for action, James! Ask if it is coming from fear or faith. 'Choose ye this day that ye will serve.' Do you serve fear or faith? For example, you can only accept disease while vibrating at the same rate as disease. Fear slows men down to the same frequency as disease and near-death. Any disease is the product of carnal thought or your ego. Disease does not exist in the Divine Mind. The Holy Spirit makes one whole. Disease is the effect of man's vain imagination. But love vibrates at the speed of light. The walls of Babylon will come crumbling down with one moment of love! Real love is selfless service. Understanding is the opposite of fear; love is free from fear. Love, being whole, leaves no room for fear. It releases without expectation of return. It is whole. It doesn't need love to be reciprocated. That is true love! Love's joy is in the joy of giving. Love is God in manifestation. Love is light. Follow the path of Love and all things are brought to you with abundance. God is love and God is supply. Follow the path of fear, hate, selfishness, and greed, and the supply vanishes."

James wasn't sure he had caught all of that. "Is this from a certain religion, like Rastafarian or something?" Maybe the Beatles were right – maybe all you do need is love, he thought, as the song wafted through his head.

"Religion is man's interpretation of God. Spirituality is man's experience of God. All that really matters is love!" Once again, he had picked up on James's thoughts. "Think of it, James! When love reigns supreme, countries will drop their arms and tear down their walls. Fear will be no more, and heaven will come to earth. Countries have boundaries.

Governments have fear. Those are the walls of Babylon. We are all responsible. Our mission is to relieve all suffering. To end hatred, we must eradicate suffering. Remember, always give energy to the solution of good, and never give energy to the problem."

"What do you mean?"

"To feel love in all moments is heaven. But to feel love at this moment is the Christ. Emerge from your chrysalis, James! Burst free from ego to God in a single instant! That is what God wants from all of us, so we can act and change the world. The disheartened are useless to God. But only the ego can be disheartened. Your ego is nothing more than habitual beliefs and preconceptions about yourself and others. As you come closer to your brothers, you approach God. As you withdraw from your brothers, God will seem distant from you. Open your heart. Let Christ in. Choose spirit instead of ego. Proclaim, 'I am here now with God' and instantly, your sins are washed away. You're in the moment, with the Holy Spirit feeding your subconscious, and you're Christ in body. All past errors are forgotten, so there is no need for guilt."

"Sounds kind of like praying." James had found himself praying a lot these days, but never in the way Charlie was describing. Most often he was asking for guidance, inspiration, and a change in what he perceived as bad luck. Usually it was he, James, who was at the center of these requests. Charlie knew how James prayed. Today, though, his prayer had reached out beyond himself, attracting Charlie's attention and touching his heart.

"Most people pray with words, but they don't pray with their heart and soul. If you need a miracle, pray with your feelings. Really pray with your feeeelings! If you are sad, and need to pray about something that is hurting you, then feel how you will feel when the bad is taken away. Feel the instant of the miracle as you pray! As Jesus prayed, 'Our Father, who art in heaven, hallowed be thy name. Thy kingdom come, thy will be done on earth as it is in heaven.' Think about those words, 'Thy kingdom come, thy will be done. On earth as it is in heaven.' He isn't saying you'll have to wait till death to enter the kingdom! He is saying that when you join God, your will is equal to the will of God, and then earth will be like heaven. It is quite a thought, eh?"

"Communion with God in a moment will bring heaven to earth?"

"You can be in communion with God all the time, just as you were as a child. We grow into adulthood with adult fears imbedded in us. Think back to when you were a child. When you ran, jumped, and laughed. When you were painting, or helping your mother to bake a cake. When you were laughing with friends and building with blocks. If you can let yourself become a child again, through the moments of the day, you will notice definite differences in your life. Your life will flow easier, worries will give way to joy, and your desires will be fulfilled."

Charlie raised his head from the guitar and looked deeply into James's eyes. "Do you want to feel your Christ within, your connection with God? To feel love at this moment is Christ, the change from ego to God in an instant. Do you want to feel your Christ within, your connection with God?"

James caught his breath. "Do it right now? How? But... yes. Yes, I do."

"Breathe. Breathe. First you need to wash away your sins."

"But how can I...?" All that came to mind was Jesus on the Cross, and young James, beating his breast while reciting The Act of Contrition.

"Easy. You do it by releasing all your worries of tomorrow, all your guilt about the past, and all negative judgment, and observe through God's eyes. Breathe. Feel the moment.

Clear your mind. Think of nothing and just experience the moment. Concentrate on your breath as a wave coming in and then going out against a sandy beach. Let go of your mind. To let go of your ego is to think of nothing. Surrender your thoughts. Surrender your ego to God. Repeat to yourself, 'I surrender. I surrender. Christ, come into my heart. Heal me. I surrender to Christ. I surrender. I am letting go. I surrender to God.'"

James stood up and closed his eyes then repeated the statements softly. Charlie watched his pupil standing before him, mouthing words that were nearly inaudible. He could see James's shoulders relax as he exhaled a large, billowing cloud of breath.

"Listen and feel with a clear mind," his instructor went on. "The only thought is the moment. See the beauty in all. Feel your presence in the moment. Listen to the sounds of silence. Feel from the heart and soul. No judgment. No guilt. No worries or plans for tomorrow. Let go of all burdens. Surrender. Feel in this moment the joy in your heart, the peace in your mind. Feel love. Feel the present state of love. Feel the Holy Ghost in you. Christ in body. Feel your connection to God…"

James opened his eyes. A sense of relief and lightness came over him. The air was fresh and crisp. Everything seemed brighter. Charlie's smile was even more radiant. James looked up at the large bricks of the water tower. He slowly raised his head upward toward the sky, seeing the tower's pinnacle. It was beautiful. He stared, feeling his breath, letting go of thought. All the tension seemed to drip from his fingers. Instantly, he felt it in his heart. He was overwhelmed by the presence of love and felt no apprehension. A soft vibration hummed in his heart. Waves of bliss washed over him. It felt perfect. Pulsations of love, peace, and joy rippled through his whole being.

Charlie's cat raised its head and eyed James boldly.

"Look who's watching you!" Charlie laughed. "He is feeling it. He is purring louder, hear that? Now, feel all the vibrations around you. Look for the Holy Spirit in others. That is when you will know your brotherhood. God's only son is oneness."

A ray of sunshine shot through the sky. The clouds softly broke, revealing patches of blue. James could feel the presence of God. He softly yielded all thought. He brought his head down and looked at all the people everywhere, walking in all directions. A jolt of fear instantly hit his body. The feeling of contentment and joy was gone. Recognizing the interloper as only himself, James ardently whispered, "I surrender my ego to God. Christ, fill my heart. I surrender all." The World of Brightness came back instantly! He observed everyone around him. He became a witness, instead of a victim, feeling the people passing by. An old lady smiled as she walked toward him. James could feel her love inside. Taking another deep breath he thought, Let go. Feel the moment. He gazed around, observing everyone, the young couple feeling angry, fighting the cold; the two ladies complaining about a rude sales clerk; the skateboarder, definitely living life in the moment as he popped his board up into the air, twirled around, and came down with both feet back on the board. Looking at all his fellow humans, James noticed something he'd never seen before. He saw beyond their physical form and right into the sparkle of their eye, all the way to their very soul, it seemed. It was like he knew them. He did not see them complaining of the cold, or the prices in the stores. He saw their trueness, their light, their Holy Spirit within. He could feel all the different waves of emotion without changing his own feelings. He felt euphoric. He looked back at the elderly woman and smiled, as he felt compassion and total love for her. She looked in his eyes too, and smiled. Her light became brighter.

James inhaled deeply, then slowly exhaled, letting go of all vestiges of thought. His breath and the feeling of completeness were all he was aware of. For just a flash of time, a vision came to him. He was a wave of energy, in an ocean of energies. Some glowed, most didn't. He realized oneness with all. An unconditional love for all — it was what God feels. James looked down at the cat. Its purr was creating a soft, gentle ripple, its heartbeat blending in perfect rhythm. James looked upon Charlie with astonishment. Flowing from him were three beautiful, colorful waves of light. Charlie's singing and guitar playing created an aural wave, his breath projected a long soothing wave, and the rhythm of his heart emitted a slow pulse. James looked out at the wave of people. He noticed that a lot of waves from the people were choppy and angry. Each person generated two waves, one from their breath and the other from the beat of their hearts. Most people created very fast waves with their shortness of breath and the fast patter of their heart. Others sent out beautiful, soft, loving waves. The skateboarder shot out a strong and exciting energy wave, traveling some distance. The elderly lady manifested warm waves of purple, blues, and yellows. Her heart seemed strong. It gave James an overwhelming sense of joy and peace, just from observing her.

For that tiny sliver of time, no longer than the flash of a lightning bolt, James became a witness, an observer of the connection between all. Each person struck him as a single wave in an immense ocean. As angry waves of people passed by, James also noticed that Charlie and the cat's wave of gentleness, compassion, and love would briefly melt the stormy waves of fear and anger for a brief moment; their waves would not be as choppy once their 'space' had been touched by Charlie's presence. James watched people walking by, one by one, and how Charlie's wave of love and spirit, would uplift everyone. If the person was happy, their wave became stronger, happier, and more beautiful. As angry-faced people passed, their waves would smooth out even if they never looked at Charlie. James looked out in the distance at the ocean of humans. Maybe because of the cold, or the heavy thoughts of the day on their minds, he could see the ocean was stormy. But within the sea of fear and anger, he could find gentle, colorful pools of sincerity and warmth in various individuals.

At that instant, the skateboarder rode his board across the long, two-foot-high cement wall that enclosed the dead flowerbed. Just before the end of the ledge, he launched into the air and performed a back flip while the skateboard continued to adhere to his feet, landing on all four wheels with its rider still on it. At that moment, the whole ocean of waves ebbed into a large ripple. Everyone seemed to look over and forget about their problems for a second. The skateboarder's friends ran over, hugging and high-fiving their newfound hero. The wave became absolutely calm. Everything seemed connected. And in that instant everyone and everything became a full body of light. Then, just as quickly as it had settled, the block of light became solid, disappearing into the ocean of human waves, only to surge back up as it was before.

Charlie was again playing his guitar, and loudly singing Bob Marley's "Get Up, Stand Up."

The Almighty God is a living man...

The lyrics were striking James with completely new meaning. The air smelled like a crisp lemon. The cold was replaced by infinity. His breath became the wind, so that when he exhaled, the wind blew strong against his back. When he inhaled, the wind changed directions. Everything around him was beautiful. Fear was replaced with awareness. The skateboarder, in an equal state of nirvana, rode his chariot with one leg in the air, horizontal to the ground, as he stretched forward like a bird. James, without thought, mimicked the athlete. He stretched out forward, extending his hands as wings, as he raised his back leg. At that moment, from a bird's-eye view, in the park-like square, with leafless trees, were three men and one woman – Charlie, James, the skateboarder, and the smiling elderly woman – living together in harmony as one. In less than one tick from a watch, the count fell by one.

"Hey, slick! What the hell are you doing?"

James came back to earth. The waves were gone. He saw as everyone stared in judgment, and he felt like a little boy who was ashamed. He lowered his leg. Keith stared at his brother, wondering if he was having a seizure. Charlie looked up at James's brother and laughed loudly, then smiled.

"Annette O'Toole," said Charlie, by way of greeting.

Keith looked down at the strange-looking man sitting on the steps with a guitar and cat. His jaw dropped. What in the hell was this?

"I'm freezing! C'mon, let's go back to the hotel," Keith urged, propelling his brother forward by the elbow.

Unaware of the revelation that had just taken place, and not even pausing to greet Charlie, Keith started to walk away. James wanted to stay, but obeyed like the little boy he used to be, following his older brother home from school. He turned back and looked at Charlie who had started playing another song. James whispered, "What are the other three keys?" No answer from the teacher on the steps.

"But what about the other three Givings?" he cried out loudly.

Keith turned back to his brother. James was five steps behind him, looking back at the Rastafarian guy.

"What's with you? Come on!" he said, baffled and annoyed.

James slowly walked away, trying to make eye contact with Charlie one last time. The song started to fade with each step until he could barely hear his friend's voice, drowned out by other voices. Charlie was still sitting next to his cat, singing another Bob Marley song.

Life is one big road with lots of signs,
So when you riding through the ruts, don't
*   you complicate your mind:*
Flee from hate, mischief, and jealousy!
Don't bury your thoughts; put your vision to reality, yeah!

All together now:
Wake up and live.

Charlie stopped strumming his guitar. James could not see the steps anymore, yet he could still hear Charlie's voice.

"Consciousness is the breath of God!" His voice seemed suddenly much nearer. "Take a moment and you will find the other three!"

James turned to face his brother, but, as he opened his mouth to speak, no words came; there seemed no way to explain the phenomenon. They walked briskly to the hotel, both not saying a word. Keith thought of the nameless soul outside of the coffee shop. James thought of the Rastafarian named "Charlie." A flashbulb went off in Keith's mind.

"Annette O'Toole! That's who played in the movie 48 Hours with Nick Nolte. I knew I'd eventually remember it!"

Chapter 10

BACK IN THE HOTEL room, Keith drew open the sheer white drapes to let in more natural light. James grabbed a couple cans of Heinekens from the honor bar. — he figured Keith could afford it — and handed one to his brother. Then, in unison, they both snapped their tabs. James's beer filled the top rim of the can with foam. Keith sat in the chair by the desk as James slurped up the suds from the top of the can before sitting down on the bed. He was eager to tell his brother all about his experience with Charlie. But as he began speaking about how he'd first noticed Charlie, he could tell that something was very wrong. He felt a strange weight in the room. Keith's eyes watered up with emotion. He lowered his head, supporting it with the palm of his hands, resting his elbows on his knees. A tear rolled down his check and his nose dripped. He quickly rubbed his upper lip with his wrist and headed for the bathroom. In the waning light, James hadn't noticed the tears. Keith found a fancy Kleenex box and pulled out yellow tissue. James could hear the nose-blowing, but thought nothing of it.

"Keith!" James called out, no longer able to contain himself. "I think I've found the answer! That Rastafarian playing guitar in the park, Charlie was his name."

Keith reappeared, wiping his nose and looking confused. "Who are you talking about?"

"I'm talking about that guy sitting on the steps at the historic water tower, playing the guitar."

"Where you were looking like a goof, posing as a statue?" Keith asked sarcastically.

"Yeah, that's right! When you came back from getting your coffee, it was the guy sitting on the steps, playing the guitar. He was teaching me about an ancient belief from Ethiopia called The Four Givings. Let me tell you, in an instant he took me to a state of pure love, joy, and peace. It was bliss! Everything disappeared, even with my eyes open. People disappeared and became vibrations. I mean, it lasted for a split second but it seemed like an eternity. Blocks of cement and buildings were still there because of their mass. But then when I let go even more, they disappeared. It was powerful! I felt God's presence. You know how people, religions, and books say that our lives are all an illusion? Turns out that our life really is a dream! I never believed it. But that moment made me think that maybe it is. Maybe there actually is another plane of reality. And it's almost like our real life, the real truth. The illusion of physical matter totally disappeared. We were all connected like waves in an ocean. We were all one."

James leaned toward Keith. He stared at him until he had his full attention. James noticed that his brother's eyes were glazed and puffy. He looked tired. James chose his words with care.

"We, I mean us as waves, we were all connected. It was like waves on an ocean."

"Then what happened?"

"I don't know. It was so beautiful and loving, but then I got freaked out when you showed up. It freaked me out and then it was gone. But I do know this: you can have complete enlightenment, right now. You can have everything that you ever dreamed of right now if you are willing. We think we know how to be successful and we think we have the answer to life

The Four Givings

but we don't know squat. All the answers were there. I can't put it together, yet, in thought. But it was like I was awakened for a second but also for an eternity. It was like we were all connected. Not by wires or protoplasm or anything like that — too limited. Almost like a puzzle. I felt connected. I saw everyone as... as they are supposed to be. I felt I knew what we are supposed to do. Why we are actually put on the earth. Charlie, this Rastafarian dude, said there are four ways to manifest miracles. To reach enlightenment there are four keys that will unlock your heart and, he said, that's when miracles will pour down. The keys are called The Four Givings.

"What are they?" Keith's sarcasm was still lingering.

"I don't know. I only have one of them. He showed me one of the keys but then you came up and I felt embarrassed. So, I left without getting the answer to the other three."

"Come on. You mean he showed you how to create a miracle in the short time while I was getting coffee? Yeah, right."

"Look, I'm serious. I've never been more serious in my life. There is something about this. It was easy. It was simple. But we have to find out what the other three keys are. The first of The Four Givings is called The Giving of the Mind. I don't know how to put it in words. I will, though. You want to try it? I think I remember…Here. Try sitting in a comfortable position. Let me see if I can remember."

"Wait. Let me get this straight. You say this Rasta guy taught you all this in the few minutes while I was getting coffee — this, what did you call it? The Giving of the Mind?"

"Listen to me. I got to remember this. What he said was that to feel love in all moments is heaven. But to feel love at this moment is Christ. Breaking free from the chrysalis is the change from ego mind to being filled with the Holy Ghost in an instant. You have to give up your ego and to allow your natural state, your true spirit, the Holy Ghost, to take over.

Then he asked me, 'Do you want to feel your Christ within, your connection with God?' He called it nirvana, the place of miracles. Charlie was saying the same thing that Jesus taught: that is, to reach the kingdom of heaven you must come through Christ. Remember how it says in the Bible 'I can do all things through Christ who strengthens me'? We are meant to have Christ in us at all times. We, as the judging God, decide every day and in every moment whether we're going to live in hell or heaven. We are to live our lives in Christ, which is to say, with Christ within us. The letting go, surrendering your ego to God, should be done daily if not hourly – or even every second, if need be! When you're filled with the Holy Ghost, only then can miracles happen. Christ in body, everywhere. For God is waiting to be received in an instant. Miracles will not only pour down upon you, they will sprinkle everyone you touch, and be felt around the world. By living in Christ, we can change our lives and other lives too, all over the world. The best way to understand is for you to try it and experience it."

Keith looked doubtful – maybe even a little bit scared.

"You want me to do this, right now? How?"

"You breathe. Just breathe. First, start taking deep breaths. Then you need to wash away your sins, your negative judgments, your guilt, your fear. Clear your mind. Let go of all your worries of the day."

"How do I do that?"

"By clearing your mind and living in the moment." James was surprised by his perfect recall. He'd been afraid he'd forget. "He called it 'atonement,' the letting go of your fear, your guilt, and your judgment. What will take its place are peace, bliss, and joy. Feel the moment."

Keith thought about the many judgments and aspersions he'd cast on his wife. He thought of the love between them.

He looked over to his brother, who was watching his every breath, then closed his eyes.

Sensing Keith's earnest willingness, James began. "Concentrate on your breath as a wave coming in and then going out. Let go of your mind. Let go of your thoughts. Surrender them to God. To let go of your ego is to think of nothing. Surrender to your true spirit. Ask for Christ to enter your heart. Clear your mind right now. Open your eyes without seeing. See the beauty in all. Feel your presence in the moment. Listen to the sounds of silence. Feel from the heart and soul. Let go. Feel at this moment the joy in your heart and the peace in your mind when you experience only the present moment. Go within. Feel the love within. Feel it. Feel the present state of love. Feel the God in you…Christ in body."

Keith looked into James's eyes. He cleared his mind and then…felt the moment.

"Repeat to yourself, 'I surrender. I surrender my ego. I surrender my sins. Christ comes into my heart.' Feel God's presence in the moment."

Keith raised his head upward toward the ceiling. He felt all the stress pour out of him. It was like a hundred pounds were lifted from his shoulders. His body tingled. For the first time in months he felt good, concentrating only on his breath, letting go of all thought.

Keith was whispering, "Let go. I surrender. I surrender to you, God. Fill me with the Holy Spirit. I hand my life over to you, my Lord. Wash away my sins. I need you. Save me. I surrender to you, God."

Instantly, he felt it, right there in his heart. It hummed in his heart! A feeling of bliss came over him. It felt perfect, like a pulsating wave of love, peace, and joy. He could feel vibrations within his body. For the first time in a very long time, he felt euphoric. Keith took another deep breath. The feeling of completeness was the only thing he was aware of. Bliss and unconditional love filled his heart, for he was in Spirit and Christ in body. It felt like…heaven.

"Rise, for I see the God in you." professed Keith.

"The Almighty God is a living man," James intoned reverently, just as Charlie had said but an hour ago.

There was a knock at the door. A voice on the other side of the door said, "Maid service." James looked around and noticed that the bed was unmade. They must want to clean the room, he thought. Keith came back to his ego. The blissful humming was gone. Sin had slithered back, guilt was grimacing, and judgment was regaining its foothold. James raised his voice to the door, asking the innocent intruder to come back in an hour.

"Did you feel it? Did you feel the presence, the love?" he asked.

"Not really." Keith said with a trace of longing in his voice. "How can you live in that state all the time? It's impossible."

"I don't know. But I think it's possible if you could let go of your ego, let go of all judgment, let go of fear, let go of guilt. I wonder what it would be like to live in joy, peace, and love. I guess it would be heaven! You would be at ease all the time – like Charlie is."

"Instead of being dis-eased," Keith put in bluntly.

"Yes. I like that. All I know is that I want you to be happy, and I don't think you are. Maybe that's why we all have the power of choosing how we'll be. They say that choice is the only power that the angels don't have. They must be exactly as they are, which is angelic, whereas we get to judge every day what is right and wrong for ourselves and choose what is best."

Keith stood and turned to the window. He looked past the cluster of buildings to the street below. Air blew up from the heater in the windowsill, warming his face. A tear welled in the corner of his eye. Keith was scared again. James watched his brother hunch over the window, his arms wrapped around his torso, as if hugging himself. The chair that Keith had just vacated cast a shadow against the wall next his silhouette. The image appeared as a condemned man carrying a cross.

"I'm dying," Keith told his brother.

"Yeah, I'm hungry too."

"Jim. Listen to me. No, I am really dying. I am sick."

"You know you really shouldn't say that! You know how powerful the words 'I am' are."

Keith turned from the window, his hands in both pockets, his head bowed. He struggled for the right words. James looked up at Keith and tried to read his mind. Keith raised his head. James could see the thin stream of a tear running down both cheeks. A shock of fear hit James in the heart. Fearful thoughts were exchanged without a sound. Keith opened his mouth to speak, his face a mask of anguish. James knew his brother was...

"I am dying. I am sick with colon cancer."

"How can that be? I mean..." James groped for words also.

"It's pretty far along. They want to start radiation and chemotherapy. But I don't think so. Not much quality of life, you know."

The room fell silent except for the sniffling of the brothers as they hugged. When the reaper knocks on your door, money and success don't mean a thing — only time becomes important, time spent with loved ones. Life is real. Death is real. Sickness is not an illusion. Or at least, that's how it seemed to Keith and James.

Chapter 11

DAY FELL QUICKLY INTO dusk. It occurred to James that Chicago always seems to be in a hurry to get dark in the evening than it does in Toledo. Keith opened the curtains further to let in any remnants of sunlight. A golden sunset poured through the window, illuminating the wallpaper. It looked very warm and beautiful, but little fingers of frost at the corners of the window let them both know it was actually freezing outside. After a good long cry and plenty of heavy talking and consoling, James went back to his room to get ready. They agreed not to talk about it anymore that night. Keith sat on the bed wrapped in his thoughts. Everything in the room seemed to be shining more brightly than before, as if illuminated from within. Enough sulking, he decided. Keith stood up and prepared for his shower.

The Italian Village restaurant was their unanimous choice, and after a quiet, ten-minute cab ride, they were there. With its old wine-cellar décor and book-thick wine list, the lower-level attracted the brothers, who were led to a table in a cozy corner. All through dinner, the conversation seemed implicitly restricted to small talk. No long philosophical discussions, nor any mention of the C word. It was after nine o'clock when they finished dinner. Outside the restaurant they flagged a cab and jumped in once again. James leaned up to the glass and told the driver a name of a bar on 43rd Street. The Middle Eastern man turned back and asked James to repeat the name, as if wishing not to hear. "Forty-third Street?" he asked incredulously.

"Yeah, that's right — the Checkerboard Club, on 43rd Street."

The driver hesitated for a moment, then flipped the meter. He looked back into the rearview mirror and then looked ahead, his brow deeply furrowed as he thought about the trip. Keith noticed the driver's apprehension.

"Where are we going?" he asked James.

"Checkerboard Club," James said matter-of-factly.

"What is the Checkerboard Club?" Keith asked, suddenly worried.

"The Checkerboard Club is an old blues club where Muddy Waters, Howlin' Wolf, and I think the Rolling Stones have played. Buddy Guy owned the Checkerboard before opening up Legends downtown."

"Sounds nice. So what's the big deal?"

"Well, it's kind of in a bad part of town — in the inner city, doncha know."

"You got to be kidding me?"

"Nope," answered James, doing his best Bogey tough-guy impersonation.

Keith looked back and saw the Chicago skyline behind them as they sped along the interstate, finally exiting at 43rd Street. The driver's eyes, which had grown to the size of silver dollars, flashed and darted in the mirror and all around. A mile down the road Keith recognized some buildings off to the left. They looked like depressed, run-down apartments.

"Don't those buildings look familiar?" Keith wondered.

"Yeah, you're right. There the ones from 'Good Times.' I think they're called Cabrini-Green."

"No, they're not," Keith corrected. "I think they tore those down on the north end of town."

"How do you know?"

James wiped the mist off the back passenger window. "It's them. There's J.J.!" James called out excitedly.

"Have you ever been to this Checkerboard Club?"

"No," said James, still affecting his tough-guy tone. "But I hear that if you can brave it, you'll hear some of the best electrified blues in Chicago. So I'm sure it's fine."

James peered forward, beyond the Plexiglas divider and salt-splattered windshield, out into the dimly lit street, looking for signs of a police car. He hoped this was a good idea. He saw only a man urinating against a building and sucking the remaining drops from a bottle, wrapped in a brown paper bag like a tight, wrinkled skirt. The driver cautiously pulled over to the curb in front of a white brick building. "The Checkerboard Club" was painted in faded colors on the side. As the driver hit the meter to total out the fare, reality set in for both Keith and James: they were being dropped off in the heart of the inner city. James paid and tipped. Without any acknowledgement or thanks, the driver tugged the wheel to the left until it made a screeching sound from the power-steering belt. Keith and James watched the green-and-white car spin wildly around in the middle of the street, then fly over a sewer grate and peel away. The street was wet and smelled of oil and burning rubber from the cab. The bar was the only oasis in sight. The sidewalks were deserted. They looked at the building, then back at each other.

"Come on, man," James urged. "Remember the secret to atonement."

"Right. When I walk in, I will give my wallet to the first guy I see."

They moved slowly for the door. As James reached for the handle, the door flew open. A massive man the size of Goliath, with a bald head like Isaac Hayes, looked down his shades at the two palefaces. James goggled at the size of the man's arm, filling the sleeve of his solid-gold suit jacket. The bouncer was dressed to the nines. He cleared his throat.

"Gentlemen, it is eight dollars apiece."

Keith gave the man a $20 dollar bill and received back four singles. Both immediately noticed that the bar was packed with black men and women; there wasn't one white face in sight. Walking farther down alongside the bar, they felt the stares of each person they passed. One man pivoted all the way around in his seat, regarding James with serious eyes while loudly sipping his cognac. Finally, they reached an open area to the left of the bar, which they discovered was where the band played. There was a small stage up front. The rest of the room was filled with black and red chairs, a few neon signs, and theatre lights hung from the ceiling, pointing toward the stage. The tables consisted of rows of narrow boards. As they entered the open room, they passed two groups of young college kids sitting at the wooden plank tables. A few of them were white, which made the brothers feel a little less conspicuous.

They found chairs against the wall under a display case. A waitress appeared right behind them as they sat down. She was very voluptuous, and with a kind face. "What do you gentlemen want to drink?"

"I'll take a Heineken." Keith was sticking with his familiar favorite.

"Budweiser," requested James.

James stretched up to look inside the display case and was delighted to find various memorabilia, including old pictures and a harmonica from Howlin' Wolf. Most amazing of all was a picture of Jimi Hendrix showing off his white right-handed Fender Stratocaster guitar, upside down. He leaned closer to see if it was signed when the beers arrived.

"Would you gentlemen like to start a tab?" the waitress inquired.

"That's fine," said Keith. "Do you need a credit card?"

"No," she replied with a small smile. "You look trustworthy."

"Thanks. What is your name?" Keith asked.

"Tamikka," she said. After she left, James pointed up at the picture of Hendrix in the display case. He leaned in closer so his brother could hear him.

"Do you see that picture of Jimi Hendrix?"

"Yes, but so what?"

"Notice how the guitar is a right-handed guitar, upside down. Hendrix was left-handed, and left-handed guitars were hard to come by, so he played it upside down. Hendrix restrung the guitar so that the thicker 'E' string was the first string on top. There's another famous blues guitarist named Albert King."

"You mean B.B. King," corrected Keith.

"No. Albert King. One of the three blues kings —Albert, B.B., and Freddie King. Anyway, Albert played with Hendrix and Janice Joplin at the Fillmore East night club. He was left-handed and played a right-handed guitar upside down, but he didn't restring it. So that means the thick E string was still at the bottom, and the little 'E' string was at the top."

"Wow! That is very interesting." It was hard for James to tell if Keith was being sincere or not.

James kept trying to engage his brother. "He did an album with Stevie Ray Vaughan."

"Oh. Well, that's good to know," Keith responded limply.

The musicians stepped up on the stage and grabbed their instruments. Each took a few minutes to warm up, playing little licks and riffs. Then one of the men grabbed his sax and an elegant-looking older black woman with blonde hair stepped up to the microphone. The colored lights hit her sparkling red dress as she nodded, signaling that she was ready. James recognized her song at once. It was an old Ike and Tina Turner song.

*I can't stand the rain against my window
Bringing back sweet memories...*

"I think Humble Pie did this song," James yelled into his companion's ear.

"Humble who?" Keith yelled back.

"You know — Humble Pie! They sing '30 Days in the Hole' and 'I Don't Need No Doctor.' by Ray Charles."

"Yes. Sure I know them, whatever. You need to get a life."

"I know! Isn't it grand?" laughed James.

Because of the small room, the band was very loud. There was no point in talking; you could barely hear your own voice. The beautiful lady sang three songs with the stage presence of a diva. For her last song, she sang a duet with a tall man from the bar that was wearing a blue pin-striped suit and matching satin tie adorned with colorful butterflies. His hair was slicked back and he had a thin mustache. When they finished, both bowed with the utmost poise and dignity that matched their musical talents. The place was up and applauding. Right after this main attraction, the brothers were startled to see, rising one by one from the bar and taking to the stage, all of the people who'd initially scared them. They were singing their hearts out! All were talented and beautiful in heart. The leader of the band, who backed up everyone, sang a few songs as well.

The highlight, in addition to the beautiful lady in the red dress, was a large, black-leather-jacketed man with a scruffy beard. If James or Keith had met this tough-looking man on the street, they'd have been scared out of their wits. But at that instant, as everyone waited expectantly, he broke into an enormous sunburst of a smile and a deep baritone version of an old Elmore James tune. The next song was "Walking Away," a Jonny Lang classic.

> ...*cry, but don't cry for me*
> *I can't take it no more*
> *That's the way it must be*
> *You can't lie your way back in*
> *Back into my heart*
> *I won't let it be broken again.*

"That's a Jonny Lang song!" James offered, still shouting. "I think his is the original, but anyway, Jonny Lang is an up-and-coming blues guitarist who's white. It shows that when it comes to music, race doesn't matter!"

James wanted to explore that topic, but the music was too good and too loud for a discussion. After the applause subsided, the big baritone said that for his final number, he was going to sing a Teddy Pendergrass tune. This time he set the mike down on a stool and proceeded to walk around the whole bar, singing a slow love song. With no microphone, but with very much feeling and tenderness, the singer's voice melted every heart in the bar. Pausing at Keith and James's table he looked into their eyes, the deep sonorous sound of his voice conveying his every emotion. Neither Keith nor James could make any acknowledgment — just a hard swallow of wonderment.

After the singer had taken his bow and was warmly applauded, he walked back to the bar and took a sip of his drink, which was awaiting him. The band followed, taking another break. By this time, the brothers realized that a couple of hours had passed and that they should be heading back to the hotel. The waitress came to their table to pick up the "dead soldier" remains of empty beer bottles. James leaned toward Tamikka.

"Hey, Tamikka, can you call us a cab?"

"Oh, that's all right," Tamikka said brightly. "John can take you home."

"Uh, Okay?" James was blinking furiously, a nervous tic of his when uncertain about what to do.

Now what did that mean? James sat down, rehashing the words for meaning. Keith looked at his puzzled face.

"What did you ask her?" he laughed, noticing the familiar eye action.

"I asked if she could call us a cab and she said that John would take us home!"

"What? Who in the hell is John?" Keith had assumed a devil-may-care manner to mask his concern.

James shrugged. "I don't know. Maybe he's the local cab guy. You know they probably use their own cabbies."

Tamikka returned with two more beers. "Here is a couple more to tide you over until he gets here. He's watching the Bull's game. It will be about twenty minutes."

"What?" stammered James.

"About twenty more minutes!" Tamikka yelled over the crowd.

"Oh?" James said, to no one in particular.

He sat and gulped his beer, trying to figure out what she meant. Keith leaned over.

"Twenty minutes. Twenty minutes to what?" he pondered aloud.

"I don't know," James said expressionlessly.

They slowly drank their beers, wondering what was about to unfold. The band resumed its playing. Tamikka approached and started to clear a table close by. After wiping it down she looked up and saw the bartender gesture toward the front door. She walked over to the Keith and James. Their old fears had definitely returned.

"Gentlemen, your ride is here," Tamikka announced.

"How much do we owe you?" Keith asked.

"Eighteen."

Because she'd given great service, they'd had a great time, and because he wanted to stay in everybody's good graces, he gave her $25.

"Just head to the front door and Stephan at the door will show you out. Thanks gentlemen."

"Thank you, Tamikka."

"Thanks."

Both rose simultaneously and screeched the chairs across the checkered tile floor. This time Keith and James nodded and smiled at all the great entertainers sitting at the bar. Keith saw the large man with the baritone voice.

"Great job there man."

"Hey, thanks."

As they approached the front door, Stephan slammed it open and held it with his full body. He pointed to a white Oldsmobile 98, its one working headlight piercing the darkness. Steam was coming up in front of the car. James cautiously started walking toward the vehicle, trying to look in to see who was inside, especially to get a glimpse of this John character. Keith passed Stephan and nodded.

"Thanks, gentlemen," Stephan said.

As James approached the car, he leaned down to see how many people were inside. There was only the driver. The front passenger window was down.

"Is it all right to jump in front?" James asked.

"That's fine," returned the driver.

Keith headed for the back as James grabbed the handle and opened the door. The light came on, showing John to be an elderly black man who looked somewhat like James Earl Jones. The car was very clean and comfortable. It smelled of cinnamon and oranges.

"How's it goin'?" James greeted the man.

"We're fine. Where do you want me to take you?"

"We're staying at the Peninsula on Superior, between Rush and Michigan."

John shook his head as a confirmation and pulled the lever down to the D position over the steering column, then looked at the face in the rearview mirror.

"And how are you, sir?"

"Fine sir, having a great time," Keith replied warmly..

Within a Chicago second, all fear and worry vanished. Every dark imagining that had built up inside Keith and James collapsed like the walls of Jericho just by seeing a kind face and greeting each other.

John pulled the long car out into the street and pressed down on the gas pedal. The car sputtered briefly then picked up speed. All was silent as Keith and James looked out the windows at the small, dark houses. James turned his head toward John.

"So, how long have you been doing this? Taking people to where they need to go."

"Oh, I don't know, maybe twenty-five, thirty years, on and off. I think the first time was when Peter Wolf sat in one night."

"Do you mean Peter Wolf from the J. Geils Band?" The band was one of James's favorites.

"I think that was the one."

"Who is that?" Keith wanted to know.

"You know, Peter Wolf? J. Geils, they did songs like 'Centerfold,' 'Detroit Breakdown,' and 'Give It to Me.' "

"Oh." Keith vaguely remembered a whistle blowing in 'Give It to Me' when, as a little boy, he tried to figure out what all the commotion was about.

"So, you go all the way back to when Muddy played at the club," James said, amazed.

"Hell, Willie Dixon, Muddy's bass player, the one who wrote most of his songs, was married to my cousin! Back in the seventies, Muddy was too big to play at the Checker. Oh, he may have come down here now and again to listen to others play. And once in a while he'd sit in for a song or two, you know. But you have to go back a lot farther to see 'The Mudd' play there."

"Did you ever see Muddy play?"

"Did I see him? Hell, I was at his daughter's baptism. Son, I am old! Not as old as Muddy would be, but I grew up around here and have lived in Chicago all my life. I remember when Howlin' Wolf would study between sets, and how he gave me the urge to learn how to read. I remember when I used to help Buddy set up when he owned the Checkerboard."

"You know Buddy? Man, we just saw him last night!" James couldn't believe his good luck. Now he'd get an inside scoop!

"Oh yeah," said John nonchalantly. "I've been to Buddy's on Thanksgiving when his mother, who is still alive, would come up from Louisiana and cook. And man — could she cook! Then we'd all sit around and play. No amplifiers or drums. Someone maybe playing' the spoons, but you knows…"

John paused, remembering. He turned down a side street, cruising past low-slung blockhouses. Keith leaned forward to hear.

"But now he lives out in the suburbs in a big ol' house. We stay in touch here and there." John sounded wistful. He paused, trying to think back in time, trying to hold on to memories of 'back in the day.'

"Hey, Muddy lived right up here! I'll take you by it. They're going to remodel it and have it open as a museum, like, where they can have tours."

"Cool! That's really cool!" James was trying not to sound too star-struck. He looked back to see how Keith was doing.

His eyes were closed and his head was tilted back against the seat. James thought he looked angelic with the flashes of streetlight illuminating his now-soft features. He wondered what his brother was really going through. Keith tended to keep things to himself, never sharing his problems. Following James's lead, John also looked back at him and smiled.

"There it is."

John pulled over to the side and pointed at a red brick two-story house. It looked a little run down.

"Four-three-three-nine South Lake Park Avenue. That's the one! I've drunk beer on that porch with everyone. Yeah, those were the good old days, with guys like Otis Rush, Eddie 'Guitar Slim' Jones, and Johnny Winter, which was before Muddy moved."

"A bluesman called Guitar Slim?" It rang a faint bell.

"You know who that is? He sang 'The Things I Used to Do.'"

"I've heard of that tune. And Johnny Winter was there?"

"He was white as a ghost," John said, chuckling at the memory. "All of us would sit on the porch and they'd play hours into the night. That's when Johnny wasn't on the juice — you know, heroin. That was right before Muddy moved out to the white suburbs."

"Muddy lived in the suburbs?" James asked incredulously.

"Uh-huh. You should have seen the faces on those white folks back then! No offense."

John continued with his story without missing a beat as he checked his rearview mirror and pulled back out onto the street. Keith looked like he was sleeping in the back. James took in every word just as he did as a boy, sitting around a campfire when someone was telling a story.

"Muddy would hang for a while, eating ice cream. The man loved ice cream. But after a while he usually would get tired, and head back inside the house. We'd keep playing. He never came out and complained. Not once. But if you were around the next morning, and sleeping, he would hose you down or pour water on you. Then he would laugh. Boy, did he love to laugh…"

John flashed a quick smile, and then seemed to turn sad. James watched the expressions on his weathered face changing as he relived his past. After a minute or two of silence, he told a few more stories about the Checkerboard, mentioning Willie Dixon and Little Walter. Their scenic driver took them past Soldier Field and the Field Museum, then over the bridge and on to Michigan Avenue.

"Muddy loved baseball," he went on. "You could always find him on the couch, during the day, watching a game." He shook his head, as if savoring the memory.

"By chance, you haven't ever heard of something called The Four Givings, have you? James asked, wondering about his quest to find the other three keys.

"No, can't say that I have. Although, my auntie used to preach about some type of Givings when I was a child but I never was much of a church going man." John replied with both hands on the wheel. "No. I can't recall. Sorry."

"That's okay." James answered with some disappointment in his voice.

Nearing their destination, they switched to some small talk about the weather and how the blues is more supported by young white guys because of the hip-hop rage. Keith opened his eyes and rubbed his face with the palm of his hand. The lights of the stores and streetlamps seemed luminescent. A minute later, they were back at the hotel.

"How much do I owe ya?" James asked, reaching into his pocket.

"What did it cost to go out there?"

"Fifteen bucks," James told him.

"Whatever you think it's worth," John responded casually.

James pulled out a twenty, thinking about the extra value of the enjoyment he received. But Keith had already beaten him to the punch, handing John a twenty, along with a five. He tapped the driver on the shoulder.

"Thanks, man!" he said heartily.

Keith scooted out of the backseat onto the street. James looked at John, switched the $20 to his other hand, and extended his right hand in friendship. John looked down. He let go of the padded wheel and grabbed James's hand enthusiastically, with a smile.

"My pleasure, sir," said John.

"No, John," corrected James. "It was definitely mine. Take care."

John's tires spun on the icy pavement. He let up on the gas to stop their spinning and then lightly pressed his foot on the accelerator. This time the car inched forward. Keith and James watched the Oldsmobile pull away. Both were thinking about how they'd gotten so worked up about the ride home. John and his ride had turned out to be one of the most memorable experiences of the trip. Then, in a quick flash, James remembered Charlie. What a day! He thought. Keith too, was thinking about the man in the street. What a day! He thought.

Chapter 12

KEITH AND JAMES STOOD on the wet, red carpet in front of the hotel, watching John drive off in his white Oldsmobile. The doorman greeted the two men and started turning the large revolving door. The wind had picked up and the temperature had dropped. James fought the wind as he moved toward the door. Keith grabbed James's elbow and turned him back around.

"Hey, I know it's getting late, but do you want to go somewhere else for one more drink?" Keith asked.

"You want to walk around outside, in this weather, this late in the morning?"

"Just one more drink."

"All right, where do you want to go?" It was obvious that Keith needed to talk.

"Have you ever been to the Billy Goat Tavern? It's the place where all the reporters from the Chicago Tribune hang out. It's also the place where John Belushi got the spin off of 'Cheezeborger, cheezeborger! No fries – cheeps! No Pepsi — Coke!' On 'Saturday Night Live.'"

"I never heard of the place but I know the skit you're talking about on 'Saturday Night Live.' So okay, let's go. But I don't want to stay out late."

"Great."

The doorman hailed a cab a block away by blowing an ear-piercing brass whistle and waving his white-gloved hand high in the air. Keith and James jumped into the back and asked the driver to take them to the Billy Goat Inn. After only a few minutes, the cab turned into a small drive in front of the Wrigley Building. James looked up at the floodlit structure in awe. It reminded him of the building where Clark Kent worked at The Daily Planet in the "Superman" series he watched as a kid. It was a white terra-cotta structure with ornamental carvings in each large stone. The driver directed the men to walk just to the right of the Wrigley Building, through a courtyard, and down some stairs to get to the Billy Goat. Between the two buildings, in the courtyard, the tourists were surprised to come upon a big bronze statue that appeared to be a man standing next to the Wrigley Building.

"I bet that statue is Mr. Wrigley," James opined, remembering the chewing-gum magnate.

James was wrong: the statue's plaque gave the name of a former Mexican President. Just beyond the statue, they took the metal stairs to the street below. The street was pitch-black. Where was the tavern? Eventually, Keith saw a neon sign that read, "The Billy Goat Tavern, Est. 1934." There were three neon signs along the long glass window. One read "Billy Goat Tavern"; the next was a neon goat's-head with the words "Born 1934"; and the last neon read "Grill and Carryout." Above the window was a wooden sign that announced "The World Famous Billy Goats, Saturday Night Live, Cheezeborger, Cheezeborger, and Cheezeborger. No Pepsi…Coke." The white head of a billy goat and the words "Butt in anytime" were painted on the middle of the bright red door.

One step through the door and they could see that the place was empty. To the right was a Wall of Fame, with photos of various Chicago Tribune reporters. In front of them was the kitchen area, surrounded by a six-foot counter, and above the counter were menus suspended from the ceiling. Photographs over the bar showed the original owner, Sam "Billy Goat" Sianis.

Most of the pictures were of Sam posing with beauty pageant queens. There also was a plaque, an honorary police award, bearing Sam's name. The tavern probably hasn't changed since the nineteen sixties, Keith thought. A man wearing an apron and holding a mop poked his head up from behind the counter. "We're closed. Sorry!" he yelled, seeing the two patrons. "Come back tomorrow." He continued mopping the floors without looking back. Keith and James looked around. The place did remind them both of Belushi's "Saturday Night Live" skit. They looked at their watches, realized how late it was, and headed back up the stairs.

"I thought all bars around here are open till 5:00 a.m.," James remarked.

"I don't know; maybe because it's more of a restaurant."

"Man, can't you just picture Dan Aykroyd behind that counter?" James grinned like a happy child.

"It's Belushi," you jackass!" Keith chided as they made their exit.

Back out on the deserted street, it seemed even darker than before. Not a cab was in sight. Keith started walking along the curb, zigzagging between the blue- and cream-colored columns that supported the courtyard above. It felt a little more open and safe than the dark sidewalk. James followed suit as they headed for a streetlight at an intersection. In the distance, they could just barely make out the words of another neon sign: Phil Stefani's 437 Rush Restaurant." Stepping up their pace, they headed nervously toward the lights. Drawing nearer, they could hear someone singing.

Sat in her boudoir while she freshened up
Boy drank all that magnolia wine.
On her black satin sheets was where he started to freak...
more, more, more...

Next to the delivery doors of the Wrigley Building, the brothers spied a street person, sitting on the ground and leaning against a dumpster. They glanced at a woman but were afraid to make eye contact. A dog snapped a loud bark at the two strangers.

"Do you see them?" James whispered.

"I can barely see them," Keith whispered back. "Looks like just a street woman and a dog. Man, its dark as hell."

In response, a conversational-sounding voice from the shadows said, "What you see is hell because fear is hell. There is nothing to fear, my friend." James looked from the corner of his eye and saw the woman petting her dog. The shadow continued in verse.

Touch of her skin feeling silky smooth
Color of café au lait...

While the sounds of the words had reached the men's ears, somehow they hadn't heard.

"Rush Street should be just up here," Keith offered reassuringly. "We can walk back along Rush. There should be a bar or a cab along the way."

Rush Street seemed safer than Hubbard, with no homeless people or dogs, but still darker than Michigan Avenue. Walking briskly with their hands in their coat pockets, neither man felt safe; Keith felt something he recognized as dread. Although it was a nice, well landscaped area, home of the Lakeshore Athletic Club, a Nordstrom department store, the Conrad Hotel, and the Jolie Fleur shop, the glaring lack of fellow humans made James feel cautious. He looked down an alley, then scanned the parking lot.

"Did you get a look at that black woman with her dog, slouched against that dumpster in the street? She scared the crap out of me. What was she singing anyway?" James asked, mainly to hear a human voice.

Keith didn't answer. He was focusing on the four large men walking toward them. Spotting the gang, James instantly calculated the location where they'd be passing the four. It was going to be right on the corner of Illinois Avenue and Rush Street, but this knowledge was of no help. As they moved closer to the approaching men, James noted that their skin was white.

"Oh, they're white. We're okay," he sighed in relief.

They slackened their pace, assessing the gentlemen approaching. James threw out a casual "Hey, how's it going?" "Hey man" was the response. Two of the four walked a little faster past Keith and James while the other two stopped directly in front of them. One was dressed all in black and had a pale, round, pudgy face, like a baby. The other wore a blue knitted cap and an army coat. He spoke up first.

"Hey, man, do you know how to get to Soldier Field?" They seemed friendly. This one had blue eyes and red hair, which stuck out oddly from his blue cap.

James retorted, "Yeah, head down this street until you hit Congress Parkway, take a left and head to Michigan. Then take a right."

James felt a prick on the side of his neck and a sharp tug on his earlobe. Keith felt something sharp against his back. The same man with the red hair and blue hat spoke. "Now do you think you could give us your wallets to help pay for our cab?" The two unseen men behind them had a strong hold on Keith and James as they stood, frozen. The baby-faced man, standing in front of James, raised his hand, and with the click of a switch, a five-inch blade appeared, gleaming under the streetlight. James thought about Charlie's words, "We are all one. We must look beyond the mask and see the Christ Child in all." The only thing to do in this – or any – situation, he thought, would be to simply let go. I must let go of my fears. Namaste! The God in me sees the God in you. As James's eyes met the blue eyes of his aggressor, all fear seemed to drain away. He could see the innocent child in those eyes. A profound calmness came over him as he said, in a manner that one might have with a close friend, "How much do you need?" Keith looked at James, dazed and confused.

One of the men behind them, now pricking a sharp object in Keith's side said, "Give it all, or we will slice you like ham, you fat old fart." James's fear instantly rushed back in. For an instant, the thought of himself being an old fart weighed on his mind. Keith and James both reached for their back pockets.

"Yah man, I am looking for my dog. Can you men help me? I lost my dog. Can you boys help, man?"

All six paused and looked toward the street. Standing on the curb, next to a bus stop sign, was an old black woman. She wore an ice white, goose-down vest, a red sweater with little blue flower trim under the vest, and a red cotton skirt. Underneath the skirt was a pair of Adidas warm-up pants with three white stripes down the sides. A small diamond earring twinkled from her nose. James thought, Charlie! But then realized it was not him. It was the street woman who had been leaning against the garbage bin and singing on Hubbard Street. She looked improbably clean for someone who'd been sitting in the street. Her hair, too, looked clean, styled in the tall, flattop 'do that Grace Jones wears, but with very long, thin braids tied with little white shells at the ends. As she came closer, everyone noticed that she was not an attractive woman: pitted cheeks, a bulbous nose, and deep wrinkles in her face suggested a long, hard life. Three white hairs stuck straight out from her chin. A large, friendly smile revealed a row of very crooked teeth. The fat-faced man with the switchblade grimaced.

"Get the hell out of here, you nappy-headed bitch — unless you want some of this!" He demo'd his weapon by quickly pressing a button, making the blade flash in and out. The man behind Keith said, "We don't know where your dog is."

Undeterred, she continued moving closer to the crowd of men while also resuming her song. Steam rose behind her head from the sewer grate in the wet street.

Gitchie gitchie ya ya da da
Gitchie gitchie ya ya da da
Mocha chocolate ya, ya, ya ya
Creole Lady Marmalade

The woman's voice rose in pitch as she extended her arms straight out like a cross. James recognized the song by Labelle. She stopped between the shoulders of two of the assailants facing Keith and James, causing the circle of thugs to be cut in half. She patted each of theirs shoulders with her hands. She wore knitted, red gloves with the fingers cut off. The two men obediently took a side-step to make room for the strange newcomer.

"Well, you are too kind," she said, smiling warmly.

Just then one of the assailants released an ear-splitting shriek. Trembling violently, the redheaded fellow stood statue-still as a small dog, a pit bull repeatedly licked his hand. All eyes looked down at the squat little tan and white animal, gazing lovingly up at his newfound friends. He then jumped up onto the chest of the pudgy-faced guy and licked his nose. Pudgy instantly raised his arm in defense, but the dog was already back on the sidewalk and walking toward the two men behind Keith and James. Keith thought, Is this girl nuts? James thought, Oh God, I am going to die.

"Bowie! My baby boy! Sir, thank you so much! You found my dog! You men are like angels from heaven, sent here to rescue my little Bowie! What do I owe you?"

Bowie returned from checking out the others and jumped up on the redhead's army coat. The man reluctantly offered his hand to the animal. Bowie sniffed his hand, and then moved forward, allowing the man to pet him. Everyone seemed mesmerized by the event. The dog went around greeting all the so-called rescuers with a lick of the hand, or by jumping up and landing his front paws on the receiver's stomach.

"Bowie, don't scare the boys!" the lady rebuked, pulling him off of Red. "He is actually a big baby."

She paused and made eye contact with the two behind Keith and James, shaking her head up and down with a large smile. She began humming the song she'd been singing in the alley.

"We are all one!" She jubilated.

Laughter rippled through the woman as she slapped the pudgy-faced man on the back of his black duster. The scene became surreal, as all the men started humming the song, trying to figure out what it was. They'd heard it before. She has no fear of these men because she has nothing to lose, Keith thought. At the same time, James was thinking, you can sense her radiant love from her eyes and smile. A sense of peace warmed the circle. Keith and James could feel the men behind them gradually releasing their grip. Keith took a step to the side to be closer to the lady. He realized that the woman was in the process of saving him and his brother. James thought about earlier in the day, with Charlie. He cleared his mind. He thought of the moment, and how great his life was. He smiled and repeated to himself, "Rise, my child, I see the God in you." He sensed the lights of the street brightening. The dog walked around the group and stood by his master. James got an inspiration. He started to sing.

Don't worry about a thing,
'Cause every little thing is gonna be all right.

The woman smiled broadly and joined in the song of celebration. James looked up into the sky. Set against the deep blue blanket of night and the dark leaves of the trees, stood a little golden finch, perched on a limb of the tree above them. To the average eye, the bird would go unnoticed, but the woman pointed at the bird, bobbing her finger. The only person who looked up and saw the bird was James.

Now James and the woman were singing together.

Don't worry about a thing,
'Cause every little thing is gonna be all right.
Rise up this mornin',
Smiled with the risin' sun.
Three little birds sit by my doorstep...

At that moment, large snowflakes started to fill the sky. The crisp air smelled like a pine forest. Everyone took a deep breath, and then all six men exhaled in unison. The woman started bending her knees, swaying in time to the music. Keith patted the side of his pants leg. Then something even more miraculous happened. Another voice joined in...Now there were three singers.

The red-headed man had joined James and the lady:

Singin' sweet songs
Of melodies pure and true,
Sayin': "This is my message to you-ou-ou'
Singin': 'Don't worry about a thing,
'Cause every little thing is gonna be all right."
Singin': "Don't worry about a thing,
'Cause every little thing is gonna be all right!"

The voices of James and the other carolers faded into the zesty evening air. Within a Chicago minute, everyone's crowns and eyebrows were frosted with snow. One of the boys shook the flakes from his hair and laughed. James looked up into the sky as more and more snow fell on them. A knowing of safety came over him and he thought, Thanks, Lord. I am so blessed!

Time seemed to have stopped as the group stood there, still-life figures set against the flying snow. Breaking the silence, the red-headed man opined, "Marley is the best."

"*Hey now, hey now, Iko, Iko un de. Jockomo feeno ai na nay. Jockamo fee na nay*," the lady sang softly. "Yes, indeed. You are all beautiful. I can see bright auras shining around all of you. Music will heal your soul. Yes, indeedy!"

"The Dead," James put in.

"Among others — yes, the original is James "Sugar Boy" Crawford. '*Hey now, hey now, Iko, Iko un day. Jockomo feeno ai na nay., Jockomo fee na nay. My grandma see your grandpa, sitting by the bayou. My grandma say to your grandpa, "Gonna fix your chicken wire."'Hey now, hey now, Iko, Iko un day. Jockomo feeno ah na nay, Jockomo fee na nay.*'"

"*Iko, Iko,*" responded James.

The woman looked down at the knife the pudgy-faced man was still holding in his hand. The blade gleamed against his all-black clothing. She reached for the man's arm and lifted it into the light so she could see. Gently stroking its blade, she said, "Is this an actual stiletto, like the kind the Nazis used? It's nice, very nice. How much do you want to sell it for? I can use it to clean my nails and cut fish." Responding to the thief's startled look, she elaborated. "You know – fish, those little guys that swim underwater and have fins? You look like you don't need a knife to defend yourself; you are strong and full of energy! May I take another look?"

The man seemed to be entranced by the lady of love. "The blade doesn't work well. I don't think it's an actual German stiletto." He started to hand over the knife. One of the men behind him said, "What are you doing, man?" The black-dressed man looked at his friend in bewilderment, then continued handing the knife over to the woman. She accepted it, admiringly holding it aloft to catch the illumination of a distant streetlight. Spinning the handle in her hand, she launched a beam of light into the night sky. One of the men said, "You Jamaicans smoke too much."

"No man. Not Jamaican," she corrected. "I am Creole. I rode my house here upriver from Orleans. Ha ha ha!"

Everyone laughed. One of the boys from behind said that he was sorry for the devastation that happened to Louisiana and Mississippi. The lady responded with a shrug of her shoulders. James could not believe what he was witnessing. Keith reached for his wallet and pulled a fifty-dollar bill from among the remaining few hundred he had and extended it to the redhead.

"Is this enough for a cab or a bite to eat?" he asked solicitously.

"You don't have to, man," said Red, obviously embarrassed. "We aren't gonna do anything to ya."

"Go ahead and take it," Keith urged. "I don't need it — really. You can pay me back next time you see me."

The boys smiled. Keith took a step forward to bring the money closer to the red-headed boy's hand. The boy accepted. The woman returned the knife to its owner.

"That is a beauty!" she continued to enthuse. "Gentlemen, you are my saviors! How may I serve you? I can't thank you gentlemen enough!"

The pudgy boy petted the dog at its master's feet. "Do you call him Bowie after Jim Bowie, the guy at the Alamo, with the big knife?

"No, I named him Bowie after David Bowie, the glam queen at the '54 Club', with the little ass. Oh, I'm bad!"

All four slowly began edging away wondering who David Bowie was. The redhead held up the fifty and said, "Thanks!"

"You are most welcome," said Keith, with sincere emphasis.

"Every day is blessed," observed their angelic friend.

She continued to smile largely as they watched the boys walk away. Then she turned her attention to singing the final verse of her song.

... Now he's back home doing nine to five
Living his gray-flannel life.
But when he turns off the street, old memories meet
More, more, more, more ...

The joyous woman turned to Keith and James. Both felt her presence strongly. She looked at them as if she could see to their souls.

"Thank you for finding my dog," she repeated.

"I think we should be the ones to thank you," said Keith. He offered his hand. James also offered his hand, and the Creole lady shook both hands at once, very energetically, shaking with both of her arms. She was genuine.

"Lady, thank you!" said James. "May I ask, what is your name?"

"Gabriel at your service," said she.

"Like the angel." Keith noted.

"Yeah man. Just like the angel."

She smiled and shook her head, making the tiny conch shells in her hair collide and clack like a wind chime. Her breath flowed out and mingled in the cold night air.

"Well, thanks, Gabriel," James said again. "You saved us. Like my friend Charlie, you just have a way of changing bad things into good."

"You are welcome, man! I am here to serve. You know, it only takes a moment to see all as one, to see one as Christ. You just got to look beyond the mask and the shield."

James longed to hear more. "Gabriel, it seems like the people on the streets are a whole Salvation Army in dreads. I mean, I think most of us tend to see just the outer layer. Take you, for example. People look at you and think you're a street person. But actually, you are an angel—"

"For a reason," she cut in. "And that's to bring hope, to bring hope by teaching love and unity."

"That's a really tall order!" Keith put in, amazed. "How do you teach love and unity?"

"By seeing the light inside me, the light in you, as one, we always experience love with everyone. You can choose that. You can choose not to see a black woman, or an old Creole, or a Muslim, or a gay man. You can see all men and women as your brothers and sisters," she explained simply.

"But how do you manage to see the real person instead of their skin or their dress? How do you look beyond what you're looking at?" Keith wanted to know.

"Easy!" she said brightly. "Just wake up every day of your life asking, 'How may I serve today?' That's the key to miracles. It is pretty simple, really!"

The word key reminded James of something very important. "When you say key, do you mean, like, one of the four keys to miracles? The Four –"

"The Four Givings. Yeah man."

James nearly burst with excitement. "You know about The Four Givings? Wow! A Rastafarian named Charlie taught me one of them just today. The first one's called The Giving of the Mind."

"Yeah man, I know Charlie and The Four Givings," she said matter-of-factly. "And so do you."

"Actually, we barely understand one," said Keith, doubting.

"What about your act of kindness?" she asked. "You gave those boys money so they can eat. And your giving was from your heart. Your heart opened up so that miracles can happen. Miracles only happen when you are in spirit, which is the greatest miracle. Only the four keys can instantly put you in spirit and allow miracles to happen. The first key you learned is?"

"The Giving of the Mind," James said, clearly remembering. "It's when you live in the moment by clearing your mind."

"Yeah man," responded Gabriel. "But it is more than that. With that key, you clear your mind, so that you see the spirit in everyone you meet; you see their light no matter what their state is. When two are in spirit, living in God, it rains miracles. A hundred in spirit is a typhoon. You ready for another one of The Four Givings?"

"Yes," said both brothers in one voice.

"The second giving is The Giving of Thy Self."

"The Giving of Thy Self?" James parroted, trying to understand.

"Yes, through charity and service."

"Wait a minute," said Keith, his critical faculty in gear. "Isn't that two keys?"

"They're both the same," explained Gabriel. "Some can give charitable offerings; others can give of their time in service. They both provide. Both help to bring prosperity to all. Remember Jesus' prayer. 'Give us this day our daily bread.' Jesus blessed the limited amount of fish and loaves, knowing of the infinite supply and abundance. Then he gave it as charity and served the multitudes. Through The Giving of Thy Self, miracles from heaven rain down upon you and all around!"

"How can that giving bring a miracle?"

"Isn't miracles something that happens or is created? Nothing happens without action. One man's action alone may be negligible. But two men can move a mountain. One man's pocket can only carry dollars. But two men can lift a chest full of riches. A helping hand or an offer of support brings hope. Prosperity spreads like wildfire. Every day ask everyone you meet, 'How may I serve you?'"

"You mean even at work?" James asked, the implications flooding his imagination.

"You should ask to serve at work, especially at home with your family, to your community, and globally. Always give to every person more than you take from them. Always pay more than they're asking for their service. In doing so, you increase the value of their service, so they may feel abundant, and in return, so shall you. And always give more in service than they can expect to pay in money, so they may know prosperity; and then so, in turn, shall you. By serving and giving to others, your heart will open wide; you will feel the connection with God through Christ in body, then and only then will miracles happen to you and to all. The giver is saying to the receiver that he or she believes in the godliness of their lives and the oneness of the universe. Your Holy Spirit is a mere reflection of a stronger power of God's love. With Christ vision from within, you raise the other from their sin and guilt by seeing their True Self, lifting them into the Light, and restoring their vision of 'One.' See Christ's face in others and you will remember God. The ego's mentality is to try to get much as possible, with a minimum of giving. That's what the ego calls a win. But can you bargain with God? Don't think that having and giving are in conflict. Understand that having is a direct reflection of giving. And that giving is the same as receiving."

The stack of bills, awaiting his return on the kitchen counter at home, flashed into James's mind.

"Wow, that's heavy. I never thought of it that way. I guess I'm afraid to give very much because I'm afraid that I may not have enough to pay my own bills."

"I love to give, but there are times when I feel that people are taking me for granted and don't appreciate it," added Keith.

"Giving creates receiving. But your gift must be offered with love. If there is fear in your heart or reluctance, the blessing will never be realized. There are two major causes of loss. The first is not being grateful for the things in your life. And the second is the fear of loss. Both place lack in one's mind. We should focus our energy on 'How may I serve? What can I offer?' Ask that of everyone you meet, and then you'll be grateful for all that you already have, and the fear of loss will be outshined. The truly helpful are not protecting their egos and so they seldom feel vulnerable. Their helpfulness toward others is their praise to God, and God will return His praise to them, for they are like Him, and they rejoice together."

As her words slowly sank in, Keith could think of nothing else to say.

"In learning to escape from illusions, your debt to your brothers, who are all human beings, is something you shall never forget. It is the same debt of gratitude that you owe God. As you learn how much you are indebted to the whole human race that abides in God you come close to Him. Only those who have a real and lasting sense of abundance can be charitable. And only those who can be charitable experience a real and lasting sense of abundance. To the ego, to give anything, implies that you have to do without it, that it is now lost to you. When you associate giving with sacrifice, you give only because you believe that somehow, you are getting something better in return, and therefore do without the thing you give."

"Wow, that's deep!" said James, dazzled in the same way as his brother.

Giving in order to get, is an inescapable law of the ego, which is always busy evaluating itself compared to other egos. So then your ego is continually preoccupied with the belief in scarcity — which gave rise to its very existence! Your gratitude to your brothers, meaning humankind, is the only gift God wants from you. To know your brothers is to know God. As it says in the Bible, '…whatever you do unto the least of these my little ones, you do unto me.'"

"But doesn't that just open yourself up for people to take advantage of you? I always feel when I accept something from someone that I'm taking it away from them. You know what I mean?" Honesty came easily to Keith in the presence of such goodness.

"Only your ego sees it that way," Gabriel explained. "People are wonderful at giving charity but are terrible in receiving gifts from others. Pride clogs our channels and blocks the flow of blessings. Blessed are both the giver and the receiver. God shines down upon a loving giver and a grateful receiver. God is both the giver and the gift, and they cannot be separated."

"I never thought of it that way," Keith admitted. "I guess we all should be more open to accepting someone's help or gift that is given to us. And we should help others. Both are a blessing to God. But where should we help? How do we know when someone needs our help? What if they
   don't want us to interfere?"

"God will always guide you to where you can be truly helpful. God will give you the ways, the means, and the words," she said, aware that the words were not her own.

Gabriel smiled, again revealing her crooked teeth. Acceptance and understanding came upon her listeners. There was silence between the three as they experienced the moment, in the cold night, a blissful clearing of their minds. The three became one, one in brotherhood, one in spirit. No other words can describe it. Bowie broke the silence by jumping up on his owner's chest.

"What is it, my little brother? You are also one with us. Yes, I know. I need to get you home to eat. Just remember this: for the abundance of all, go through all your days asking, 'How may I serve? What can I offer?' Always give others more value in your service than remuneration that you get from them. Likewise, pay them more for their services than they were expecting. The truly helpful are beyond offense because they are not protecting their egos. Their helpfulness to others is their praise to God, and he will return his praise to them for they are like him and they can rejoice together."

Bowie the dog replied to his master with two barks. Gabriel grabbed both of their shoulders and smiled. James placed one hand on Gabriel's extended arms. Keith just stood there, feeling awkward.

"It's time for me to go. Take care, my brothers. And until next time, remember — it just takes a moment to see the Christ in someone when they are receiving your gift, your service. But remember your responsibility, being a holder of the keys. Your debt is to serve and help all. I think you can pull it off. You two seem like smart men."

"At least one of us is," Keith guessed.

Gabriel cut in sharply. "We all have that part – that dark side of the moon – that is turned away from the Light. Now listen to me carefully. Why are some children born into luxury and ease while others are born into hunger and privation? Why have one child, receive a world of opportunity, and the other child receive only toil and pestilence? It is because we travel many worlds, wearing many faces. We are drawn back by unfinished business, desires, and debts from our past lives. We learn from each lifetime. But this time around, we need to pay back our debts from past lives of spiritual blindness. It is time we pay our karmic debt for past-lifetime mistakes."

Gabriel bent over and gently placed Bowie between her legs on the ground, her skirt acting as his tent.

"This is taking the Giving of Thyself to a global level. I don't care what your burden is, if it is cancer, Aids in Africa, heart disease, missing children, the homeless, or genocide in Darfur, what ever your burden is, do something, always move towards the solution instead of dwelling on the problem. Get involved with your family, your local community, and your global community. Ask yourself, 'How may I serve?' By focusing on the solution, and taking action to remove the problem, your burden will be diminished and miracles will be unlocked."

Gabriel took a few deep breaths and paused to watch the snow fluttering in the lamplight. "Whatever burdens your heart, then pick up your banner and pay homage. Jesus said, 'If two of you shall agree on earth that they shall ask, it shall be done for them of my Father which is in heaven.' When man is living in desperation, he becomes doubtful and fearful. But when someone offers unwavering help, hope turns into reality. By always focusing on and giving energy to the goal of everyone having food, education, proper shelter, or disease free living, and by offering charity, or asking 'How may I serve?' you are saying to your brothers, 'I am here for you.' Always give energy to the solution, never to the problem. Because you will feel too helpless and the problem then expands from our vision of lack."

Gabriel began to walk away. The dog ran ahead, knowing his dinner was waiting. James felt an urgency to know more.

He reached out and grabbed her arm as she was turning away.

"Gabriel."

The Creole women turned back around, her braids swinging from the motion and their beads and conches tinkling.

"Yeah, bumble bee?"

Time to cut to the chase! James's mind raced with anticipation. "What about the other two keys, the last of The Four Givings?"

"Practice the first two keys, the Giving of the Mind and the Giving of Thy Self, and the other two will just come. Behold your role within the universe. To each one of you, God gives the grace to be a savior to all. When first you look upon a brother as he looks upon you, you see the mirror of yourself in him. And in this single vision, you see the face of Christ, and you understand that you look on everyone as you behold this one brother. For there is Light where there was darkness before, and now the veil is lifted from his sight."

"What veil? How can there be a veil over the face of Christ?"

"The veil is the space between you and your brother maintained by an illusion of yourself that holds him off from you and you from him. The sword of judgment is the weapon that you wield before this loveless abyss that seems to keep your brother at a safe distance — safe for your ego, that is. But only holiness is seen with holy eyes that look upon the innocence within and expect to see it everywhere. And so they call it forth in everyone they look upon. This is the Savior's vision; he sees his innocence in all that he looks upon and sees his own salvation everywhere. He brings the Light to everything he sees and beholds the likeness of God in all your brothers and sisters. The Light sees no past in anyone at all, and thus it serves a holy and wholly open mind, unclouded by old concepts, and prepared to look on only what the present holds. It cannot judge because it does not know. It is all in the book, 'A Course in Miracles'."

"But…What?" blurted James.

"Oh, honey child, I have to feed my dog. Just remember what I told you about the Giving of Thy Self. Of everyone you meet, simply ask, 'How may I serve? What can I offer?' I know, James, that right now you have money on your mind. But money, like health or any other miraculous circumstance is not a goal. It is the natural result when you are on purpose. Find your purpose and help with the karmic unfolding of the world as you nourish the poor. If you ask anyone on the street what religion they are, they will most likely proudly say 'Christian.' But then ask them how they feel about poor people. Most will offer a gloomy answer because deep down they have been taught to resent them. Is that Jesus' teaching? Is that how Christ would act?"

James said "No." Keith listened.

"No, it is not. Throughout the Bible, God always takes the side of the oppressed. Fighting for the liberation of those who are oppressed is an important responsibility of our faith. As Christians, with Christ within us, one of our greatest responsibilities is to protect the poor and feed the hungry. It is our duty from God. Remember what it says in the Book of Matthew 25:41-46, 'Then he said to those at his left hand, "You that are accursed depart from me… for I was hungry and you gave me nothing to drink. I was a stranger and you did not welcome me, naked and you did not give me clothing. Sick and in prison and you did not visit me." Then they… replied, "Lord, when was it that we saw you hungry or thirsty or a stranger or naked or sick or in prison, and did not take care of you?" And he answered them, "Truly I tell you, just as you did not do it to one of the least of these, you did not do it to me."' First, daily, hourly, by the minute, find your Christ within, live as Christ. Then go out into the world and search for the Christ in others. When you see the Christ within them, they will feel it. Help and serve others. Light their lanterns. Then together we will be fulfilling our spiritual duty. Our duty is to protect the weak and feed the hungry. That will end hunger. That will end hatred. That will end terrorism. That will end tyranny."

"Got it, right," said Keith. "But isn't that supposed to happen during the Second Coming?"

"Don't make the mistake of the apostle Paul, who believed that we should not do anything, because he believed the return of Christ would happen in his lifetime. All he had to do was look within to find it. We are the Second Coming when we accept the Christ within and see it in others. We are all looking for the Light within. What most of us don't yet understand is that to find it, we must see the Light in all others. If we are willing to risk ourselves for a moment, let down our guard and look into the eyes of another — friend or foe— seeking the flame, the spirit within, then we will find ours, and only then miracles will trickle down from the heavens like these snowflakes we see falling all around us." She turned her face to the snow, letting it melt on her skin. "That is the Second Coming. The other two keys are on the key ring with the others, inside your heart. Feel, and you will find them."

"But what about…" James didn't know how to formulate his thought.

After patting her goose-down vest with both hands, Gabriel quickly turned and continued on her way. The men looked at each other, and then turned to watch the retreating back – and tail — of Gabriel and her dog. She turned back and bowed, lifting her red skirt that would normally show undergarments but only revealed her black warm-up pants. She then turned back around, skipping along with her dog, not caring what anyone thought. She started to sing another song.

She keeps her Moet et Chandon in a pretty cabinet.
'Let them eat cake,' she says, just like Marie Antoinette.
A built-in remedy for Khrushchev and Kennedy.
At any time an invitation you can't decline.

Caviar and cigarettes,
Well-versed in etiquette,
extraordinarily nice,

she's a Killer Queen…

As the song faded into the night, the realization set in that they were alone again. They decided to head back to the hotel via Michigan Avenue because it was more lighted. Walking along in silence, both reflected on all that had just happened, trying to take it all in. James grasped the Tiffany's box in his coat pocket. A revelation came to him about himself.

"You know, there is one thing that's bothering me," he began, looking genuinely troubled.

"Oh? What's that?"

"Well, I never thought of myself as being prejudiced."

"So?"

"Well, it's all bullshit. I am a bigot." He could feel his face reddening.

"You are not a bigot." Keith offered.

James was not convinced. "Think about when we passed the garbage bin and were both afraid to make eye contact with the black street lady, who ended up being Gabriel. And then, just a minute later, we thought, Hell, I take that back! I said that we were going to be safe because the four men coming toward us were white? Why would I think that the whites would be any safer?"

"Yeah, okay. You're right. You're a bigot," Keith said blandly.

"No, I am serious! C'mon! What about when we went into the Checkerboard Club? When we walked in, I was scared because all I saw were black faces. But the thing is that we had a great time. All the people that I was afraid of ended up being local performers and were entertaining and friendly. It was my hang-up, my problem, my own limitation — not theirs. I can't believe that just before we got mugged we thought we were safe because those guys were white. I think that I am better than everyone else because I read all these spiritual books, and listen to all the inspirational tapes, and I think I have the answers, but let's face it – it's all bullshit. I don't know anything."

"I see what you're saying and I agree. You don't know anything." It occurred to Keith that the same might also apply to him but then he quickly dismissed the thought.

"Maybe, we should try to change our prejudices. Maybe the way to start is to contribute like Gabriel said to. Don't be part of the problem, become the solution." replied James.

"I'm willing to donate if I know it's going directly to the cause. But who do you trust? I don't know if I can give money to those organizations because only a tiny percent makes it to the country. Then you hear about the food being stolen and sold on the black market. Who do you trust?"

Keith and James were so deep in conversation that they finally realized that they'd passed their hotel. They turned around and noticed that they'd walked right by Tiffany's without even thinking of their experience there. The two men stood across the street from the corner where the skateboarder rode in the water tower park, earlier that day. They looked up at the Chicago Water Tower. The stone building was illuminated by lights shining against its cream-colored stone.

"Who do you trust to give money to?" James echoed his brother's thought. "How do you know that the money will make it to the children that need to be fed? Who do you trust?"

Keith looked up and pointed to the sky, above the pinnacle of the stone tower. Breaking through the clouds, the full moon shone down on them. Flurries of snow continued to fall. The water tower appeared medieval.

"The answer is right up there!" Keith said, still pointing.

James suddenly realized that this was the same place where he'd met Charlie. Looking down at Charlie's steps, he hoped to see the Rastafarian playing his guitar with his cat sitting next to him. The steps were empty. He turned, looking for the boom box on the park bench. It wasn't there. A vision of the skaters appeared in his head. As the snowflakes brushed against his face, he felt that moment in a flash, but then it was gone. He turned his face back up, trying to see where his brother's finger was pointing to.

"What, the old Chicago Water Tower? Are you talking about that – or about God? What? What is it?"

"No, not there, way up there." Keith was pointing beyond the tower to some lighted floors on a high-rise building. The snowflakes landed softly on his hand as it pointed upward. James looked closer. He could not see anyone up in the upper floors. There were just a few lights on, spread across different floors.

"What? What?"

"Do you believe in this Givings crap enough to put your money where your mouth is?'

Chapter 13

THE NEXT MORNING FOUND Keith and James with their bags in the lobby, preparing to check out. The clerk printed out the long receipt. Keith reviewed the charges and signed the bill for both rooms.

"Is there anything else, Mr. Kerrigan?"

"Yes, can you provide me with an envelope?"

She reached under the desk and pulled out a manila envelope with a gold Peninsula Hotel insignia in the upper left-hand corner. He folded the bill and stuck it into his back pocket, then placed the Peninsula envelope into the inside breast pocket of his fleece jacket. James grabbed his bag and waved farewell to the nice lady. Once through the revolving doors, their faces were again blasted by the cold wind. It stung their cheeks, instantly turning them red. Keith handed a ticket to the valet, asking if they could leave their bags with him while they went for a coffee. The valet said he'd take care of their bags and have the car waiting for them. As they walked, James kept sliding on the new dusting of snow, his hands stretched out like a bird. He'd run a few strides then use his shoes as skis.

"You're going to fall on your ass," Keith warned.

"No way man, falling is not part of my spiritual path."

When they arrived at Starbucks, both ordered a double latte and an almond biscuit. After doctoring their coffees, they went back outside. Keith looked around for the man he'd met the day before. No one was around except for a couple of pedestrians walking their dogs. Keith told James about his experience with the street person outside of Starbucks. Describing how the man had touched him, he again thought about what Gabriel said and remembered his new desire to help others.

"Let's put your money where your mouth is. Let's see if you really believe in this Four Givings idea," said Keith

"What's that?" James figured Keith was about to tell him what he had in mind while pointing up at the skyscraper the night before.

Keith folded his biscuit in the napkin and put it in his pocket to free up his hand. Then he took some bills from his wallet. He counted out two hundred and forty-nine dollars. He stuffed a five-dollar bill into his front pocket for tolls on the way home, returning two hundred and forty-four dollars to his wallet.

"I have two hundred and forty-four dollars," he announced. "How much money do you have?"

James reluctantly pulled out his wallet. He opened it and shuffled through the bills.

"I don't know. About eighty-three bucks."

"That's it? You mean to tell me you came to Chicago on what, a hundred dollars?"

"I'm not working, remember?" said James defensively.

"Okay, so listen up. This is what we're going to do. We will pool our money and take it over to Oprah's building and leave it for her."

"What building?" asked James, his mind reeling at the prospect of giving his money to the cause.

"The one right across from the old water tower, the one I pointed to last night."

"You want to just leave money at the front desk? What are you, nuts? Why don't we wait until we get home and donate it on her Web site or by phone?" James had a pretty good idea of what would become of his money at the front desk.

"That would take away from it. By having a record of your donation, it takes away from your belief of this voodoo stuff. Don't you want to stay anonymous?" Keith asked. He continued, "By dropping it off we're demonstrating faith that it will get to her. Also, if we go to the Web site, they'd ask us for our information. Don't you think that would jinx us? If you believe in this voodoo, you must think that when people do something kind and then tell others about it, the blessing is weakened and somehow diluted. And I know you. Once you go home, you wouldn't do it."

"Hey! I'm just frugal," James bleated. "And besides, I'm out of work!"

"Just take the money out of your wallet and give it to me. Maybe this is the ticket to getting your next job, if you can have a little faith! Otherwise, you might as well not worry about the other two Givings. Remember what you've said now that you think you're enlightened: live in the moment, give offerings, and you will open the way to miracles. You said it yourself. Now let's see if you can believe in it."

"Do I have a choice?"

"No. I don't even believe in this crap but I am willing to try it."

"All right," said a resigned James. "I will do this even though I think we're nuts."

"You talked all this crap about letting go of your ego, and letting go of your fears. But it looks to me like you're full of it. Up until now, you haven't practiced any of it! You are so blessed, yet so blind. You know if you do what you say, your life will change for the better, as long as you believe it will. Don't fret about the money that you are missing. Because you know that will jinx the blessing. And you better not think of the personal rewards that it will bring you, either. Just like your two buddies told us, always just focus on the blessing your service or charity will provide. You know that Giving of Thyself stuff. Think about what this will do for a hungry child. Maybe you can visualize the recipient, playing with a new baseball, or eating well, smiling, wearing nicer things, getting a better education. Think of those things."

Keith took a step closer. His eyes squinted in the sun and his cheeks were flame red. The cold breath rose from his mouth like the steam coming from the manholes in the streets.

"How does that make you feel?" Keith inquired.

"Ah, I guess pretty well," James admitted.

"Now go ahead and give me your money before I kick your ass."

James extracted the eighty-three dollars by turning his wallet sideways, trying not to spill his coffee. He looked at the empty wallet in one hand, and a few dead presidents in his other hand, flapping in the wind between his fingers, just under his cup of latte.

"All of it?"

"All of it."

Putting the wallet away James noticed, written on the side of his Starbucks cup, a message. He paused to read the caption silently to himself. Then he read it aloud to his brother.

"The Way I See It, Number 178: The measure of genuine civilization, it has been said, is the quality of life for a nation's poorest and least privileged people. By that measure, we are barbarians. Our current level of inequality cannot be justified or sustained. It was written by Robert W. McChesney, the author, media critic, and professor at the University of Illinois at Urbana-Champaign."

As he looked in the direction of Oprah's building, James fanned the money between his thumb and forefinger. He looked down at it one last time, and then handed it over to Keith. Keith regarded the small sum and shook his head. He stuffed it into his wallet, took a sip of coffee, and stepped against the forceful wind.

"Come on," Keith urged. "Let's get going."

Keith walked briskly, ten steps ahead of his brother. James ran up to Keith, and then shuffled past, making two ski-tracks in the snow. Leaning his weight just a little too far back, he lost his balance and WHAM! He landed on his back.

"You and your spiritual path. Huh?"

Keith helped his brother up by the arm. James eased up slowly, feeling the pain in his bum. The pain stung in the cold. A white icing of snow clung to his pants. He briskly brushed off his rear end.

"Ouch! Damn, that hurt!"

Back at the hotel, they found their rented SUV in front of the stone lions and revolving doors. The valet retrieved the luggage, then opened the hatch and placed the bags in the back. Keith tipped using a five-dollar bill he had in his front pocket. Inside the car it was toasty warm. It felt good to finally be out of the wind and cold. Gripping the steering wheel with excited anticipation, Keith pulled away from the hotel. James looked over and noticed that the gas light was on.

"We'll have to stop and get gas," he told Keith.

"Yeah, we better get gas before we make our drop-off at Oprah's."

"Oprah!" James mocked gently. "Listen to you. We'll probably be arrested!"

Chapter 14

KEITH SWITCHED THE RADIO over to FM. James searched the buttons on the radio. There was a station that was only one notch from being tuned in. It was a good song. He pushed the "stereo" button and the static disappeared. Just ahead, on either side of the street, loomed two impossibly tall skyscrapers. James craned his neck, trying to make out the tops of the buildings, but could not. The large red canopy at the main entrance must be to keep tenants dry while awaiting transportation, he figured. Keith parked the car across the street from the glass doors and canopy. He reached for his wallet and took out all of the money that his brother and he had put together. James looked down at the pile in his brother's hand.

"All of it?" James asked for the second time.

"Giving this money is a sign of your faith in this crap. Besides, I still have five dollars for tolls, McDonald's takes credit cards. So we're fine."

"Are you sure she lives here?" asked a worried James.

"Yes, I think so."

"You think so! You don't even know if she lives here and you want to give her the last bit of our money. I'm not even working!"

Keith counted out the $327 dollars, and then stuck the money in the hotel envelope. James stared upward, looking for a sign of Oprah in the windows of the towering building.

The glare from the sun shined against the glass, precluding any sighting of this myth, this legend called Oprah.

James made one last-ditch effort. "She may not even live in Chicago. I heard she bought a new house."

Keith thought, just for a flash, that maybe he should hold some back. Nope! The word instantly popped into his mind. Keith turned down the radio. Feeling oddly sneaky, he looked in the review mirror to see who was walking along the street.

James was on the same wavelength. "They probably have us on camera. I can just see it now: we'll be on 'Hard Copy,' a couple of stalkers hanging out in front of a famous celebrity's place."

"You keep going to the fountain of life with a shot glass in your hand instead of a bucket."

"Quit looking and talking in the mirror and let's get on with it."

"This will prove if your bullshit theories are worth anything," Keith said.

Wash away my sorrow
Wash away my pain
With the rain in Shambala…

As James surveyed every window for witnesses, Keith licked and sealed the envelope, addressing it To: Oprah Winfrey. Keith jumped out of the car and ran across the street. He knocked on the glass door under the canopy. A man, who appeared to be a security guard, greeted him at the door. The band, Three Dog Night, continued to play in the car.

How does your light shine
In the halls of Shambala?
How does your light shine
In the halls of Shambala?

James watched his brother through the car window. The man Keith was talking to in the lobby wore a blue blazer and gray pants. James felt scared. He was afraid of what people would think if he never again got a job. It was possible that he wouldn't make any money that year. But does that matter when there are children homeless and hungry? he thought, forming each word in his mind. Here we are doing something good, and instead of enjoying it, I am worrying about myself! He continued to think of the good that this little bit of money would do for some hungry child. I wonder if I gave away all my money, if it would really come back to me. An instant reply inspired. Not if you were just giving to get. The sun was shining between the tall buildings. The wind howled off the lake. Steam rolled out of the sewer as a lady pushing a grocery cart crossed the street. James took a deep breath, letting go, letting go of all thoughts. Instantly, he felt peace and enjoyed the moment. His mind was empty, spacious. He felt blessed. He felt his spirit, Christ in body. He knew that everything was going to be okay.

> *I can tell my sister 'bout the flowers in her eyes,*
> *On the road to Shambala.*
> *I can tell my brother 'bout the flowers in his eyes,*
> *On the road to Shambala.*
> *How does your light shine*
> *In the halls of Shambala?*
> *How does your light shine*
> *In the halls of Shambala?*

"Namaste," said James to the world around him. "May the God in me see the God in you."

Keith handed the letter to the security guard. The man looked down and noticed that the envelope was from the Peninsula Hotel.

"Will you deliver this envelope to one of your tenants? It is very important."

"But I...I don't..." the man began to stammer.

"Please just take it and make sure it gets to her," said Keith, eager to be done with the transaction.

"I don't know if I should. I'm kind of new here and we have to be careful..."

"Why would anyone think this little envelope would do harm? And who would harm Oprah? Tell me one person on this earth who doesn't love Oprah! You love Oprah! I love Oprah! We all love Oprah! Heck, Will Smith kissed her on national television, in front of his wife and everybody! Even he loves Oprah."

"But I... As I said, I'm new and I have to send it down to the mailroom to get it scanned. And they're closed on Sundays. I'm not allowed to take any packages."

"Well, that's fine, but can you make sure that it's delivered?"

"But I'm not sure if ...Oprah? Did you say Oprah? What makes you think that she lives here?

"A friend of mine told me that she lived..."

"Listen pal, this is the John Hancock Tower. We have no tenants here, only offices. She does not live here and I do not know where she lives. Sorry"

The man handed the envelope back to Keith. Keith reluctantly accepted it back.

"Okay then. Thanks a lot."

Keith looked back at the man shaking his head as he opened the glass door. The man said in disbelief, "Oprah? Boy you must be crazy."

Keith felt discouraged as he walked back across the street, dodging a passing car. James was looking through the door at the guard, who was looking at his brother while talking into a walkie-talkie.

"What was that all about?"

Keith set the envelope down onto the center console next to his coffee mug. "I guess I was wrong. She doesn't live there. Maybe she does live in a house."

"I knew it, you and your big ideas. Oprah!"

Keith slammed the car door and quickly accelerated, almost burning rubber. He went around the block then turned the car left onto Michigan Avenue. They looked at all the places they had walked past over the last two days. Keith looked over to the window ledge at Starbucks where he'd met Angel. The spot was empty now except for a pigeon on the windowsill and a few more, pecking at the sidewalk.

Chapter 15

AT EACH CROSS STREET, Keith quickly scanned for signs of a gas station but no luck. He finally spotted a Shell station sign a block down through an alleyway. Keith quickly stopped the car and turned left down the alley. The SUV whizzed passed a man next to a garbage bin. James glanced over but did not get a good look at the man. When the car came out of the alley into an open parking lot, Keith noticed that the gas station was boarded up. He drove into the parking lot, through an opening, between two yellow metal poles. The lot was surrounded by the yellow poles with cable running through each pole, acting as a perimeter. He stopped the car and scanned the sky for any other signs. He saw flurries against the all-gray backdrop of clouds. James jumped out of the car, "Stay here. I'll be right back." James slammed the passenger door.

"Where in the hell are you going?" Keith desperately yelled but it was too late. He looked back and saw his brother jogging back to the alley. A man came up with a squeegee and spray bottle and gestured with his hands, asking Keith if he could wash his window. Keith shook his head in agreement and then turned back, looking for his brother, wondering what was going through that head of James.

James slowed down to a walk when he reached the alley. Something inspired him to look for the man they passed in the alley. In the distance, the alley ran between two buildings, where he saw the man resembling Charlie. But then again, it could just as easily have been Gabriel. He looked over at Keith and saw a man washing the windshield. Keith stepped out of the car and approached the man.

"How much do I owe you?" Keith asked.

He could hardly believe his eyes. It was the nameless face from the day before, outside of Starbucks. The man instantly recognized Keith also, and cheerfully waved his chapped hand.

"You owe me nothing." said the man. "This is my payback to you for being so kind to me yesterday. It's all I have, but it's my way of thanking you for your thoughtful gesture."

"Yesterday, I forgot to ask you your name. What is your name?"

"Angel."

"Well, thank you for your service, Angel. But please, let me offer you something. Have you eaten?"

"No".

"Will you at least take my biscuit?"

Keith reached into his pocket and handed the breakfast dessert to the homeless man. His leathery blue hands reached out and took it. Gingerly unwrapped the napkin as if it were a Christmas present, Angel looked up at Keith with tears in his eyes. He took a big bite of the sugar-sprinkled cookie.

"Thank you. You are a very kind soul. Your family must be proud."

The man was shivering as he held the bottle of windshield cleaner and the squeegee in one hand and his breakfast in the other. He vigorously took another bite and handed the biscuit back to Keith. Keith hesitated at first, and then grabbed the offering. He took a bite also. Their eyes met in wholeness.

"You are a very appreciative man," said Keith, bowing slightly. "It's my honor. As far as my family, it is just my wife and I. I had a daughter but she has passed."
Angel felt Keith's anger spewing out of his body. Keith realized he was spilling his guts out to a stranger.
"I'm sorry. I'm burdening you with my troubles."
"That's fine. It's nice to be confided in. I remember when my daughter used to confide in me. Those moments were some of my fondest memories." Angel wore a yearning, far-away expression.
"Your daughter, do you see her much?" questioned Keith.
"No. I lost her many years ago."
"I lost my daughter, Linda, at the World Trade Center in the 911 attacks," Keith said quietly.
"My daughter was in a car accident. Her boyfriend was speeding."
"I'm sorry."
"I am so sorry for your loss. You have other children?" Angel asked.
"No, no more children, just my wife and me."
"Oh. May you and your wife find peace again," Angel prayed.
"Isn't it strange that we both lost our little girls? My daughter died in the towers. Your daughter died in a car accident." Keith thought it must be a coincidence.
"Oh, I'm sorry. I should clarify. I didn't lose my daughter in the car accident."
"May I ask how she died?"
For the first time, Keith saw pain in Angel eyes. "The report said it was an aneurysm, but that wasn't what killed her."
"I don't know what you mean," Keith gently prompted.

"It was the hate. The hate that she held inside is what killed her. Ever since the accident, she could never find it in her heart…" his voice trailed off.

Keith bowed his head, waiting for Angel to reveal the cause of death. After a moment, Angel composed his thoughts and spoke.

"She could never find it in her heart…to forgive. It was the fear, and judgment that killed her."

The words struck a chord deep within Keith's heart. He raised his head, fighting the tears he hoped this stranger would not notice. Of the entire staff of doctors that Keith had seen, in their clean white waiting rooms, not one could tell him why his illness was there. They could only tell him how to kill it before it could kill him. And now this homeless man had answered it on the cold asphalt of a gas station. A golden finch fluttered its wings to gently land on the cable between two poles. Those doctors could never tell me what caused it, he thought.

Keith's face crumpled. He looked away, looking for James, but he vanished in the alley across the parking lot.

Angel continued. "You see, we always carry our banner, by which I mean our ego, high above all others, and we raise our sword in vengeance, meaning judgment, so we don't have to look at our own fearful projections, delusions, deceits, or feel our own wounds, by which I mean guilt. As long as you have someone to blame, you do not have to ask for mercy. And when mercy cannot be given… "

"But tell me, why does this happen? Why does God let things like this happen?" Keith queried.

"I cannot answer that. But, I will say what a very wise person once told me. She said, 'In this life, or any of our past lives, if we ever act as the aggressor against anyone, we will fall victim of aggression. If we ever have oppressed another, we will witness oppression, at another time. If in any lifetime, we did not help the sick or poor, we will fall victim to sickness, we will witness deprivation."

"I have a hard time believing that the reason my daughter died was so that she could learn a lesson from a life before."

"Maybe, the lesson wasn't for her, but rather for you. God uses angels in many ways so that we may learn grace through love, charity, mercy, and ..."

"The giving of mercy," Keith interjected.

"Yes, that is right."

"The Giving of Mercy," Keith repeated, as if it were a mantra.

"Let me tell you what I know," Angel began with a smile, his face suddenly aglow. "Man has the power to forgive and neutralize his mistakes. Go into silence. Find peace with your perceived enemies and with yourself. Only then can you be healed. What a man says of another can be said of him. What a man wishes for another human being, he is wishing for himself. If you wish someone bad luck, you are sure to attract bad luck to yourself; if you wish someone success, then success will be yours. Use your words only to heal, to bless, and to prosper. All sickness and unhappiness come from the violation of love. Bless the ones you hate. You then outshine their vengeance. Bless those you do not understand. Send love and goodwill to all these people and they are stripped of their power to hate. When you change your thought, your adversaries will change theirs. It is the law of grace and forgiveness that frees man from the law of cause and effect, the law of consequence. When you are no longer shaken by man's cruelty, he will cease to be cruel. No man is your enemy. No man is your friend. Every man is your teacher. Man's hate, resentment, and criticism boomerang back in the form of sickness and sadness. Bless any adverse situation! Let go of your worries. Ask for the grace to not be disturbed by it, and the legs of the adverse situation will collapse from its own weight. Hate, and even mild dislike, causes your blood to literally bubble with poison. It is the cause of all sickness and failure. You can only see through and eliminate fear by walking up to what you are afraid of. It will then fall to its knees. By the way, criticism brings rheumatism, did you know that? Unloving thoughts cause unnatural deposits in the blood. Guilt settles into your joints. Tumors are caused by jealousy, hatred, and fear. Every disease is caused by a mind not at ease. I say to you, love your enemies, and bless those who curse you; do well to those who hate you, and pray for those who persecute you. Man's only enemy is himself. There is peace on earth for he who sends goodwill to all beings."

"Come on, you think that all diseases are created by your thoughts? Bull."

"Disease can also be born from your environment, or family history, or immoral acts. But do not discount emotion. Your thoughts, feelings, and emotions will affect your body, in a positive way, or a negative way. Be aware of your emotions. Your health depends on it."

The man paused briefly, then continued, "Give no response to an inharmonious situation; it will disappear from your path. 'Resist not evil.' as it says in the Bible. Otherwise, your fear is only feeding and enlivening it. Pray with an open heart: 'I put this situation into the hands of God. I give thanks that it is now harmonized and removed from my life.' The Bible states that the battle is God's battle, not man's battle! Repeat this: 'I cast this burden of lack on the Christ within, where it is consumed, and I go free!'"

"But you don't understand. I lost–"

"Know your role within the universe," Angel cut in. "When first you look at another being as he looks upon you, you see yourself mirrored in him. In this single vision, you see the face of Christ, and you understand that you look on everyone as you behold this one brother. And whenever you fail to see the face of Christ in another being, simply know that 'I am the Christ within, consuming this burden of fear and lack.'"

"I am the Christ within..." Keith began, trying to remember the rest.

"Consuming this burden of fear and lack — and I go free!" Angel finished.

"The Christ within consumes this burden, and I go free," said Keith tentatively, still not convinced.

"I am in the presence of grace," Angel added.

"I don't feel any different," Keith said frankly.

"Someday you will feel it. And on that day you will forgive."

"Is that why you're here?" Keith asked shyly. "I mean, living in the streets. Is it because you can't forgive?"

"No, that's not why I am here. I am here to tell you what is – 'what's what,' if you will! You believe that your brothers are guilty because you only see the past and not the Sons of God. The guilt that remains in you hides the Father. You condemn others, believing that in doing so, you are freeing yourself. What you don't yet know is that you can easily free your brothers from the past and lift the clouds of guilt that bind their minds to it. And in this freedom you'll find your own. See no one then as guilty, and you will affirm the truth of guiltlessness in yourself. Guilt makes you blind. While you see one spot of guilt within yourself, or within another, you cannot see the light within. Shrouded within your guilt, the world seems desolate and dark. You've thrown a dark veil over it and cannot see it because you will not look within. Don't be afraid to look within! Find the present. Look upon it lovingly. And with that, I'll jump down from my soapbox. Once again, to answer your question, the answer is 'no.' I live here in the streets because I needed to ask for forgiveness first, before I could start to forgive. And where else could I have met you? Be safe, my friend!"

Angel shook Keith's hand with both of his and placed a rectangular object in them. Stepping backwards, Angel raised his hand in farewell. Keith looked down at his gift. It was a tattered book, its front cover missing and its binding cracked. Keith suspected the glue had cracked from exposure to the freezing temperatures. Blocks of pages were no longer bound to the spine of the book. A dry-rotted rubber band held its pages together. Keith held it gently, gazing at the torn cover page. It read A Course in Miracles by Helen Schucman and William Thetford.

Keith opened the car door, looking on the backseat for his favorite blue Notre Dame sweater. It occurred to him that he didn't get a chance to wear it on the trip. He reached back and grabbed it. Folding it quickly, he reached into the front console and grabbed the envelope. He handed the sweatshirt and the envelope to Angel.

"Angel, it's cold. Please take this. I want you to have it to keep you warm. May you remember me, and every time I see the words 'Notre Dame,' I will remember you. It will be our connection." Keith did not mention the envelope. The man standing in the windy cold accepted the gift. He lifted it in the air as a gesture of happy acceptance.

"Thank you. Thank you, and take care, my friend."

He looked at his new friend one more time as Angel began walking away.

"Angel, thank you. Take care…"

Keith hopped into the driver's seat and started the engine. He watched the man turn around and continue walking through the empty lot and onto the sidewalk. He waved for the last time, even though Angel never turned back around. He gently placed the book in the console between the front seats. It was the first time in a few years that Keith felt good about himself. He felt joy in his heart. The radio turned on a second after the engine fired. The synchronous words of Don McLean's "Vincent" were not lost on Keith.

With eyes that watch the world and can't forget
Like the strangers that you've met,
The ragged men in ragged clothes,
The silver thorn of bloody rose
Lies crushed and broken on the virgin snow.
Now I think I know, what you tried to say to me
How you suffered for your sanity
How you tried to set them free.
They would not listen, they're not listening still
Perhaps they never will.

Angel walked across the parking lot towards the empty gas station. He looked down at the gift he received and noticed the envelope. He read the inscription. "Oprah?"

James ran toward the black man, almost slipping again on the fresh-fallen snow. The buildings encasing the alley were of the old red brick style, with rickety iron stairs running up along the back. There were a couple of green Dumpsters on either side of the alley. In the distance, newer buildings with modern silver exteriors could be seen at the end of the alley. A suspended glass walkway connected the two buildings. James blasted through each cloud of breath as he ran. When he caught up to the man, James noticed that he was wearing a long gray overcoat made of wool, and white Nike tennis shoes. In his hand was a red-and-white-striped box of popcorn. James gently grabbed the man's shoulder, hoping to be greeted by a familiar face. When the man had turned all the way around, James placed both hands on his shoulders to get a good look. The man smiled. He looked at his face. The face was unfamiliar. The man had short dreads and was quite a bit younger than Charlie and Gabriel. It appeared that the young man had a large set of teeth with a bit of an overbite.

"Sorry," James said, embarrassed. "I thought you were someone I knew."

James quickly released the man's shoulders. He was totally winded after the run. He realized that he wasn't twenty anymore. Even after drawing in a large breath, he still was huffing. The man replied with a pat on James's back.

"Hey, no need to be sorry," said the amiable young man. "You recognized me as your brother as you were seeking out a friend. More people should see others as their friends. Who knows, maybe we are friends, yet waiting to happen. It just takes a moment. We are all one!"

James could hardly believe his ears! Was every vagabond in this town a wise man?

"Well, I'm sorry for rushing up on you."

"Again, no need to be sorry when showing friendship to a stranger. It takes just a moment to let go and surrender our egos. Then we see each other as one."

"Yeah," said James, nodding his head vigorously, "you're right. It just takes a moment. I met a…uh… friend yesterday. I thought you were him. He taught me that thing…you know… that thing you guys do…"

The man just shook his head yes, trying to understand what this newcomer was talking about.

"You know, where you let go of everything. Oh! And you ask, 'How may I serve?' 'What can I offer?' Yeah, that's it."

"Oh, yes. To surrender! Good. Good!" said the new friend.

"Those are the first two keys. But I still don't know the other two! I need to know the last two keys. Some people I've met here have told me about the Giving of the Mind. And I know about the Giving of Thy Self. What are the last two, do you know? I need the last two of the Four Givings. Can you tell me?"

"Ah!" exclaimed the man. "You are searching! You have discovered the first two keys. Yes, sure, man. I can tell you all about The Four Givings. You have already shown that you know the third key. It is the easiest to remember. It is the 'forgiving' of The Four Givings."

"Is there a name for the third key?"

"Yes, man. You cannot condemn the Son of God in his parts. When you see others as guilty, they become witnesses to your guilt. Casting guilt and blame brings darkness to all. Always look within to see the Light. The at-one-ment heals. Giving and asking for mercy shines away the darkness. It is known as the Giving of Mercy."

"The Giving of Mercy," James repeated, letting the words sink deep.

James mentally reviewed the phrase several times so as not to forget. A golden finch landed on the garbage bin next to the two men. "Which way did he come from?" James wondered as he spun his head in each direction. The man fed the bird a tiny piece of popcorn as it sat on a cardboard box at the top of the pile in the garbage bin. The bird ate the BB-size treat as another piece between the man's fingers awaited him. The little creature then relieved the man of his second kernel. "Forgiveness heals," he remarked, looking up from his feathery friend. "In forgiving, the fires of hatred and judgment are extinguished. And by humbly asking for mercy, your pain and guilt recede, and eventually vanish."

"Okay! So what's the fourth key?" James felt that time was of the essence. Keith would be leaning on his horn any minute now!

The man smiled enigmatically. "When you are ready, I will tell you! Let's talk about the third key. The Giving of Mercy is the easiest to remember but the most laborious, the hardest.

Many know of this key, but few can unlock the heart with it. To forgive someone is hard. To ask for forgiveness is harder still. Whether you are the transgressor or the victim, both are heavy crosses to bear. When you forgive another, or ask for forgiveness, the inner Christ vision raises the other from their sin and guilt. By seeing their true Self, lifting them into the Light, you restore their vision of the One."

"But some people don't deserve forgiveness. My brother lost his daughter on 9/11. Those terrorists don't deserve forgiveness. Everyone knows they're merciless – even to themselves!"

"You think that the forgiveness is for them? You think that they receive the miracle just because you forgive them? How can a terrorist be blessed by the miracle of your forgiveness when they did not ask to be forgiven? When they find it in their hearts, and ask for forgiveness, only then will the blessings fall upon and enfold them."

"But you know, there are the everyday problems. If my best friend screws me over, or my son doesn't get his ass out of bed and go find a job, am I supposed to forgive because I will benefit? The thing is, I can forgive these people till the cows come home, but they'll still keep on doing what they're doing, and I'll keep on getting pissed. Am I supposed to forgive forever? Look at all the crap that has gone on recently — the earthquakes, the tsunamis. Don't you think that's God's way of showing he's fed up?"

"Judgment is not an attribute of God. We're the only ones who can imagine and cling to the illusion of damnation. That best friend who screws you — sure, you can forgive him, but I never said that you'd have to continue hanging out with him. And as for your daughter dropping out of school, or your son not working, how does that affect you?"

"But they're screwing up their lives! Of course it would affect me. No parent likes to see their kids in pain!"

"Has it occurred to you that maybe that's the spiritual path they themselves have chosen? But are they screwing up your life?"

"What? Are you kidding? Yes! They'd be costing me money, and embarrassing me to death, so yes — I'd definitely call that 'screwing up my life!'"

The man looked unimpressed by James's implied predicament. "You can forgive them if you think that you are really hurt by them. After that, if you feel you will still be hurt, choose not to support them."

"You mean kick them out?" James had heard of "tough love," but how could it fit in with The Four Givings?

"Yes. We're here to experience and to learn. You're holding them back from experiencing and learning. Let them screw up. It is a blessing!"

"We would worry too much. We wouldn't have a moment's rest."

"So, you're telling me that you worry now because your kids left school and don't have a job. You're worried that they might screw up and need your help. Are you afraid of helping them?"

"No."

"Then which way is helping? Letting them stay in the nest, or letting them fly? They may fly quite well. They may learn that they need to get a job. They may come back and be serious about school. What opportunity!"

"You're nuts," James blurted without thinking. "But before I can forgive them, don't the transgressors have to ask for forgiveness or mercy before I, or any victim for that matter, can forgive them?"

"If you forgave someone but they would not ask for mercy, would your willingness to love them be any less, or would it be condemned?"

"No," said James, vaguely aware of something new stirring in his heart.

"And if you asked for mercy," the man persisted, "but the person you were petitioning could not forgive you, would your plea be in vain?"

"No. But I wonder how it would go if you couldn't ask for forgiveness to their faces. I mean, because you're too ashamed, or they live far away." James was thinking of his stepson.

"You truly ask for mercy from your heart, not from your mouth. Why do you think we have prayer?"

James furrowed his brow and searched for a good answer. "So I can pray to God and ask for forgiveness. Do I ask God for forgiveness? Do I pray and ask God to have the person forgive me? Should I pray for the person? Ask God to bless him?"

Just as James had, the man chose his words carefully. "The healing will start at the very moment your prayer is launched, but the wound is deep. It may take many prayers for mercy before the wound finally heals. But there is a better way. Your wrongdoing from years past is dead, but your guilt continues to breathe life into it. If you cannot correct the wrongdoing, then remove it by a kind act today. Perform an act of kindness for someone you know, or a random act of kindness for any person. When you serve others, all is forgiven."

"That seems like a long haul! Isn't there some way to speed things up?"

"Hah! You Americans love your instant oatmeal!" The man laughed good-naturedly. "If you cannot pray daily until healed, and need relief instantly, then make your request for mercy directly to the person in question. Then, and only then, can you be healed instantly and permanently."

"What happens when I'm the one doing the forgiving? Can I forgive someone without letting the person know?"

"Yes!" said the man joyfully.

"I can see that we carry the burden of guilt whenever we do harm to someone. That is our cross to bear. But what is the cross that I carry when I haven't forgiven someone who has harmed me?"

"It's the cross of hatred and judgment. To forgive someone, it doesn't take prayer. You simply forgive them and see them as your brother again."

"But how do I know the hatred and judgment are really gone? How do I know I'm not fooling myself?" James sensed that this was the crux of the matter.

"You'll know it's over when your heart quits hurting when you think of them." The man smiled radiantly. "If it still hurts, then hand it over to God. He'll know what to do with it! Ask God to help you to forgive."

The man paused to hand the bird another piece of popcorn. The bird bobbled its head to the right, then to the left, and finally reached for the corn. James looked back at the parking lot. His brother was still talking to some man.

"Is there someone you need to forgive?" the man casually inquired.

"I don't know. There was this kid when I was little who punched me in the jaw because he thought I called him a bad name."

"What was the bad name?"

"I can't tell you. It's not nice."

"Sure you can," said the man, suppressing giggles. "Don't be scared."

Although innocent, James felt his face flushing at the memory. "Well, he thought I called him the N word, you know. But I swear to you on the Bible that I didn't call him –"

The man laughed out loud as he dug for the last few kernels of corn at the bottom of the box. His mouth was wide open as he laughed, showing all of his teeth. The laughter was loud and seemed to roll along the alley, between the buildings.

"He punched you because he thought you were a racist."

"Yeah, I guess so."

"It sounds like he was the racist."

"I guess so," said James, still shaken by the memory. "But I'm not sure if I have been carrying a cross because of it."

"Why would you even mention something that happened so long ago if you were not still carrying a burden? The burden is that you were probably afraid of black people from that day forward, and may not have extended a hand to one in need, or seen them as your brothers. That is a burden! But you can forgive him. True forgiveness, like true love, is without judgment. Most of us tend to forgive by looking down on the transgressor as we grant something like amnesty. When Jesus said, 'Father, forgive them, for they know not what they do,' he did not focus on what they did. He did not mention any particular act against him; rather, he focused on the forgiveness of our Father. That is true forgiveness, without judgment of the act, where you see the Christ within the transgressor. You look upon them without paying attention to the past."

James shook his head in agreement. The black man turned the popcorn box upside down and shook the remaining crumbs onto the ground. Watching from the box atop the garbage bin, the bird fluttered its wings, gently lifting into the air, then slowly floated to the ground and made its way to the scraps.

"That is all I have, my little friend."

James watched the kindness of this man. He watched as the man bent down and picked up the few kernels on the ground and held out his hand, waiting patiently as the bird made its way over to him. A revelation came to James: I really do judge a man by the color of his skin. Last night proved it. I don't think of myself as prejudiced, but the Checkerboard Club, and the mugging last night showed otherwise. I am a bigot.

The man rose from his squatting position while the bird looked around for any other scraps of charity. The man threw the empty popcorn box into the bin. James grabbed both of his shoulders and looked at him until he had his full attention.

"I'm sorry," he said, inches from the man's face. I'm sorry for anything that anyone has done to harm or try to shame you. I'm sorry for any thoughts I have had that judged or feared any black person. I hope you can forgive me. I'm sorry for any time I have used the N word. I'm just so very sorry…".

The man seemed to feel worse for James than he felt for himself. "No forgiveness needed from here!" he said brightly. "I think we all want to feel important, and one way we do that is by always looking for an opportunity to be offended. To me, nigger is just a word — just like 'bastard,' 'fag,' and 'Screw you.' I have two choices: I can hate you for it or I can dismiss it. I choose not to be burdened by it, and not to burden you with the burden of guilt. We are all one. We have brought it on to ourselves, together, as one. Your sin is mine, and mine is yours. But now you need to forgive yourself. You need to let go. Just as my black brothers need to let go. We brought on slavery, too. We, people of Africa, also have engaged in violence and slavery. Look at what is happening in Darfur, and the Congo, today. So we are not so pure and innocent ourselves. We have carried our cross too long. Black men and women need to forgive whites for prejudices, bigotry, and violations of their rights. It is keeping us down. Many of my black brothers love to carry their weight around their necks, showing whose life has been more of a hell. Those brothers who have forgiven the white race for their transgressions have moved on. We also need to pray for forgiveness for inhuman acts towards whites. There will always be prejudices until we can put down the shields those we hold up to one another. It is the only way that we, as humans, can grow spiritually."

"To paraphrase Bob Marley, who was himself quoting from Haile Selassie: 'Until the color of a man's skin is of no more significance than the color of his eyes, the rule of international morality will remain a fleeting illusion to be pursued but never attained.'"

James's new friend, who had memorized all of Marley's song "War," began to sing:

> *And until there are no longer*
> *First-class and second-class citizens of any nation*
> *Until the color of a man's skin*
> *Is of no more significance than the color of his eyes*
> *Until the basic human rights*
> *Are equally guaranteed to all,*
> *Without regard to race —*
>   *There's war.*
>
> *Until that day,*
> *The dream of lasting peace,*
> *World citizenship,*
> *The rule of international morality*
> *Will remain but a fleeting illusion*
> *To be pursued,*
> *But never attained.*
> *Now everywhere is war, war...*

"And that great statement, my friend, goes for people of every skin color. You are quoting Bob Marley — what a trip!"

"We have friends who judge others," said James, suddenly wanting to air all his dirty laundry.

"For example, we saw a mixed-race couple, and our friends commented that it wasn't fair to their kids to 'put them through' all the trouble. But I'm wondering now what they really meant?"

"Your friends' judgment of the other couple is blocking so much health and prosperity that would otherwise be theirs. Their river of life is clogged with debris. If the mixed-race couple feels fear because of their situation, aware that they are being judged, then their river of life also becomes obstructed. Of course, if you go along with your friends' judgment, or don't stop to question it, you too are blocking your river of life. So when someone casts a judgment, just say, 'Is that so?' Make no judgment of the situation. It requires no feedback! Just move on, and flow with the river of life."

"It's like Tom Cruise getting upset when he was talking with Matt Lauer about Brooke Shields using antidepressants," added James, an avid student of popular culture. "He should have said, 'Is that so?', and left it at that."

"And we should do the same for Mr. Cruise, instead of judging him," the man put in sagely.

"I guess pretty much all I ever do is judge, label, and belittle others too. I think I probably only approve of people who are like me, or people I can understand." It was a sobering – but honest – thought. James felt the exhilaration of truth.

"We believe that our happiness is dependent on other people's actions and behaviors," the man went on. "By casting judgment on others, the judge is asking God to continue to experience the event. He's solidifying it! Unwanted things cannot jump into your reality without being invited. Freedom from your fears will never be experienced if you continue to try to control the behavior of others who are unlike you, or who you don't understand."

"So every time we judge another, we're asking God to let us continue experiencing this judgment?" The irony was staggering.

"Yes."

"But why would that be? You'd think that God could figure out what we're REALLY asking for!"

"It's because of our guilt. When we feel guilty, we attack. Guilt is the root of judgment, attack, and condemnation. We attack another, thinking that they are undeserving of love, and that they deserve damnation. This way, we can continue to believe that we are separate from them, the condemned. We can also feel very, very superior in every way! And by damning them, we, the attacker, believe that we escape our own condemnation. It's all very ridiculous when you think about it!" The man was trying not to laugh. James, he knew, was not amused.

"I have a son whose name is Michael." James began haltingly. "My biggest regret is that I didn't support Michael the way I should have. I feel guilty."

"What do you mean your guilt?" Although he knew what it was, and had just been speaking about it, guilt — actual, living guilt — was a foreign concept to this man personally.

"Yes, my guilt for being so mean to Michael. It eats at me. I'm afraid there were times when I wasn't a very pleasant husband or stepfather. I have been so verbally abusive that I'm ashamed. And I'm afraid that Michael will do the same when he has kids, and all because of me. I don't want him to! I want him to have a happy life! I want to tell him that I screwed up. I really do love him. I hope that he will never be mean like I was mean to him. I want to take it all back. But how can I? It is water over the dam now and there's nothing I can do about it."

The man's eyes softened as he prepared to give hope. "You're right, you know. You can't take it back. It is water over the dam. But what you can do is let it go. You said yourself that it was gone! So how do you make sure it's gone? By telling him you are sorry, and meaning it through and through. Until then, it will be with you. You need to apologize. That's what you need to do to free yourself from it. And mark my words — he will forgive you! And in that moment, you will become as one."

"I can't," said James hopelessly.

"You can. You can pray about it. Ask for forgiveness from God. Ask for courage to meet with your son and ask for forgiveness."

"Do I have to meet with him? How about a letter? Or can't I just ask God for his forgiveness?"

"Yes, you can," said the man soothingly. "But in person, if you ask for forgiveness and he forgives you, both your hearts will open at once, and miracles will flow, the greatest miracle is present. As it says in the Bible, 'Wherever two or more are gathered in my name…'"

James closed his eyes and sighed. He felt like he would collapse any minute. He felt the burden.

The man immediately picked up on it. "The guilt in your heart is so heavy! I can feel the weight. When you feel guilty, the ego has violated the laws of God, but you have not. But until you change your mind about those whom your ego has hurt, the at-one-ment cannot release you. While you feel guilty, your ego is in command because only your ego can experience guilt. Then you condemn others, thinking you're taking the blame off of yourself! This does not need to be."

"I feel weak, as if it were taking all my energy."

"When you give up this voluntary dispiriting, you'll see how your mind can focus and rise above fatigue and then heal. The habit of truly engaging with God and his creations is easily formed if you actively refuse your ego mind and practice the first key, the Giving of the Mind. The problem is not concentration. It is the belief that no one, including you, is worth constant effort. Please raise now, my friend, that I may see the God in you. Oh, yes! I see you as reborn!"

James opened his eyes and looked at the man, who was smiling broadly. The two men lay their hands on each other's shoulders. Their thought became one in Unity.

"Excuse me. I forgot to ask you your name. My name is James."

"Hi, James, my name is Matthew."

He leaned over and extended his hand to James. James looked down, and then met Matthew's hand in friendship. They both smiled, seeing in each other the light of God. James broke the handshake first as his ego pushed for control.

"What about the fourth key, The Fourth Giving?"

"James, you are eager to learn. But I'll tell you what my grandma told me back in Manhattan."

"Manhattan? You're not from Jamaica?"

"No, James, I am not."

James looked him up and down. "But you are a real street person, right?"

"No, James. I am here going to the university. I grew up on the Upper West Side. My father is an Ambassador from Republic of Cape Verde," Matthew said humbly.

"No shit? Darn!"

"Sorry to disappoint you," chuckled Matthew.

"No, no! I just thought you were one of those cool Rastafarian Gandhis running around here."

"Sorry, I…"

"Oh, never mind, it's me just talking," said a very embarrassed James.

"Okay. But once you unlock your heart with the third key, the fourth will be presented. I wish you well, my brother. Take care."

James thanked him and turned to walk away. Matthew reached out and they shook hands a second time. Both whispered, "Unity." The man waved, then turned around and resumed his walk down the alley.

"I hope we all can find peace," James called after him.

"To know peace, teach it, so that you may learn it," Matthew replied cheerily.

James couldn't reply. He ran the words through his head: To know peace, teach it, so that you may learn it. Before Matthew was out of earshot, James urgently raised his voice and yelled, "Do you think he will forgive me?"

Matthew stopped in his tracks and paused. The bird flew ten feet above Matthew's head before landing on a low-hanging wire.

"Listen to me," called Matthew. "Of all the words I've thrown around here, please remember this, and remember it always. Your son, Michael, will forgive you if you ask him to. But his act of forgiveness, without judgment, will bless him like a tidal wave. It will bless all others like a ripple in a stream. It will bless you like a pebble in the sand because your guilt will not allow. And your asking for forgiveness will bless you like a tree; but for all others, including Michael, it will bless like a forest"

Matthew thrust his hands into his pockets and turned around. Just above him, still on the wire, the yellow beauty, startled by Matthew's footsteps, flew away. At the same time, Keith was driving up the alley. James looked back, hoping to catch one last glimpse of Matthew. He had disappeared. James jumped in and Keith continued down the alley, passing the garbage bin. By no coincidence, Keith had tuned into Kansas's "The Wall."

To pass beyond is what I seek; I fear that I may be too weak.

And those are few who've seen it through to glimpse the other side.
The Promised Land is waiting like a maiden that is soon to be a bride.
The moment is a masterpiece, the weight of indecision's in the air.
It's standing there, the symbol and the sum of all that's me.
It's just a travesty, towering, blocking out the light and blinding me.
I want to see.

Gold and diamonds cast a spell; it's not for me, I know it well.
The treasures that I seek are waiting on the other side.
There's more than I can measure in the treasure of the love that I can find
And though it's always been with me, I must tear down the Wall and let it be
All I am, and all that I was ever meant to be, in harmony,
Shining true and smiling back at all who wait to cross
There is no loss.

Chapter 16

"GUESS WHAT THE THIRD key is?" James asked his driver.

"Forgiveness," replied Keith.

"How did you know that?"

Keith smiled. "Lucky guess, I guess."

"It's actually called the Giving of Mercy. But yes, you're right. It's about forgiving and asking for forgiveness. A guy I was just talking to said that giving forgiveness is for your healing, not theirs. You ought to try it."

"Yeah, as if that will happen. Letting go of the ego, I can understand. Giving service and charity makes sense too — which happens to be your problem, by the way! You're concentrating so intently on the lack of work that you're blocking everything, keeping abundance away. But forgiving? Some people just can't be forgiven. Sorry."

A few minutes later and the car turned onto the ramp for the I-90 expressway. Keith's pride ran deep. He thought about what Angel said about his daughter, that she could never find it in her heart to forgive.

"I'm bummed out that we didn't find out what the last key is, the fourth giving of the Four Givings," James said disappointedly.

"Well, maybe it will come to you someday." said his brother.

"You know, on my eighteenth birthday I became 'saved' or 'born again.' I remember it vividly. I acknowledged that I was a sinner, which to me means that you have hurt yourself or others at the direction of your ego. Then you ask for Christ to come into your heart. You actually surrender your ego. I remember the sensation of the presence of the Holy Ghost, and the filling up of Christ in body. It was an awesome feeling. The problem is that we then go on saying we are Christians and yet continue to cast judgment on everyone else. What I think needs to take place is that we try to always surrender our egos and ask Christ to come into our hearts daily, hourly, or as much as we can. As the scriptures say, 'I can do all things through Christ, which strengthens me.' Then there's something about, uh, 'where there is neither Greek nor Jew, uh, something, something, barbarian, Scythian, bondman nor freeman, but Christ is all and in all.' Or how about, 'If there be, therefore, any consolation in Christ, if any comfort of love, if any fellowship of the Spirit, if any bowels and mercies, fulfill ye my joy, that ye be likeminded, having the same love, being of one accord, of one mind.' Philippians, man. Huh? Pretty good, huh?"

James reveled in his self-proclaimed brilliance until he looked down at the center console of the car.

"What happened to the envelope full of money?" James queried.

"Oh, I forgot to tell you. I donated it to that street man who washed my windows."

"You did what?"

"I donated it. He was the same guy that I met outside of Starbucks yesterday. His name is Angel."

"Are you frickin' nuts? I barely can pay my bills and you gave the last of our money away!"

"What? Giving it to him is the same as giving it to Oprah. He definitely is in need."

"In need of what, more booze, or more drugs?"
"I don't think he is like that. Besides what happened about all that crap about the four gifts?"
"The Four Givings!"
"Whatever. What about that crap that it will come back to you, tenfold?"
"Beautiful! That's just great! Nice touch, Einstein! That's just great. That's just frickin' —"
Before James could say another word, both men looked up and saw the slowing traffic. The procession of cars began clumping into lines. He could see the fifty-cent tollbooths up ahead. The reality set in instantly. A horrific feeling nearly overwhelmed him. Oh shit! YOU gave all of our money away!
"Do you have a couple of quarters?" asked Keith, dimly aware of their predicament.
"No. Don't you remember? You gave it all away!"
"I kept a five-dollar bill for the tolls."
Keith started frantically checking his pockets after stretching his body out like a plank. James grabbed the steering wheel to help his brother move into a lane to pay.
"Uh-oh."
"Uh-oh what?"
"I gave my last five dollars to the doorman. We have no money."
"That's frickin' lovely," observed James.
The two searched every pocket and every surface for coins. James looked in the console, between the seats, and on the floors in the back. He came up with some quarters left from before. Keith found a couple in his pockets.
"Here. Here are two more. We have a dollar in quarters," Keith announced.
They pulled up to the booth. They had enough for this one and the next, but was there another toll down the road? Keith

and James tried to remember how many booths there had been on their way to Chicago. Keith pulled up and lowered the window. He looked at the two coins in the palm of his hand. God help us! he thought, throwing them into the plastic basket. The car continued along, seemingly on auto-pilot as the men contemplated their dilemma. It seemed like an hour, but was actually only a few minutes before they reached the next toll. As Keith again rolled down his window, a blast of wind blew into the car, smacking them both in the face. Keith threw their last two quarters into the basket. The barrier rose into the air. They both looked forward. It felt like they were about to cross the Sahara, but for them, a Sahara of asphalt and snow. Keith pushed down the gas pedal.

"What are we going to do now, Mister Let's Give All Our Money Away?" James asked in his most sarcastic tone.

"I can't remember if we have any more fifty-cent tollbooths before we get to I-80/90."

James rolled his eyes. "Even if there aren't any more fifty-cent booths, we are going to need money for the turnpike."

"You would think that this has happened before. They have to have some way to accommodate. Maybe there is an attendant. Don't you think?"

"Do you want to take that chance? For the turnpike, we just need to take a ticket. We can stop at one of the rest stops. They have ATMs," Keith said, waves of relief suddenly washing over him until he looked at the fuel gauge. The red light blared back at him.

"I think there's at least one more fifty-cent booth. I guess we're going to have to get off somewhere and find an ATM."

"I think we have to get off now. We have a bigger problem."

"Now what's the problem?"

"We are out of gas."

"You are brilliant! How in the hell can you make all that money with that melon you call your head."

"You were supposed to remind me."

Their fear of not having money, or not having any gas, was replaced by the fear of getting off at the next exit. They looked ahead and could see clouds of smoke belching into the air from the steel mills. The neighborhoods consisted of dilapidated houses, burned-out buildings, and abandoned cars. The next exit appeared. It was the downtown exit for Gary, Indiana.

As if reading James mind, Keith made the decision, "We don't have a choice. We need to get money."

The car drifted onto the ramp as both men clenched their teeth and knuckles. At the end of the ramp, they looked left and then right, simultaneously. The wind blew against the car, strong enough to rock it. The sun blinded their view. James pointed to the right by tapping on the window.

"I think I see a station over there to the right, between those old buildings."

Keith turned right. About a quarter mile down the road they came upon another abandoned gas station without any pumps on the island. As they started to pull in they realized that the station was all boarded up.

"I can't believe our luck. Two gas stations in a row shut down?"

"What now?" asked James, replacing his sarcasm with the voice of fear.

"We'll just head farther down the road."

I've looked under chairs
I've looked under tables
I've tried to find the key
To fifty million fables
They call me The Seeker

I've been searching low and high
I won't get to get what I'm after
Till the day I die

The Who song blared through the speakers. Keith pulled out of the abandoned gas station and headed south on the desolate road. The pavement was white from the rock salt used to melt the snow. The area was very depressed. About a half mile up the road they came to what appeared to be a business district with old brick buildings still acting as storefronts. There was a beauty salon, a thrift shop, and a specialty boutique with a large poster of a nude female hanging in the window, but there was no sign of a bank or a convenience store. Another half mile down the road they found their oasis — a gas station with a green neon sign reading "ATM." Keith triumphantly pulled the SUV into the station and up to the side of the island next to the road. The passenger side of the car was closest to the street. He passed the first gas pump on the island and drove up the next one in line. He didn't want to block anyone from getting gas: Reduce all possibilities of confrontation, he thought. It was a good decision because a Mercury Grand Marquis pulled in behind him.

"You've paid for everything, so I'll go in and get some cash," James offered. "Besides, your silly white ass with your designer clothes will definitely get us mugged. Do you want anything?"

"Want anything? Yeah, how about getting out of here alive!"

Keith looked for something to release the door for the gas tank. He found a little black lever with a drawing of a white gas pump, next to his seat, on the floor. James jumped out and wrapped his coat tightly around him to protect himself from the wind. Keith got out of the car, inserted his credit card in the slot, removed the pump handle from the carriage, and inserted it into the gas tank. Watching his brother briskly walk into the station, he was also dimly aware of a little old lady getting out of the car behind him. He watched her as she slowly pushed her way against the wind to the glass door of the station.

In the store, a few customers milled around in the cramped area. James walked around the candy rack to the back corner, but no sign of any technology. He looked around but could not find an ATM. He thought: What should we do now? The only thing to do was to ask someone. He got in line and waited behind a younger man wearing a Cub's baseball cap. He noticed that it still had the price tag on it. James looked around to see if there were any more for sale but didn't see any. After the man had purchased his soda and a candy bar, James noticed that he'd walked out without paying for the hat, and the attendant didn't say anything. He stepped closer to the protective glass window that was about two inches thick. A hole in the glass shield allowed conversation between the patron and the cashier.

"Hey, man, do you have an ATM?"

"No, cousin, it was yanked out of here a year ago."

"Do you know where there is one?" James was trying to sound casual.

The guy looked James up and down, as far as the shield would allow. The counter came up to James's stomach and the bullet-proof glass that extended to the ceiling was pretty scratched up. With one glance, the clerk concluded that this man must be lost.

"You might try Lakeshore Drive."

"Ah, thanks. Appreciate it."

The man looked impatiently for any item that this lost white guy might be purchasing. "Otherwise, don't waste my time," the man mumbled. James turned around quickly, almost knocking over an elderly lady standing in line behind him.

"Oh! I'm sorry, ma'am."

James stepped aside and headed for the door. He looked outside, searching for a street sign. Then he remembered that Lake Shore Drive runs along the lake in Chicago and is the address of some of the wealthiest homes in America.

"Ah, that is funny!" James whispered. "What a funny guy! He is hilarious!"

He was startled by a tap on the shoulder. James hoped the clerk hadn't heard him! Whirling around, he came face to face with the elderly woman who'd stood behind him. Her finger was still extended from tapping him on the shoulder. As she moved from her tip-toed stretch back to the ground, James noticed that she was rather short. The lady was a little overweight, with peppery gray hair and appeared to be in her late sixties. She was dressed nicely, wearing fashionable clothes that one might see on a businesswoman. He guessed that she must have just gotten out of church. She wore a red pillbox hat with a small lace veil that covered just one eye. Her coat was red and double-breasted, with large red buttons. Her gloves and shoes matched her red coat.

"Excuse me, sir," she said pleasantly.

James looked down into brown eyes and dark brown skin. He could tell that she was beautiful when she was younger. She wore silver-framed glasses. Her smile and eyes lit up her round, wrinkled face.

"Ah, yes, ma'am. May I help you?"

"No," she smiled. "Actually, I was hoping that I could help you. I overheard your conversation. The closest ATM machine is down on Central Avenue and Tennessee Street. If you head down 11th, it will turn into Central Avenue. Do you know where that is?"

James looked up to the ceiling, trying to mentally map the directions to the unknown location. He also caught sight of his brother, leaning over the car with its hood extended in the air. Oh shit, I hope we didn't break down!

"No, ma'am, I don't know where that is," he said, worried now on two fronts.

"You're not from around here, are you?"

"No, ma'am, I'm from Michigan."

"Oh!" she said in what struck James as a sympathetic tone. "You are a long way from home! You need the money to go home?"

"Ah, well, sort of," he frankly admitted. "We just need to get some money to pay for the tolls. Once we find a rest area, we can get more money at an ATM."

Without missing a beat, the elderly lady reached into her purse. "Please, let me help you. Here…"

The lady started to pull out a rhinestone-studded change purse from her red handbag. James realized what she was going to do. He blushed as he raised his hands in protest.

"Oh, no ma'am, please! I cannot accept any money from you. I…"

"And why not, pray tell? I'm sure you would help me in the same circumstance. Besides, I believe it always comes back tenfold. Here, c'mon…"

She held up a five-dollar bill in her red-gloved hand. James looked at the offering in front of him, but hesitated. She shook the bill, insisting that he take it. He looked down at her bright brown eyes. She whispered, "Take it." James slowly met her hand with his. Accepting her charity, he whispered, "Thank you." He embraced her extended hand lightly, thinking, *This lady is our savior.*

"Thank you," he repeated. "How may I ever repay you?"

"Like I said, I have been paid many times over. No need. My life is full of miracles."

James shook his head in agreement.

"Miracles, I seem to have been hearing a lot about them lately."

Such a gracious and timely offering — from a stranger! Once again, a small miracle has been laid upon him. He wanted to tell her about the Giving of Thy Self, and how her offering had blessed him in more ways than one, but he wasn't sure that she'd understand about the Four Givings. It might even seem like he was preaching to her, she whose generosity didn't need any instruction! He smiled as he softly hugged her with just his hands upon her arms. He didn't know if he could wrap his arms all the way around her to fully embrace her. She reached closer to him and hugged him back.

"Heaven knows I don't get hugged by cute men all that often!" she chuckled. "I am so blessed. Thank you."

"Thank you, ma'am, I will never forget this. You are a saint."

"You are most welcome," she said emphatically. "I pray that God guides you home safely."

"He already has. I promise."

"Take care, sir."

She slowly pushed the door, struggling against the wind with the full weight of her body to open it the remaining few inches. James helped his angel from God by reaching over her head and pushing against the glass. With the bill still in his hand, he paused to watch her walk away. He then looked at the money and thought to himself: Most people in this world are good. Thanks, God! We are blessed.

Keith returned the handle back onto it's carriage as an elderly lady crossed over the island of gas pumps. As she laboriously opened her car door, a man from the car on the other side of the island yelled to her, "Hello, Mrs. Goodwin!" and waved. Before stepping into the car, she turned around and waved back. Keith grabbed the wet squeegee out of the bucket of dirty water then walked in front of his car. He nodded to the lady as he walked back. She continued to stand, supporting herself against her car as she spoke to the man on the other side of the pump. Keith started to wash his windows, wetting down half of his windshield with the sponge side of the washer. He overheard their conversation.

"Mrs. Goodwin, did you buy a new car?"

Keith scraped the wiper-blade side of the washer across his windshield as he listened for her answer. A familiar pain resonated in his body.

With one leg now in her car, Mrs. Goodwin yelled back, "Yes it is! I just bought it. You know, I needed one for so long. I prayed to the Lord and gave thanks for all the blessings in my life. I even gave thanks for things I needed but didn't yet have, including this car! Well, He answered my prayer with a big bonus from work. You should try it. It confirms your faith. Praying with gratitude is so powerful!"

"Praying with gratitude for things I need. Hmmm," considered the man. "I'll have to try it."

Astonished, Keith strained to hear the rest.

"You'll be amazed when you start to believe that God gives you everything you desire and you relate to it with a feeling of deep and profound gratitude. I'm talking about being truly grateful. True gratitude, or gracious attitude, draws the mind into closer touch with God, from whom all blessings flow. Clear your mind and fill it with gratitude! Be grateful for everything in your life! Gratitude will lead your mind to the Source of all things. Being grateful keeps you in harmony with creative thought, and prevents you from falling into competitive thought."

"Well, that's pretty interesting, Mrs. G. The way my life has been going, I guess I need to pray and be thankful for the things I do have. But sometimes, it's just hard with the way things are. Not having money or a job, you know?"

"Yeah, I know the feeling! But when you give your attention to something that you want, and you say 'yes' to it, then you're placing it in your path, synergizing the vibration of your creation to the vibration of the physical effect. In just the same way, when you look at something that you do not want and you say 'no' to it, then again, you're putting it in your path, synergizing the vibration of your damnation with the vibration of the physical effect. I know that may sound a little complicated, but it's really not at all! You just have to be constantly aware of the kinds of thoughts and feelings you're putting out there."

"But how do I not think about the lack in my life when it's right in front of my nose"?

"'Draw nigh unto God, and He will draw nigh unto you.' If your gratitude is strong and constant, God's message will be strong and constant. The action and reaction is equal. The things you want will always move toward you. You can give thanks for not only the blessings in your life, but also for the blessings you want to come into your life. Give thanks with perfect faith. When you can wish without worrying, every desire will be instantly fulfilled. Jesus said, 'I thank Thee, Father, that Thou hear me.' Gratitude keeps you aware of your connection to God. Without gratitude, you begin to think dissatisfied thoughts regarding things as they are. The moment you permit your mind to dwell on lack and unhappiness, you begin to lose ground. To dwell upon the inferior is to become inferior, and to surround yourself with inferior things – like my old junk of a car! This new one suits me much better, I must say!"

"Sounds good," said Mrs. Goodwin's friend.

"Faith is born of gratitude. The grateful mind continually expects good things, and expectation becomes faith. Praying graciously for all the blessings you already experience in your life will open you to new opportunities. The preacher this morning told another story from a book titled, The Game of Life and How to Play It by Florence Scovel Shinn. It is about a pauper begging for food who met a traveler along a road, who stopped him and said, 'My brother, I see that you are poor. Take this gold nugget, sell it, and you will be rich all of your days.' Well, the pauper was overwhelmed by his good fortune and he took the large gold nugget home and put it in a safe place. Just knowing that he had that gold to depend on made him feel lucky and prosperous. He raised the nugget into the air and he praised God for his good fortune, stating that his life was so blessed, and he gave thanks. All that week, every day, he looked at that gold nugget and praised God for his blessed life. The next week, he found a job. Because of the job, the man felt there was no need to sell the gold at that time. He carried it in his pocket to remind himself of his turn in fortune, and that his life was so blessed. Years passed, and he became a very rich man. One day he met a man on the road of little means. He stopped and said, 'My brother, I see that you are in need. Take this gold nugget, sell it, and you will be rich all of your days.' The needy man eagerly took the nugget to a gold dealer to find the value and to sell it. The dealer discovered that the nugget was made out of brass. The depressed man felt discouraged and spent the rest of his days homeless. The moral of the story is that the first man became rich through feeling rich and being thankful, thinking the nugget was gold. As Scovel Shinn points out in her book, 'Many a man is building for himself, in imagination, a bungalow when he should be building a palace.' Many men go to the fountain of life with a shot glass instead of a bathtub. Opulence! When you desire riches, you must be rich first in consciousness. Don't be ignorant of the fact that gifts — in addition to being what they are, expressions of love – are also investments. When you become as ungenerous as a miser, your hoarding and saving will naturally lead to loss. Your abundance is inexhaustible when you begin to fully trust in God's unlimited supply. 'According to your faith be it unto you.' 'Faith is the substance of things hoped for, the evidence of things not seen.' If you can trust, have faith, just enough, no bigger than a mustard seed, miracles will fall upon you. If you can believe, your supply is unlimited, your health and energy are inexhaustible, your heart unfailing. Opulence! 'According to your faith be it unto you.' By giving praise and thanks, your faith will be strengthened. You just need to take your first step by daily acknowledging and enjoying the blessings in your life, praising your life, and giving thanks. The Grace of God will fall upon you. Get in the habit of constantly saying, 'I am blessed.' When you give thanks and praise to God, the Christ vision from within raises you from your sin and guilt. You see your True Self, lifting you into the light and restoring your vision of 'One.'"

"'I am blessed!' I like that! All right, I will start praying and giving thanks. Looking at that beautiful car of yours, and your smiling face, have convinced me."

"Please keep in mind, though, that we have a responsibility to God. That is why it is so important for us to help and heal the poor and the sick, so we do not continue to look upon poverty and disease saying, 'What a shame,' and then continue on with our lives with that vision in our heads, feeling helpless. We need to feel strong and know that we are changing the world so that all are fed, all are educated, and all receive medical care, so that one day there will be no memory of poverty and disease. If you want to have faith in your abundance and prosperity, give something back, help someone out. That shows faith in your future. The money will come back tenfold in one form or another."

"That makes sense. You are such a role model! I will do that."

"I am here now, thankful, blessed in the grace of God. By giving thanks for everything you have, you become free of your covetousness and envy. The appreciation of others, and the appreciation of yourself, is the best way to connect, to be closer to your Creator. It removes your wanting, and your perception of not having. My preacher calls it one of The Four Givings. The four keys to be closer to God! Give praise and thanks for your blessings. He calls it the Giving of Gratitude! When you are in a state of gratitude, the river of life will flow abundance to you, and miracles will begin to appear!"

With that, the elderly lady got into her car, waved at the man, and shut the door. The man waved and yelled, "Have a nice day!" James came out of the store with a can of Coca-Cola in his hand and watched her driving away in her shiny new car. He ran across the lot and over the gas-pump island as Mrs. Goodwin's friend returned the pump to its holder. The wind blew James's coat open as he ran around the grill of the SUV.

"Damn! It's cold," he blustered, jumping into the car.

"Did you get the money?"

"Well, sort of. They didn't have an ATM machine but this older lady overheard my conversation and gave me five bucks."

Keith's mouth dropped open. "You mean the older lady who just left?"

"Yeah, I guess."

"Well, that was sure nice of her! It will at least get us past the fifty-cent tolls, but we'll still have to stop at one of the rest areas to get more. Did you thank her?"

James snapped open the top of his soda can and took a sip.

"Yeah, of course I thanked her."

"Did she buy you the soda too?" Keith teased.

"No. I bought it using the five dollars."

"You mean to tell me that the lady just gave you five dollars from the bottom of her heart so you can make it home, and then you go ahead and spend it on soda pop? You're unbelievable."

"I was thirsty, all right? God! What's the big deal?" James asked defensively.

"You took charity and then you blew it," Keith shot back. James couldn't tell if he was angry or just teasing him. It felt like a little of both.

"We still have three dollars and some change," James said, trying to mollify him. "Besides, I didn't want to ask the guy to break a five-dollar bill to get quarters without buying something. He wouldn't have liked it."

"You big sissy, what are you scared of?"

"Listen to you. You were just whining about getting out of here alive."

James reached into his pocket and pulled out all the change.

"I have three dollars and ninety-five cents, so there!"

"Unbelievable."

"At least I didn't give away all of our money to a bum."

Chapter 17

KEITH BACKTRACKED TO THE expressway and then drove until he finally reached the I-80/90 turnpike. The five dollars were not needed. There were no more fifty-cent tolls. Keith rolled down his window and grabbed the ticket from the turnpike booth. They drove along in silence, each lost in thought about all that had happened. Finally, they reached a rest area with a gas station, a few restaurants, and a convenience store. After using the bathroom, they stopped in the store to find an ATM. James found it first and took out sixty dollars. Keith followed, taking out two hundred dollars. Their next stop was the food court's Burger King. Wanting to even out all the treating Keith had done over the past few days, James bought his brother's lunch. Carrying the food and drinks back to the car, he stepped cautiously over the ice as the wind whistled in his ears, pushing him along. Keith turned the heater on full blast and positioned himself right in front of the vent.

 James began distributing the food to his brother. He put his drink between his legs, then handed Keith his pop. Keith did the same, placing his drink between his thighs. James handed his brother the white cardboard box, housing the sandwich. Keith grabbed the burger with one hand and kept the other hand on the heater vent. James placed two sets of fries in the console cup holders. Keith pulled out of the parking space and started back on their journey.

"Well, everything worked out okay. I guess we should be thankful." James said thinking of the minor crisis they thought was a catastrophe.

"Oh, that reminds me! Guess what I found out?" Keith could hardly believe that a burger and fries had made him forget the most important thing of all.

"That it's hard to hide the fact that you're gay?" guessed his wise guy brother.

"I'm glad to see that The Four Givings is really working for you. Never mind, I won't tell you."

"Alright, I'm sorry. What were you going to tell me?"

"What I was going to tell you is that I know what the fourth key is to the Four Givings."

"How did you figure that out? Did you meet some Rastafarian or Creole at the ATM machine?"

"No. It was at the gas station in Gary, Indiana. And it wasn't a Jamaican. It was that elderly lady there who told me. Well, she didn't actually tell me. I overheard her telling the man pumping gas next to her."

"You mean that nice lady who gave me the five dollars? I can't believe it." It figures, James thought, that the giver of the money would also be the giver of the fourth and final giving.

"Believe it. That is if you want to believe in this voodoo crap."

"It's crazy. God gave us the four keys" – James snapped his fingers – "just like that. Maybe there is a connection between all of us and God. So tell me, what is the fourth key?" James felt a surge of suspense that went beyond any movie-theater variety he had known.

"Well, the lady came out of the gas station while you were thinking of yourself and buying a pop and –"

"I told you that I had to get quarters," James interrupted defensively.

"Anyway, she mentioned to the man that we should always give thanks to God for all the blessings we've received. It confirms our faith. Giving genuine thanks for everything we have leaves no room for covetousness or greed, and it cures envy. She said that. And guess what?"

"What?"

"She actually said that her preacher refers to it as one of The Four Givings. The keys to enlightenment! There's your fourth giving: Give thanks for your blessings. The fourth key is called the Giving of Gratitude!"

"Wow! This just blows me away! Now we have all four keys to creating miracles, The Four Givings. One, giving up or surrendering your ego; two, giving charity or your service to others; three, forgiving and asking for forgiveness, and finally, number four, giving thanks."

James pulled down the visor to look in the small mirror then he continued with his thought, "You know, even before the fourth key came our way, I had an insight. It just suddenly struck me that we all seem to be of two minds: the 'Aware Mind,' being love, and the 'Ego Mind,' being fear. The Aware Mind expresses, which is the love, the godlike mind, the Holy Spirit, spirit in body connected to God. And the ego mind can only express what it is — namely, fear and guilt, masked as special ness and an assumed superiority to other egos. The ego is kind of like the Devil. I suddenly knew for a fact, without even knowing why, that unlike egos, God does not judge! God is all love! The devil is your ego, which makes decisions based on fear. Does that make sense to you?"

"I don't know, it's kind of voodoo, mumbo jumbo talk." Keith challenged.

"My God, you don't believe in this? You don't believe that we can decide to live in that aware, loving, peaceful, joyous mind, without fear, without guilt, and without judgment. The Holy Spirit is Christ, expressing in body. Or, we can choose ego, the judging, fearful, competitive, and guilt-ridden Devil. The problem, of course, is that as we go about our daily business, we choose the ego mind 90 percent of the time. All I know about percentages," said James, his mind suddenly razor-sharp, "is that whatever you think about a majority of the time is going to be attracted to you. Most people are so scared that they tend to dwell on the negative, or they suspect somebody's trying to rip them off or deceive them. People seem to think from the side of lack. Instead of going to the fountain of life with that bucket they go with a puny ol' shot glass. I believe it is our birthright to be successful."

Keith tried not to be so pessimistic by adding, "Have you ever heard that if you collected all the money in the world, and distributed it evenly, it's said that in a matter of a few years, the money would end up back with the people who originally had it?"

"Yeah, I can see that happening. But getting back to The Four Givings, we need to let go of our egos by quieting our minds, or by helping others, or by forgiving ourselves and others, or by giving thanks. I see them all as invitations for the Holy Spirit to take over. When we quit thinking about the worries of tomorrow, or the regrets of yesterday, and we allow this moment – now! — To just be as it is, we are living in God. When we forget about ourselves in the moment, or help others through service, or being grateful, it clears the way for the Holy Spirit to enter. And when we forgive someone, or they forgive us, we see each other as brothers in Christ!" James stated excitedly.

James paused, waiting for his brother to comment but Keith remained silent so James continued, "When we are grateful for all the blessings in our lives, God communes with us. This state can be represented by a dove, which is also a symbol of peace.

To live in Christ means to turn on that faucet of everlasting love, pick up the receiver and guess who's on the other line! Surprise! It is God! We just have to surrender our egos by acting daily on The Four Givings. It's that wonderful freedom that knows no fear, no guilt, no pain, and no judgment. All is love, joy, and peace. You are then opening your heart for miracles to show up in your and others' lives."

"In the Buddhists' view, there is no actual opposite of love, joy, and peace. They believe in harmony. They don't need an opposite." Keith added even though he still wasn't committed to this new philosophy.

"The only thing that I don't get…" James pondered out loud, "Is that these four keys will unlock miracles in our life. I got that. But they talked about that we will see the greatest miracle of them all. I don't know what they mean."

"Mean what?" Keith looked over questioning.

"I don't know what this greatest miracle is. Charlie mentioned it, do did Gabriel, and Matthew. You know the guy in the alley."

For a moment, James forgot about his guilty feelings toward Michael, he forgot that he was not working, he forgot about all his fear-based prejudices, and, for a moment, he forgot that his brother was dying. For a moment, Keith forgot about his daughter's death, he forgot that he hated so much, he forgot about the problems with Jillian, and, for a moment, he forgot that he was dying. At the same time, unknown to the brothers, bits and pieces of a Marley song was wafting through both their minds at once.

And you should know,
You should know by now.
I like it. I like it like this, I like it like this.
Satisfy my soul, whoa, yeah.
You satisfy my soul.

Every little action is a reaction.
Oh, can't you see what you've done for me,
Oh, can't you see what you've done for me?
Oh yeah. I'm happy inside, all, all of the time.

Chapter 18

"LOOK! YOU CAN SEE the gold dome of Notre Dame University! That means we're halfway home," said James.

Keith looked at the glittering dome and thought of Angel and the Notre Dame sweater that he'd given him. Angel's words rang in his head: "It was the hate. The hate inside that killed her. Ever since that day, she could never find it in her heart to forgive."

"Hey! Would you mind if we stop again and go to Notre Dame?" Keith asked.

"Are you hungry again?"

"No, I just wanted to pick up another sweater or something from the bookstore. Is that okay?"

"Yeah, I know where the book store is. I've been to it before a football game. Maybe I'll look for the stadium." James said, thinking aloud. "Let's go."

Keith got off at the next exit and drove onto the Notre Dame campus. They could see St. Joseph's Lake and, in front of them, above the tree line, the spire of the Basilica of the Sacred Heart. Once again the wind blasted their bodies. James grabbed his coat from the backseat. Keith zipped his jacket all the way up to his neck. The sidewalks were mostly clear of snow except for a few patches of ice where there was a low spot in the concrete. James jumped over the ice patches. Keith just walked around them in the snow. As they passed between buildings, the wind subsided. Ahead lay the Eck Visitors' Center, crowned by James's beloved golden dome. Keith wondered out loud about the figure at the top of the dome; James raised his arm and pointed straight ahead. He explained that the figure was the Mother Mary and that Notre Dame means "Our Lady" in French. "I think we just keep walking straight until we're parallel to the stadium off to the left. As I remember, the Hammes Building, where the bookstore's located, should be one of the buildings on the right-hand side."

Keith looked ahead to where his brother was pointing. I'm at my crossroads, he thought. The entrance to the basilica was very inviting to him.

"Hey, would you mind going ahead without me? I want to go into the church for a minute and look around."

"Do you want me to go with you?" asked James, momentarily missing the point.

"No, no. I'll catch up with you."

James had an idea of what his brother needed to do. He searched for the right words.

James added a quick, wordless prayer that his brother would find this miraculous giving – this may take some time!

"I'll meet you back here."

Keith shook his head in agreement but said not a word. He squeezed his brother's shoulder, then turned and headed for the Minster. James watched his brother as he mounted the steps of the church. He wondered what was going through his head. He knew that Keith had gone through a lot, but he couldn't make sense of the urgent need for this unplanned stop. Keith threw his head back and looked way, way up at the belfry. The white cross at the top of the steeple stood brightly against the dark gray clouds. He walked up the marble steps, grabbed onto the golden handle to a heavy wooden door, and passed through the stone archway. He was expecting to hear the door creak, but it opened silently. Keith peeked into the church. It appeared empty, so he quietly slipped in, pressing his hands behind him against the door to prevent any loud slam that might disturb a priest or someone praying. The sight of the beautiful architecture took him by surprise — it was as if he'd been transported to a heavenly realm. Keith had never been to Europe, but he imagined this to be very close in magnificence to the Sistine Chapel, or to Westminster Cathedral. At the entrance of the church stood a large gray marble bowl that sat on a pedestal and the stand was of hand-carved wood, with a golden dove flying upside down along the base. It reminded Keith of a large birdbath, but he figured it must be a baptismal font, or used for holy water. The base of the stand was surrounded by green marble tile, with white swirls, in the shape of a hexagon. Carpet surrounded the tile, spreading behind the oak pews and all the way up the nave. Keith lifted his head in awe. White columns, topped with gold leaf, appeared on each of the far sides of the two groups of pews. Above the columns were white-pointed arches. Light streamed in from the stained-glass windows, splashing colors over the top of the pews. Angelic murals, set against dark blue and golden backgrounds, adorned the ceiling. The church was long, with rows of pews on either side. The main altar glistened in gold-leaf tributes to various Christian saints. It was about two o'clock in the afternoon, and, aside from the two altar boys extinguishing candles from the Sunday morning masses, the cathedral was empty. Keith walked down the aisle and sat in a pew about seven rows from the back. He pulled down the kneeler and assumed an upright kneeling position. Gazing up at the saints floating on clouds above him, Keith took in such a deep breath that it caused him to shake like a crying child. The altar boys exited through a side door, leaving Keith completely alone in the church. He smelled a strange spice. Frankincense, he thought. He closed his eyes and folded his hands as he placed his elbows onto the pew in front of him. He gently laid his forehead against his thumbs and began to pray...

"Heavenly Father, in Christ I pray. Lord, thank you. Thank you for all the blessings you have poured upon me. I feel so blessed. I don't know what I have done to receive your gifts. The job and home that I have, and my wife...

Lord, I pray for Jillian's health. I pray for my wife. I pray for my brother and sister. Be with my brother James. We both know he is out there sometimes. Help him find what he is looking for.

There is so much hate in me. Lord, forgive me for my hatred. My pain is deep. Forgive me for anytime that I may have hurt someone while climbing the corporate ladder. Forgive me for any joke that may have offended anyone. Forgive me for not standing up for others in the name of righteousness. I ask for forgiveness.

Lord, I believe I am dying. My stomach aches, my heart hurts. I am weak. I try to keep up a positive front, but I want to cry. I am scared. I don't know what to do. I always seem to fix everything for everybody but I can't fix this. I can't fix this! How, Lord? How? Show me the way."

Keith hands squeezed tighter. His eyes welled with tears and he clenched his teeth. He leaned back against the pew and opened his eyes to the blue- and-gold ceiling with the mural of angels and saints.

"Lord, my God, I know I am to forgive. But I can't. I can't forgive them. I can't forgive them for taking her away from me. I hate them. I hate them. They killed my daughter! I love her and miss her so much. I love her. I can't forgive them for what they have done! I want to die! God forgive me! Forgive me! I can't forgive them for what they did. I can't find it in my heart. I hate them all. Forgive me...Show me the way, Lord."

Keith, alone, in the Presence of God, sobbed like a child. Tears rolled from his cheeks and fell onto his knees. He pointed his hands upwards, and then rested them on his heart; he raised his head again but then closed his eyes. Warmth fell upon his face. The light coming through the stained glass increased. Rainbows of light filled the cathedral.

"Lord, I am a sinner. I have sinned against Thee. I surrender. I surrender to the Holy Spirit. I recognize Christ as my Lord and savior. May Christ enter my heart! Wash my sins away through your grace. I surrender to the Holy Spirit. "

Keith opened his eyes. He cleared his mind and let go of thought. He felt the moment. How may I serve?

He listened. His heart filled with the Holy Spirit, Christ within, in communion with God. Revelation fell upon him. He felt the Presence of the triune God, the Father, the Son, and the Holy Spirit. It filled him to overflowing.

"In Christ, I pray, Amen."

A rainbow appeared, stretching across the ceiling and arching all the way below the keystone of the arch, coming to completion at the altar.

Outside of time, Keith tasted eternity.

Chapter 19

KEITH PUSHED OPEN THE heavy door with his back, his hands in his pockets. The sun, now shining through cumulus clouds, bathed the marble floor of the church entrance, making it whiter than white. The air smelled fresh and crisp, and tickled his nose. Still in that one moment, he walked in God's arms. James was sitting on the bottom two steps, enjoying the sunshine on his face, looking into the sky. Keith bounced on each step as he made his way downward. James turned around on the step and then stood up. He looked at his brother and noticed the white trails of dried tears on his brother's red cheeks.

"You're okay?"

"I'm fine, Brother."

Keith hugged his brother on the bottom step. The bells in the tower rang two times for the top of the hour. The brothers walked across the campus, patting each other on the back and going out for air football passes, pretending to be the quarterback and wide receiver, as if Knute Rockne were watching. James caught the final air ball by slamming onto the hood of the rented SUV. Keith unlocked the car as James rolled off the hood. James looked across at his brother. He seemed relieved. He seemed happier, but James figured it wasn't his business to ask. They returned to the turnpike and

The Four Givings

headed east again. Keith never mentioned the church all the rest of the way home.

And as we lie beneath the stars
We realize how small we are
If they could love like you and me
Imagine what the world could be

If everyone cared and nobody cried
If everyone loved and nobody lied
If everyone shared and swallowed their pride
Then we'd see the day when nobody died
When nobody died...

    The Nickelback song rang into the speakers. The remaining drive through Indiana flew by without much conversation. All of the excitement began to wind down and exhaustion began to set in. Keith paid the Indiana toll when they reached the Ohio-Indiana line. A few miles down the highway, the Ohio Turnpike started, and another booth appeared. Keith grabbed the ticket from the machine, and then continued to drive into Ohio.
    "Wow," said James. "We're almost home — just one hour."
    "Hey, do you mind if we listen to the radio for a while?" Keith asked.
    "Sure, go ahead."
    James scanned the offerings until he found a station coming in from Toledo. The news program was starting at the top of the hour.
    "Is this all right?" James wasn't sure Keith wanted to hear the news, which had to be bad news.
    "That's fine. Turn it up. I want to hear this," Keith said cheerfully.

In its report, "AIDS in Africa," the UN agency examines three potential scenarios for the continent in the next 20 years, depending on the international community's response. Researchers determined that even with massive funding and better treatment, the number of Africans who will die from AIDS is likely to top 67 million in the next two decades. "What we do today will change the future," concluded the report, drawn up by some of the world's leading experts on HIV and AIDS. "These scenarios demonstrate that, while societies will have to deal with AIDS for some time to come, the extent of the epidemic's impact will depend on the responses and investment now."

"Wow! Sixty-seven million will die from AIDS," James said, shocked. "We have to do something —"

Africa has been hit harder by the HIV/AIDS virus than any other region of the world. More than 17 million Africans have died from AIDS and over 25 million are infected with the HIV virus, approximately 1.9 million of whom are children. Every day, 8,000 people die and another 13,000 contract the HIV virus, nearly 1,800 of whom are children. In poor countries, there are approximately 6 million AIDS patients in need of lifesaving medicines, but only 700,000 currently have access. More than one billion people, including half the population of Sub-Saharan Africa, live on less than one dollar a day.

In other news, According to recent estimates, at least 400,000 people have died in Darfur since the genocide began in February of 2003. It is impossible to know what the final number will be, however, as the genocide is still taking place today. There are approximately 3.5 million men, women and children in the western Darfur region of Sudan trying to survive the Sudanese government-sponsored campaign of violence and forced starvation. These innocent victims are *essentially on life support, their continued existence dependent on U.S. and international humanitarian aid and the presence of African Union peacekeepers. Despite the best efforts of the under-funded and under-manned African Union peacekeeping force, attacks have increased in recent months, leading to tens of thousands of new arrivals at refugee camps in Darfur and across the border in Chad. 2.5 million people have already been driven from their homes in Darfur, Sudan. The refugees now face starvation, disease, and rape, while those who remain in Darfur risk displacement, torture, and murder. The President's next year's budget provides only $441 million for UN peacekeeping operation in Sudan...*

"That is where we should be sending out troops and spending our war chest on." James exclaimed.

"It is not a strategic region for our national security." Keith replied.

"You mean there is no oil there." James added.

...Moving now to the War on Terror, the cost of the war in Iraq will reach $320 billion after the expected passage next month of an emergency spending bill currently before the Senate, and that total is likely to more than double before the war ends, the Congressional Research Service estimated this week.

"We could have put an end to hunger and starvation with that chunk of change!" said James indignantly. "If I were president –"

The analysis, distributed to some members of Congress on Tuesday night, provides the most official cost estimate yet of a war whose price tag will rise by nearly 17 percent this year. Just last week, independent defense analysts looking only at

Defense Department costs put the total at at least $7 billion below the CRS figure.

Once the War Spending Bill is passed, military and diplomatic costs will have reached $101.8 billion this fiscal year, up from $87.3 billion in 2005, $77.3 billion in 2004, and $51 billion in 2003, the year of the invasion, congressional analysts said. Even if a gradual troop withdrawal begins this year, war costs in Iraq and Afghanistan are likely to rise by an additional $371 billion during the phase-out, the report said, citing a Congressional Budget Office study. When factoring in costs of the war in Afghanistan, the $811 billion total for both wars will far exceed the inflation-adjusted $549 billion cost of the Vietnam War.

"Could've cured AIDS with that money, too," James slid in bitterly.

But according to one of the world's leading economists, that is just a fraction of what Iraq will actually wind up costing American taxpayers. Joseph Stiglitz, winner of the Nobel Prize in Economics, estimates the true cost of the war at $2.267 trillion.

"If you remember, the White House's own economic adviser, Lawrence Lindsey, was fired for predicting, in September 2002, six months before the invasion, that the total cost of the war might reach between $100 billion and $200 billion. Do you remember that?" James's recall for such details had been honed by frequent debates with many of his pro-war friends.

… The death toll for the American and coalition forces has passed the 3000 mark…

"I think that the death count for Iraqi civilians is somewhere around sixty thousand people," James went on.

"The dollar cost of this war and sixty-three thousand lives is a hell of price to pay. That is a hell of a price! We can't even give one percent of that to Africa to save millions of lives. Our priorities are screwed up."

"Listen to you getting all righteous!" countered Keith. He continued, "Screw the Iraqis. Screw all of them! This war has to continue on. We cannot pull out before the job is done."

"What is that job? Define it." James questioned.

"The job, plain and simple, is to end evil in the world, to end terrorism. And who are the terrorists? Easy: The Muslims are."

"But why do you say that? We need to be asking, ''Why do they hate us?' And that is easy to answer. One reason could be that we, as a country, have a mission statement called the National Security Strategy, also known as the president's own doctrine. It states that the United States will do everything in its power to maintain military supremacy and we have the right to take preemptive action against any country, even though we do not have sufficient proof of any aggression against the U.S. Sounds a little like the Roman Empire days of oppression and what Jesus was standing up against. No wonder they hate us."

"First of all," began Keith, inhaling deeply, "I have read the thirty-five page document, and are you aware that it states that our mission is to support Palestine in its efforts to become a democracy? And we are to support Sub-Saharan countries in Africa to promote democracy? Have you read it? It's easy to sit on the sidelines and bitch about our ideologies, but go put on a uniform and go drive around in Iraq. Go up to the insurgents and tell them you're sorry. See how long you keep your head. Has it ever occurred to you that to stop terrorism, you first have to create a democracy, so that freedom will spread? Did you ever think that maybe the best strategy is to take the fight over into their backyard instead of ours? You've noticed, of course, that we haven't been attacked again."

James leaned over, his eyes suddenly bugging out, and stabbed his temple with his index finger to make his point. The vein in his temple protruded and his face turned red.

"Screw you. Wasn't Russia or China our enemy thirty years ago? Then our enemy was Vietnam. Looks like now we have replaced it with Iraq! Where ever we need a country's resources, or if one of our corporations may gain from our occupation, we go in, saying it is because of democracy and freedom. Have you ever heard of the Military Industrial Complex? We have to keep the war machine producing, so we get the citizens buy-in by scaring them, and then we force our "liberation" at gun point. Fear always needs an enemy."

"If we don't protect our interests, we become victims. Think if the oil-rich countries decided to hold us hostage by not supplying oil. What would happen to your way of life? How will you get to work? How are you going to heat your house? It would cripple us, our economy, our safety, and our freedom. We have to take military action to protect our way of life." Keith stated loudly.

"But do you know why half the world hates us?" James asked.

"Yes," said Keith smugly. "They hate us because they are heathen extremists who don't want democracy because then they will have to give everyone equal rights. They are afraid of our free way of life."

"They hate us because we constantly force them to submission by occupying their country or by supporting other countries. Perfect example is Palestine. In 1947, Britain partitioned the land for Israelis and Arabs in two equal pieces, even though the Arabs made up two-thirds of the population. In 1948, Israelis declared a Jewish state, and started a war called the Israel War of Independence, which forced seven hundred and fifty thousand Palestinians out of their homes; they had to live in exile in neighboring counties, sleeping in tents. In December of 1948, a UN resolution was adopted, affirming the right of the Palestinians to return to their homes and property, but it never happened. By 1949, Israel had bullied its way in and grabbed 50 percent more land than the original UN partition. Even that wasn't enough. Israel started the Six-Day War in 1967, then conquered and moved into Sinai and the Gaza Strip, then conquered the West Bank from Jordan, and finally the Golan Heights from Syria. And how was all this accomplished by such a small country? Because the Arabs didn't have any major artillery — but Israel certainly did because they were, and continue to be, funded by the United States! Every bomb destroying Palestinian houses had our country's stamp on it, and our tax dollars behind it. Then, once again, the UN stepped in and drafted Resolution 242, stating that Israel shall withdraw from territories conquered. But it never happened. Then the UN produced Resolution 338, again mandating that Israel shall withdraw — but it never happened! Then there were the Camp David Accords, yet again ordering Israel's withdrawal — but it never happened! Then, once again, the UN adopted Resolution 465, calling for Israel's withdrawal from existing settlements in Arab territories occupied since 1967. Hundreds of thousands of Palestinians are homeless, having lived in tents for many years in neighboring countries, even though they have deeds to their original land. The Palestinians in the occupied West Bank, Golan Heights, and Gaza Strip, are treated as sub-humans. All water infrastructures from the Jordan River, for example, go to the Israeli homes, but Palestinians cannot even drill a new well because it may take water from the Israelis."

"Wow!" exclaimed Keith. "What a perverted distortion! First of all, it was Egypt, Syria, Lebanon, Jordan, and Saudi

Arabia that declared war on Israel in 1948. They ganged up on Israel so of course we were going to help!"

"Yes, with American bombs and bullets."

"And guess what? Israel gave the land back after that war and was starting to pull out of occupied territory when the Palestinians started to crank up their terrorist acts. They are the ones who want to stage war! Also, the UN resolution gave Jerusalem to Israel, but Jordan still held half of it. So Isreal had every right to take Jerusalem, the Gaza Strip, and the West Bank, because it is their biblical right. God said it was to be their land of milk and honey. We must protect and defend Israel because the Israelis were the first to believe in democracy, and they are the chosen tribes of God. It seals our faith that we must defend them from Arab oppression. Look at any map. There are twenty-two Arab countries and Iran, which is not considered Arab, surrounding Israel, fifty people to one, all wanting to kill them. For thousands of years, Israelis have lived under slavery and oppression. They have been occupied and enslaved by Egyptians, by Romans, and by Germans. It is our God-given responsibility to safeguard them. Don't you agree that we are to help the oppressed? Did you forget the six million Jews that died in Nazi concentration camps?"

"It is our responsibility to protect the poor and stand up for the oppressed. Nothing against Israel, but they are not oppressed!" James was staggered by their differing viewpoints, but determined to hold his ground.

"Oh, did you forget about the Nazi Holocaust, just as the President of Iran did?" returned Keith.

"Look," said James, trying to be patient. "You have Palestinian children throwing sticks and stones, while Israel soldiers open fire with machineguns and 50-mm cannons. Read about the hundreds of Palestinian civilians massacred in cities. For every Israeli citizen killed by a Palestinian terrorist,

Israel kills 50-100 Palestinian citizens. President Carter writes that for every Palestinian accused of attacking Israel, twelve innocent families lose their homes. Israel bulldozes Palestinian houses because they are too close to Israeli settlements or because of "security" issues while Israeli settlements are being built in the occupied territory funded by the United States. Each Israeli settler has the privilege of using five times the amount of water that a Palestinian is allowed to use, yet the Palestinian pays four times more for the water. There are Israeli swimming pools next to Palestinian villages where drinking water has to be hauled in on tanker trucks and dispensed by buckets."

"Oh sure, the Palestinians are victims. What about the victims in Israel? The Palestine Liberation Organization, Hamas, Islamac Jihad, Fatah, and all the terrorist groups' main goal is the destruction of Israel, don't you know that? They kill, mainly targeting buses, restaurants, and open-air gathering places in every major city. Do you know how many of thousands of Israeli people have been killed, and wounded by Palestinian terrorists?. And let us not forget the people killed at the U.S. Embassy, and the Marines killed in their barracks, in Lebanon."

"But what about —"

Keith interrupted. "You ungrateful bastard, Israeli and American Jewish citizens have done more for the United States than any of our other allies. If we let the terrorists control Israel, then we are defeated. And I guess you think that the people in Iraq were not oppressed under Hussein. We freed them from tyranny. War is the only way to deal with terrorism. Quit feeling sorry for the terrorists!"

James barely knew where to begin. It seemed to him that his brother had been completely brainwashed. "War is not God's choice. Christ is not coming down from the sky. Christ will come from within, at any moment; our Savior can come only from within. Charlie told me that to really know our brothers we should look for the Holy Spirit in each person, no matter what their state is or what they do. I'm looking now, Keith, but I can't find yours. I just see hate."

"And I just see nothing but judgment from you. Oh my God! You like to sit on your high horse and think 'Love is the answer.' These people treat their dogs better than they treat their women. Their women are enslaved. They kill in the name of Allah. They have beheaded innocent people. Don't you get it? They want to kill us, all of us, all over the world. Until we deal with these terrorists, no place in the world is safe. My daughter was burned and crushed in mortar. Do you remember your niece? Did you forget the death count for 9/11, and that one of those numbers is your niece? What about the terrorist attacks at Yemen, India, Indonesia, Kenya? Want me to keep going? Hamas recently called on all Muslim nations to 'teach the American enemy a harsh lesson.'"

"What about forgiveness?" James asked, hoping to get back to basics.

"What they did cannot be forgiven," Keith stated flatly. "I hope God kills them all. When the last Muslim fanatic falls dead, then maybe, we will have peace on earth."

"All of them dead? Do you know that Israeli tanks, supplied by the U.S., killed 19 civilians, mostly women and children, in Gaza City?"

"It still doesn't top the highest toll — 29 Israelis killed by a Palestinian suicide bomber at a Passover gathering in March 2002," Keith fired back. "Are you advising that we not help our only ally in the region? Think, for once in your life, what my daughter, your niece, had to go through. Did you ever think of her once? Did you ever think how she had to die? Did you? I think of it every day. Did she burn to death? Did she suffocate? Was she trampled? Was she smashed by steel and mortar? You're still a naive little kid with Mom still wiping your ass. Grow the hell up. We have enemies out there who'll kill you. And you want to hand them flowers."

Except for the news on the radio, the car was silent as they traversed the snowy white plains of Ohio. James stared out the window, his head against the glass as Keith drove with both hands on the wheel. He tried to feel what his brother was feeling. Not having any biological children himself, he could not imagine what it would be like to lose a daughter. A half-hour later, Keith pulled into James's driveway. The bump as the car lifted onto the asphalt made James's forehead slam against the glass. The SUV came to a halt in front of the garage door.

> *Rick Weiss of The Washington Post reports that scientists have discovered a tiny genetic mutation that largely explains the first appearance of white skin in humans tens of thousands of years ago, a finding that helps solve one of biology's most enduring mysteries and illuminates one of humanity's greatest sources of strife. The work suggests that the skin-whitening mutation occurred by chance in a single individual after the first human exodus from Africa, when all people were brown-skinned. That person's offspring apparently thrived as humans moved northward into what is now Europe, helping to give rise to the lightest of the world's races. Several sociologists and others said they feared that such revelations might wrongly overshadow the prevailing finding of genetics over the past 10 years: that the number of DNA differences between races is tiny compared with the range of genetic diversity found within any single racial group.*

"We're all flipping 'One,'" said Keith, figuring that James would understand his meaning. He pressed the radio button changing the station.

James grabbed his CD case, stepped out of the car, and shut the door without saying a word. There was no shaking of hands or hugs, unlike two days before, or even two hours before on the steps of the church. James went to the back of the car and raised the hatch. Standing in the back with the hatch raised, James was blasted by the music.

Forgive, sounds good.
Forget, I'm not sure I could.
They say time heals everything,
But I'm still waiting

I'm through, with doubt,
There's nothing left for me to figure out,
I've paid a price, and I'll keep paying

I'm not ready to make nice,
I'm not ready to back down,
I'm still mad as hell
And I don't have time
To go round and round and round
It's too late to make it right
I probably wouldn't if I could
Cause I'm mad as hell
Can't bring myself to do what it is
You think I should

James picked up his bag from the back, and then slammed the hatch door. He walked along the passenger side of the vehicle, then around the front, but did not turn his head. Keith watched his brother as he passed in front of the car, raising the bag by throwing the strap over his shoulder. A moment later, James stepped into his house and was gone. Keith felt very cold and alone again. A sharp pain punched him in his midsection. The angry strains of Dixie Chick's "Not Ready to Make Nice" followed James into the house. He set his bag down on the table. Karen greeted him and asked about the trip, but James did not respond. He felt drained. He used the bathroom, then walked into the bedroom and collapsed onto the bed. Karen entered a few minutes later. She sat on the bed next to her husband, bent over, and kissed him on the cheek. On the tip of her nose, she felt the wetness of a tear from her husband's cheek.

Keith drove around for a while, trying to block out the weekend and his conversation with his brother. But instead, the trip triggered thoughts about his life, his marriage, his family life, and the loss of his daughter. His world seemed to be spinning out of control and he didn't know how to stop it. Unable to take any more sadness, Keith pushed another button on the radio. The news show was ending just before the top of the hour.

> *And finally, on a lighter note, Tom Cruise met with Brooke Shields and her husband to apologize for bringing her into the televised conversation he had with NBC's Matt Lauer. "He came over to my house and he gave me a heartfelt apology," Shields, 41, told Leno. "And he apologized for bringing me into the whole thing and for everything that happened. And through it all, I was so impressed with how heartfelt it was. And I didn't feel at any time that I had to defend myself, nor did I feel that he was trying to convince me of anything other than the fact that he was deeply sorry. And I accepted it."*

Keith stopped at a convenience store before returning to his sister's house. He bought a pint of milk to coat his stomach, and then filled the tank of the car so he would return it on full at the airport in the morning. That night, with few words spoken about the trip, he and his sister Diane watched "Desperate Housewives" over Chinese take-out. Early the next morning, after a piece of toast and some small talk with his sister, he said a quick good-bye and was off for the airport. Pulling off the sheets from the bed where her brother had slept for two nights, Diane noticed three small stains of blood, the sizes of a dime, a nickel, and a quarter on the pillowcase.

Chapter 20

ELEVEN MONTHS PASSED BEFORE time healed the wounds that angry words can sear into one's soul. The brothers didn't talk over this long period of time, but that was not unusual. Even before the trip to Chicago, months would go by with no contact between them. James thought about his brother and everything he was going through with his cancer, but he never found the courage to call him. During that time Keith read the book given to him by Angel called A Course In Miracles. And every morning, alone, he prayed. In his prayers, he cleared his mind and invited the Holy Spirit. He gave thanks for all the blessings in his life and for things he wished would come to him. Not material items or worldly adventures. He prayed for health, for peace, and he prayed for joy. He prayed for understanding. He prayed for acceptance and the ability to quit being offended. Keith chose not to have any radiation or chemotherapy. He began to mend fences with Jillian. She still spent most of her time away. James tried to practice The Four Givings as much as he could. He greeted others silently with 'How may I serve?' He surrendered to Christ often. Frequently, he witnessed the Holy Spirit in others. In those moments, he knew that the seeming stranger was actually his brother. He enjoyed moments through the day. He prayed for forgiveness. He tried to stop being offended all the time. James contributed money as often as he could, and, for the first time in his life, he donated his blood every few months.

The weather on Christmas Eve changed from mild fifty-degree temperatures in Toledo to blistering cold, with an eighty percent chance of snow. The forecast was calling for six to seven inches by Christmas morning. The last task of James' day was finding CDs for the nieces and nephews who still lived in town. The store was filled, wall to wall, with people. Over the crackling speakers The Little Drummer Boy did his annual rup-a-bum-bum thing, as James hummed along. After grabbing a few CDs, he headed over to the tool department. He wanted to find some air tools for Michael. Over the summer, his stepson had found a job at a mechanic's shop. James too had landed a job, another project-management contract, so money was flowing back in. This Christmas seemed special, what with the forecast of snow and the steady income. It was a good feeling. James finished his shopping, and then waited twenty minutes in one of the long checkout lines. He greeted the weary cashier with a "Merry Christmas" as he placed the tools and CDs on the counter. After the transaction, as James grabbed his bags, she barely whispered a "thank-you." Empathizing with her plight, he just smiled at her when she looked up. She broke a smile and said "Merry Christmas." Mission accomplished, James hurried toward the exit. The moonless night blackened the sky and snowflakes were beginning to swirl in the wind. He could hear the clanging of a bell. It was a man dressed up as Santa Claus collecting money for the Salvation Army. James didn't look over. He figured that he'd made enough contributions over the past month at every store he visited.

"Merry Christmas!" cried the Santa.

"Merry Christmas to you too," James answered warmly.

James opened his wallet. He had two twenty-dollar bills and three ones. He wondered what might be a proper amount to give. James grabbed all of the dollars and folded them small enough to fit into the little slot in the red pot. He stuffed the dollars into the slot until they disappeared.

"Thank you for your kindness," said Santa.

"Thanks for your service," James replied.

"May you and your family have a Merry Christmas," Santa added.

"Merry Christmas, Santa."

James jogged across the parking lot. There was a light dusting of snow on the ground and on his car. He unlocked the door with a button on his key, and then jumped in, throwing the shopping bags onto the passenger seat. The leather was hard and cold. He pressed two buttons to turn on the seat and steering-wheel heater, then turned the ignition key. The starter made a slow grinding noise. The engine didn't start. He tried the key again. This time there was no sign of life from the starter. The radio was on but he didn't think to turn it off to save juice. He tried again, to no avail. He noticed that the dashboard lights were shining dimly. The battery was about dead. Just to the left of the front of his car, a little golden finch landed, and then walked, bobbling along the cold steel rail. "Hate this car, I hate it!" James roared. How humiliating. At that moment, a bright light shined through the icy windshield. He moved his head a little to see around the ice. It was the headlights of a large truck, but he could only see the silhouette of the driver. He opened the door and got out. An old Chevy truck, spotted with primer, was parked right in front of him on the other side of the guardrail. The driver-side door of the truck opened and the dome light came on. It was Michael with his pet dog, Deacon.

Michael stood in the falling snow, smiling at his stepfather. Then he reached behind his bench seat and pulled out a pair of black and red jumper cables. James jumped up and down on the icy blacktop trying to generate some body heat.

"Jim, sit in my truck and get warm," advised Michael. "You're not dressed for standing out in this weather. It will just take me a moment."

James obediently opened the passenger side of the truck and jumped in. Michael's dog jumped up on James lap and licked his face in greeting. The truck was very warming compared to outside. Large snowflakes bombed the windshield reminding James of the Asteroids video game. He watched Michael raise the hood of his truck and connect the large alligator-teethed clamps to the battery terminals of the truck. Then he hooked up James's car. Michael returned to the truck, the door squeaking as he jumped into the driver's seat. He pressed his foot against the gas pedal, revving the engine a few times before letting the engine idle. All was silent in the truck except for the humming of the motor. Michael petted his dog. James stuck his hands in his pockets and looked down at the floor, feeling awkward about what he was going to say.

"Thanks for coming to my rescue."

"That's okay."

A long, uncomfortable pause of silence blanketed the truck cab. Finally, James found the courage to seek redemption.

"I realize that I haven't been much of a father to you," he began abruptly. "You know, you've done a lot on your own without my help. And I've been thinking lately about how it was for you when you were growing up…I was always on your ass. I never cut you any slack. I was always worried about what other people would think instead of caring what you thought!" He paused, his cheeks now blazing. "I just want to tell you that I'm sorry. I'm sorry, Michael. I'm sorry for the time I yelled at you when the Christmas tree fell over. I'm sorry for everything. Most of all, I am sorry for that day in the kitchen, on 9/11. I am sorry for hitting you and your mother."

"Yeah, I guess you were a jerk sometimes. But you did some cool things too."
"You know I love her, your mom."
"I know you do."
"And I love you too."
"I know."
"But do you forgive me?" He held his breath.
"Yeah, I forgive you."
"Do you want a hug?" James asked, awkward and overcome.
"Nah, I'm good."
"Good."
The car became silent again. Both were reluctant to discuss any specifics. Finally, Michael jumped out of the truck, high-stepped over the guardrail, and got into the car. With two pumps of the accelerator, and one turn of the ignition key, the car started like a champion. Michael returned to the truck and opened the driver's-side door.
"I think you'll be all right now. You probably just left your lights on. You might want to put the charger on the battery when you get home."
"Thanks for the help," James said, immediately sensing the understatement.
"You're welcome! I'll try to check on it Christmas morning. If you still have problems, I'll pull the battery."
"Thanks again for the help."
Deacon barked out loudly, then raised a paw and set it on his master's shoulder. James began to step back out into the cold air. He paused, still sitting with one foot on the snowy ground. Michael reached out to shake his stepfather's hand. As James extended his hand, Michael grabbed it and pulled him closer to quickly hug him. It was over in a flash. But the warm feeling rushed through James's body. He was forgiven,

truly forgiven! James continued out the door. He stepped over the rail, then hopped into his car.

James watched Michael pull out of the parking lot. He felt so proud. "That's my son!" he heard himself saying. James gleamed and beamed as he drove home. He felt like he could fly. He felt the weight of years of guilt and judgment lifted from his body. Inside and outside, his spirit sang with newly liberated joy. He whispered, "I and I." Turning up the stereo, he welcomed U2's wise commentary:

I believe in the kingdom come.
Then all the colors will bleed into one
Bleed into one
But yes, I'm still running.

You broke the bonds and you
Loosed the chains
Carried the cross
Of my shame
Of my shame.
You know I believe it.

But I still haven't found what I'm looking for...

Christmas Eve, in the afternoon, Keith tried to call his wife but she didn't answer. He left her a short message in her voice mail. She was visiting her parents in Phoenix for the holidays and was due back the day after Christmas. He turned on the TV as he finished dressing. He hadn't slept much the night before and now the sun was shining high above the California hills. He lounged around for most of the day, mainly working on his laptop. He didn't have any more presents to buy. Over the past few weeks he'd picked up a few little gifts for Jillian and he'd mailed some Christmas cards to family members and old friends; that was about the extent of his holiday preparations.

Tired of being cooped up in the house, he decided get out and enjoy the little bit of sunlight that was left. Walking in a park up in the foothills, he found himself thinking about his life and what was the right way to live it. He walked several miles into the setting sun; he received no life-changing answers. By the time he was back at his car the sun had dipped below the California Mountains. The sky was an orange glow. The temperature began to drop. Keith drove down the winding road. He could see multicolored Christmas lights sprinkled across the foothills from mountain estates. In the canyon, it was now dark. Keith's Mercedes headlights popped on, glaring against the brush and rock, as he made a wide turn. Just ahead, around the next bend, he could see flashing red taillights. A group of people were standing next to their car, with its trunk up. Keith steered his car to the left, over the yellow line, to avoid hitting them. His headlights lit up their frightened faces. It was a family of four, a mother, father, and two children. Keith noticed that the mother and one of the children, presumably her daughter, wore white hijabs, the linen headscarves that some Muslim women wear.

"Damn towel-heads," he muttered, continuing down the canyon road. "Get the hell out of the road!"

Keith accelerated, barely braking into the next curve. He came out of the turn, again pressing the pedal to the metal. The engine responded at once with increased speed. Racing down into the canyon, running from his fears, Keith threaded through its twists and turns like an Olympic skier. His headlights splashed crazily through the trees at each turn. Two red beams flashed at him in the distance. His instinct applied the brakes as the beams magically metamorphosed into the form of a white-tailed doe. The deer raised its head to the oncoming light but stood its ground on the yellow lines. Keith applied the brakes harder. The rear end of the car released to the right toward the edge of the road. Keith envisioned the canyon's edge as he slid toward the trees.

"Christ, help!"

The tires slid in the gravel, swinging the car around one hundred and eighty degrees. Frozen, Keith watched the trunk of a pine tree racing toward the driver's-side door. His fingers dug into the steering wheel. The car slammed into a sandbank, stopping instantly. Dirt exploded across the hood. Keith's head slammed against the window but the glass did not break. The engine stalled. Sand flew everywhere, clouding his vision. Keith panted, his chest heaving up and down as he realized that he was alive. Consciously trying to slow down his breathing, he began to get his bearings. The dust settled. His lights were shining off the edge of the road into space. Along the canyon road in the distance he could make out headlights, and two flashing red lights. It was the stranded travelers, just two turns back. The headlights from his car timed out after the engine stalled, and darkness fell upon him. He regarded the distant lights through the windshield. They reminded him of the lighthouses along the bay. He watched as another set of lights rounded the bend by the stranded car. The lights swerved away from the two stationary lights to pass around the obstacle. Another set of lights repeated the process, moving around the stranded travelers but never stopping. The two cars continued down the canyon, passing swiftly by Keith a few seconds later, just as disinterested in the second disabled vehicle as in the first. The deer passed in front of the car and stopped. It turned its head to the distant lights, then looked at Keith. The animal resumed its walk to a patch of grass by the pines. The stars shined in the black sky above the edge of the canyon. And the words came to him.

How may I serve?

Keith sat there, gazing across the canyon at the headlights of the broken-down car under the stars. He tried the ignition and the headlights went back on. Shifting into Drive, he began to pull out of the ruts by backing up and quickly moving forward a few times before the tires gripped the mud. Pulling back onto the road, Keith drove slowly back in the direction from which he'd come. He pulled onto the shoulder alongside the broken vehicle. There was barely enough room for two cars. A sign on a metal pole designated this "Point of Interest." Keith could see that the car was running with its lights on and the front tire was flat. The faces of the two children, standing off to the side, appeared frightened. The parents were back by the trunk and could not see Keith as he walked in their direction through the chilly night air. One of the children spoke up in a Middle Eastern language, alerting his parents to the intruder. The father poked his head around the car and looked up at the strange man coming toward him. The man appeared startled and scared. Keith sensed their fear. It was rather dark out but Keith could tell that the family was definitely Muslim. The man uttered words of halting English.

"Please... Do not hurt us."

"Hello!" said Keith, trying to sound harmless. "Do you need some help?"

The man stared into Keith's eyes as Keith raised a smile.

"Yes, help. No tire."

Keith didn't quite understand what he meant but continued walking to the rear of the car. As he drew closer, the man's wife lightly screamed, then dashed over to her children.

"Sorry to scare you," was all he could think of saying.

"Scared? Yes I am" said the Middle Eastern man.

"Please don't be scared. I am not going to hurt you."

The man shook his head up and down, expressing that he understood. He turned to his wife, who now was standing behind her children with her arms around them, and said something in their native tongue. She also shook her head in response.

"I cannot get the…"

The man paused, searching for a word but could not find it. To compensate, he pointed his hands into the open trunk, then raised his arm up and down quickly, acting as if he were jacking up a car.

"The jack, you can't get the jack out."

"Yes! Jack!"

The man pointed to a panel that was open on the right side of the trunk. Keith stepped closer to see the panel as the man stepped back, giving him some room. The jack was mounted on a bracket inside the panel. Keith tried with both hands to loosen the wing nut that held the jack, but it was screwed down tightly. He stared at the contraption, trying to figure out the logic of its design. It came to him. Keith pulled out the tire iron that had slid behind the jack. He then stuck the flat tip of the tire iron into the slot of the nut and was able to loosen it. After a few turns, he could move the nut with his fingers. The jack dropped off the mount easily once the wing nut was off the mounting screw. The man clapped his hands twice showing his approval. Keith held up the nut and showed the man how the tire iron fit into the slot of the nut for leverage. The man moved his head once again in agreement.

Keith walked back to the flat tire, which was on the front driver's side. This was the tire that was closest to the road. The man followed behind stopping at the driver's door to turn the car off. Keith got down on his knees, feeling for the official spot for the jack. Lights shined from a car coming around the bend. The Middle Eastern man stepped into the road, protecting Keith by waving his hands and motioning to the oncoming car to move over. The car obliged by slowing down and moving into the other lane as it passed by. Keith thought, Well, at least he'll get hit before I will. Immediately, though, his ego was overcome by another inspiration: How may I serve? Keith's fear subsided, and the feeling of danger never returned. He jacked up the car and removed the tire, all the while exaggerating his motions to instruct the man in how to change a tire. Keith started to lift the flat tire off the lugs to switch it with the good tire in the trunk. The stranger grabbed the flattened tire from his hands before Keith was up off his knees, returning quickly with the new tire. He bent down next to Keith, wearing a large smile. Keith watched the man lift and mount the new tire onto the lugs. The man then screwed on the five nuts by hand. As he started to tighten the nuts with the socket end of the tire iron, Keith pointed with his finger, in a star pattern, instructing the man to skip every other lug nut, so that the tire would be mounted evenly. The man shook his head once again in acknowledgement. Keith lowered the jack and showed the man how to reinsert it onto the bracket in the trunk.

"Thank you, sir. I thought no help would come. We just moved here from Morocco after living there for eighteen years. We were told by our friends that most Americans hate Muslims, especially Iranians... Please don't hate us."

"You are Muslim?"

"Yes, I am."

Keith looked at the man and thought about how he should respond to the man's fears. The man seemed timid. He didn't look like he could do harm to any living thing.

"Don't worry. I don't hate you. But you do have to be careful. Some Americans may be prejudiced against you."

"But please, they must understand that my father and I fled from Iran in the year nineteen seventy-eight, and if I returned to Iran, I would be killed. My father was a scientist, as am I, and owned a company in Iran during the Shah's regime. When the country was overtaken by Ayatollah Khomeini and

Muslim clerics, my father's company was taken over. So even though my father and I have nothing to do with the former regime, I would be killed as a traitor."

"Didn't this country, the United States, back the Shah of Iran?" Keith asked, dimly remembering the Shah's face on magazine covers and in newsreels.

"Yes, but he was a murderer. His secret police, SAVAK, tortured and killed innocent Iranians in a brutal campaign that was equal to that of Hitler's SS."

"So is that why Iranians hate us, or all Muslims for that matter?"

"I am Muslim but I don't hate Americans. Not all Muslims hate Americans. I only hate all of the hate. Believe me. I have always wanted to visit America. I also understand why so many Americans hate Muslims, because of what happened on that September day."

"Yes." He shook his head in agreement with the man, but more with himself.

"Yes. I lost my daughter there, so I guess, I am leery of Muslims, to say the least."

"You lost your daughter on 9/11?"

"Yes."

"And you still found it within your heart to help me? You must be a very enlightened and forgiving man." The man studied his rescuer's face in amazement.

"Not really. I actually passed you at first, but then I turned around."

"Well, all I can say is thank you. Thank you for finding mercy in your heart after such a loss."

"You are welcome," said Keith with total honesty.

"Your kindness is our blessing. Thanks be to Allah, in Muhammad's name, and peace and blessings be upon you. Do you know that Muhammad was the most merciful person in all of history? He was merciful to his family, followers, friends, and even enemies. He was merciful to the young and old, to humans and to animals. Those who persecuted him in Makkah and killed his relatives and his followers were later defeated in battle. When they were captive under the Prophet Muhammad, he forgave them. He did not ever take revenge or retaliate. He was the most forgiving person. The Qur'an, the most fundamental scripture of Islam, teaches sanctity of life, not violence.

"You don't say," said Keith in a condescending tone. This guy doesn't know when to shut up! He thought, his blind prejudice making a slight comeback.

Now very inspired, the man went on. "The Qur'an enjoins peace, justice, and compassion as basic tenets for all of humankind, and condemns violence and aggression in all forms. 'Say: O my Servants who have transgressed against their souls! Despair not of the Mercy of Allah: for Allah forgives all sins: for He is Oft-Forgiving, Most Merciful.' That's from Al-Zumar :53. Muhammad believed that forgiveness means to look beyond the error, and to look for understanding."

"That's nice. But why is it that Muslims hate Americans and terrorize our communities?"

"Please know, not all Muslims are extremists who hate Americans. The religion of Islam as described in the Qur'an was given to our Prophet from Allah. Allah, who is our One Creator and is just, omnipotent, and merciful, teaches Muslims to love and have mercy, to donate regularly to charity, and to reject racism. Sheikh Muhammad al-Ghazzali, the late Muslim thinker, said: 'You can find some people who describe themselves as belonging to religion, and they display all the physical manifestation of religion. However, they are sick at heart and defective in thought. You can be sure that these people are as far away from religion as the sickness of their hearts and the defectiveness of their minds.' Karma will be their retribution."

"I just wish I could learn to forgive."

The man motioned for his wife to come over. She reluctantly came forward, her arms spread across her children's shoulders. The father shuffled the children to face the stranger, then stood behind them, next to his wife.

"Sir, before we came here, we were all scared because we heard of the hatred. And we are still fighting that demon of fear. But for eight months, we knew we were moving, so we prayed. I prayed to Allah that you in the West would accept us. I prayed that Americans will learn to understand the hatred of Muslims. I prayed that I could learn to forgive the Western atrocities against our people. My brother was shot by a member of the SAVAK police, from a rifle and a bullet, both bearing a U.S. stamp. My cousin was killed in 1988 when a United States Cruiser ship shot down an Iranian airbus killing 290, mistaking the airline plane for a fighter jet. My daughter — who cannot speak English, so she does not understand — visited France and was stripped of her clothes, and tormented on a schoolyard. So I prayed that you would be accepting, and understanding of my family. The only answer we received from Allah, was 'Accept, and they shall accept; understand, and they shall understand; forgive, and they shall forgive.' And finally, my heart echoed the words, 'It starts with me.'"

The man hugged his family a little closer. He patted his daughter's cheek softy. Keith noticed a tear falling from the man's face.

"So as a family, we prayed that you would learn to understand us, and forgive our people for atrocities against you. It starts with us. I cannot expect you to accept and understand us. I cannot expect you to forgive the pain and loss that you have felt because of fools from our land. I only can say to you, as my brother in spirit, I am truly sorry for your daughter. I am sorry on behalf of all Muslims for your pain. I pray that I might understand someday. I pray that I will accept everyone

I meet as my brother. I pray that someday you can see me as a friend and not an enemy. I pray that you can find forgiveness in your heart."

The man reached out his hand in friendship.

"My name is Tazim; it means honor."

"Keith. My name is Keith."

Keith extended his hand and shook Tazim's hand. Tazim placed his other hand on top of Keith's wrist as their arms shook. Once they released hands, Tazim raised his arm to his wife and pointed to her.

"Keith, this is my wife, Farah. Her name means happiness."

Farah smiled and slightly bowed her head but did not say any words. Keith replied by bowing his head. The two children smiled. Tazim opened his palm to the sky, then pointed to his son.

"My wife's English, not so good. This is my son, Hasan; it means beautiful or good."

Hasan waved his hand and smiled. Keith raised his hand to gesture his hello.

"Hello," said the little boy.

Tazim repeated the gesture, first raising his arm with open palm to the sky and then pointing to his daughter.

"This is my daughter, Mahasin; her name means virtues."

Mahasin smiled and waved. Keith waved by moving his fingers up and down.

"Thank you for helping us," she said. "You are our angel."

"You are welcome. You have a very nice family, Tazim."

"We just moved to Pleasanton. I'm starting work as a scientist at Lawrence Livermore National Laboratories. I hope that we may see you again sometime so we can see your nice face."

"I hope so too. You must be very smart if you're working for the Department of Energy." Keith hoped he wasn't being too frank.

"Thank you. I enjoy my work. Well, I am rambling on and probably keeping you from your dinner. May I say, thank you again, and Merry Christmas."

"Merry Christmas. Or should I say, Merry Ramadan?"

"Ramadan is over," Tazim politely corrected, "but thank you."

"Oh, I am sorry. Is it Merry Aid then?"

"Do you mean Eid? When we gather on that day, we pray for forgiveness and strength of faith. And Allah has promised those who approach Him with sincerity that He will welcome them with forgiveness. In the purity of his prayers, any true Muslim would be ashamed to hold any ill will toward his brothers. The idea is to pray not only for Allah's forgiveness, but that you yourself may forgive all those who have wronged you. And when you forgive others, the blessing of forgiveness is mercifully granted by Allah, and widely exchanged between the Muslims. So that's our Day of Forgiveness. Oh, I'm sorry! I'm rambling again. But I did whole-heartedly mean what I said about your loss. On behalf of the Muslim community, let me say that I am deeply sorry. We will pray for you, Keith."

"And I will pray for you and your family, Tazim."

Keith and Tazim shook hands one more time. The rest of the family waved as they walked to the other side of the car to get out of the cold air. Tazim opened his door, then hesitated before getting in.

"Keith, thank you! There is a saying my grandmother would tell me when I was mad. She would say, 'Fill your soul with love for everyone. See the unfolding of God in everyone you meet, including those whom you have learned to hate, and then you will be healed.' She believed that healing was through forgiveness. I hope that we both can find forgiveness in our hearts."

"I hope that we can too."

With a tint of golden glow in the horizon, another set of headlights coming around the bend, blinded the two men standing along the gravel shoulder. As the car slowed, the driver put on his hazard lights. The blinking yellow lights of his Toyota illuminated the jagged rock wall of the mountain on the inside brim of the road. The passenger-side window descended as a bearded man turned on the dome light over the rearview mirror. A younger, black-haired man was in the driver's seat. The bearded passenger was middle aged, wearing a black suit, a white shirt buttoned at the neck, and a broad-brimmed black hat. His beard had two braids on each jaw. He appeared to be an Orthodox Jewish man of the cloth.

"Good evening, brothers. May I offer my assistance?"

"No need, Father, I mean, sorry, uh, rabbi," Keith stuttered gauchely. "I think we have it under control."

"Yes, this nice American man has helped me to change my tire."

"Glory is to Hashem! It is a blessing when a stranger extends his charity and service." intoned the rabbi in a deep voice.

"Indeed!" agreed Tazim. "I am truly blessed, my brother."

Tazim opened his car door and started the ignition to warm his family, patiently waiting inside. The rabbi caught sight of the man's wife and daughter wearing the customary hijabs, and both he and his companion waved. The family waved back as Tazim closed the car door. Keith looked at the two men. It struck him that their respective religions and cultures had been at odds for thousands of years, and yet here they were, regarding each other with a vision that went way beyond their physical senses. Keith let out a chuckle.

"Keith, you are smiling!" Tazim observed while standing in the doorway of his car. "I can see your teeth shining from the dome light." He closed his car door.

"Oh, I am sorry. It's nothing," Keith said shyly.

"Hey! No need to be sorry for a smile, my friend," exclaimed the rabbi. "What is your merry thought that brings humor on such cold a night?"

"Well, I was just thinking that our meeting here tonight is strange — strange in a good way, I mean. Your governments and cultures have been fighting for years, yet you both seem to look past all the conflict."

At this time, a deer came down to cross the road. The animal stopped in the middle of the pavement to sniff the yellow line then looked up at the yellow flashers and the two bright headlights shining towards him. The deer looked at the two men standing between the cars, and then looked at the two figures in the vehicle with the bright lights. A calming sense filled the moment. The deer continued on to his unknown destination by trotting across the remaining pavement and disappearing in the brush. It may have been the angelic presence of the animal or the presence of a Jewish holy man, but something changed. The two men, Muslim and Jew, felt oneness.

"It seems that all my life, I have been learning how to hate," Tazim said quietly. "But I do not wish to hate any longer. A friend of mine in my country, who was a Jewish student at the university, taught me many things about Judaism. My friend's skin is like mine. His fears are equal to mine. His desires for his family beat in a heart just like mine. The hatred that we have been taught from the political podium is simply the fear and manipulation of our leaders."

"I too was taught to fear my brother of the same skin, taught this from our temples of worship!" confessed the rabbi. "But being a man of faith, over the years I've studied all of the world's major religions, and our two religions have more similarities in their teachings than there are differences. We share passages from many of the same scriptures. It's just our warped interpretations that brought on all the intolerance and hatred. It finally occurred to me that to put an end to this misery, it all starts with me! I must extend my hand in friendship."

"I too must extend my hand in love," said Tazim, reaching out. "We are all brothers; we are all Sons of Allah!"

"Yes, we are all Sons of Hashem!" rejoiced the rabbi.

"I guess we're all one, one in God. If only everyone else had the same awareness. If only the armies of Palestine and the armies of Israel were aware of this one simple reality!" Keith was surprised at his eloquence.

"If you look closely," the rabbi put in, "it's obvious that, while they follow two different ideologies, they are both the same army."

"I don't follow you," Keith said, puzzled.

"I know what this holy man is saying," Tazim began to explain. "All armies in the world are the same. They are all the armies of Babylon, the armies of the powerless."

"What armies of the powerless?" Suddenly their words weren't making any sense to Keith.

"Well, no one believes that God would leave his sons and daughters powerless, right?" asked the rabbi.

Keith couldn't imagine where this was leading.

"I think this must be our only hope," said the rabbi. "If we choose to see all of God's children as our brothers and sisters, then I believe the means to see that light will be given to us. And I believe that what you said, sir is true. This healing of nations does start with just one man seeing no religion, no nation, and no color, only seeing the power of God."

"So maybe the question is," Keith jumped in, still inspired: "Are we willing to exchange the world of sin that we dreamed up, for what Our Heavenly Father sees?"

"Say! That's what just happened now between you and me, Keith!" Tazim said excitedly. "When you pulled up and offered to help, at first I was very scared for my family. I saw you as my enemy. But when you looked beyond your old world and gave yourself in service to me, then my fear diminished, and look what happened – a whole new reality!"

"Hang on. What is this reality you're talking about?" Keith asked.

"The truth is that we are all descendents of the same family. Like the biblical twin brothers Jacob and Esau, Israel and Palestine — the truth that we are all brothers."

"You mean to say that Israelis and Palestinians are descended from the same family?" Keith had never heard or read anything about this.

"Yes, from the parents Isaac and Rebekah," the rabbi happily informed him. Their twin sons were named Jacob and Esau

"This makes us all brothers." Tazim offered.

"We are all related?" Keith asked, knowing the answer.

"Yes, brother" Tazim and the Rabbi spoke at the very same time.

"Wow!" exclaimed Keith. "Too bad my brother isn't here!"

"But we are!" The rabbi shot back.

The men laughed with their newfound brothers. Tazim and the rabbi shook hands through the car window. Keith stepped back in awe, taking in the spectacle. No need for forgiveness, because there was no thought of the past. There was only the present, this moment of unconditional brotherly love.

"Assalam alaikum!" cried Tazim.

"Shalom aleichem!" responded the rabbi and his driver as they both raised their hand to gesture.

"Wa alaikum assalam!" Tazim replied.

The two men in the car replied in their native tongue, "Aleichem shalom."

"Peace be with you?" questioned Keith.

They looked at Keith and raised their hands in a gesture of friendship — an open palm.

"Peace be with you," repeated the men.

"And also with you," prayed Keith.

Chapter 21

TAZIM SMILED AT THE young driver sitting next to the rabbi as the Toyota pulled away, the rabbi waving his good-byes. Tazim shook Keith's hand one more time without a word spoken. Then he opened his car door and climbed in with his family. They all turned and waved back at their rescuer as they drove away. Keith stood there for a moment in the crisp air, taking in the night sky full of stars. The moment of bliss was replaced with time. Keith got into his car and headed for downtown Pleasanton, a quaint California town with a lot of specialty shops and restaurants, all lit up for the holidays. The streets were busy, and it took some time to find a parking space on the main street by his favorite Italian restaurant. Dodging last-minute shoppers with their arsenal of shopping bags, he squeezed through the door, and then worked his way past the waiting people to the hostess. Keith could not believe the crowd considering it was Christmas Eve. He thought most people would be heading home to their families. The waiting time for a table was thirty to forty minutes, but the hostess pointed to an empty stool at the bar. There was no wait and he could eat dinner while sitting at the bar. It was private and hidden in the corner by the television, a perfect sanctuary for someone all alone on Christmas Eve.

Keith ordered his meal to go, veal parmesan with a side of spaghetti, along with a diet coke to drink while he waited. The

The Four Givings

bartender, looking perplexed, took the order and returned a moment later with the soda. Keith was a frequent customer and usually he would order three or four bourbon and cokes while he waited. Keith glanced around the dining room and watched the families. Some looked very happy and were having fun. Others seemed sad or frustrated. How can anybody be sad when they're with their family on Christmas Eve? They don't realize how blessed they are! He thought.

On the overhead TV, the news was airing the story of a homeless man delivering Christmas toys to children in a Chicago orphanage. An anchorwoman interviewed the man delivering toys. Keith leaned closer to try to listen over the waves of voices in the room. The homeless man's eyes were crystal-blue – a perfect match for the Notre Dame sweatshirt that he wore. When the food arrived, Keith tipped the bartender substantially, saying "Merry Christmas.".

To Keith's relief the traffic of cars and frantic shoppers seemed to have died down. All the way home, his food kept steaming up the passenger window. He could smell the tomato sauce. The house was dark. Keith grabbed the two white bags as he got out, and then opened the garage door that entered into the kitchen and fumbled for the light switch. He took off his jacket and threw the keys on the counter, then grabbed silverware out of a drawer and a plate from the cupboard.

Over the past few months, his living room had become his dining area. He justified it by thinking that it was only him most of the time, and that he's not messing up a place setting at the table. Besides, the TV kept him company as he ate alone. The room was lavishly decorated. Keith gingerly set his plate on the couch, found the remote control between the cushions, and turned on the television. Scanning the menu for something of interest, he settled on the color-enhanced version of It's a Wonderful Life. Carl Switzer, the childhood star who played Alfalfa in "The Little Rascals," was turning the key that opened up the gym floor as Donna Reed and Jimmy Stewart danced on the edge. Keith finished his dinner, and then laid the plate on the coffee table in front of him. A dangling strand of spaghetti from his plate bridged onto the glass tabletop. Keith picked up the strand between his thumb and forefinger, wiped the splat of sauce off the table with his palm, and ate the piece of pasta. He removed his shoes and stretched out on the couch, stuffing the pillow under his head.

Jimmy Stewart's George Bailey was wearing an old football uniform as he walked Mary, played by Donna Reed, back to her home. "I'll give you the moon," he tells her as they stroll beside a white picket fence. For some reason, Mary was wearing a bathrobe, and George stepped on the bathrobe wrap, disrobing her. At this point, despite the possibilities for George, Keith drifted off into a deep sleep, dreaming...

"... To my big brother, George, the richest man in Bedford Falls!" All the donors burst into "Auld Lang Syne." Someone brushed the Christmas tree and a little bell on one of the branches began to jingle. George Bailey's youngest daughter, who was being held in his arms, pointed to the tree: "Look, Daddy! Teacher says that every time a bell rings, an angel gets his wings." George grinned broadly, and said, "That's right, that's right." Then he looked upward and, giving a wink said, "Atta boy, Clarence!"

Keith woke up just as the bank examiner was joining in the singing. A sense of fear came over him. He tried to remember what he'd been dreaming. It felt like he has been sleeping for a year. It was hard to differentiate what was a dream and what was reality. He eased his head back down onto the pillow and stayed there most of the night, waking only briefly to the sounds of movie classics. He would open his eyes for a minute or two, watching the old movie stars in black and white. With all of his strength, Keith crawled into his bedroom. He was able to collapse his body onto the bed. He labored for air, drawing each breath around his teeth, collapsing his cheeks. He felt he could not take another breath. Laboring to breathe, like a child gasping after a good cry, Keith cleared his mind and opened his eyes. Keith pictured Tazim and his family. He saw the man not as a terrorist, not as a Muslim, but as himself. He saw a man who was scared, a man trying to provide for and protect his family. He felt for a moment a small sense of release. Keith prayed openly.

"Lord, help me to understand. Through You, I choose to hate no more. I choose to hate no more. I pray that Linda… I pray that she understands. I forgive the men who killed my daughter. I forgive them and I pray, Lord, that the hatred in their hearts will soon be extinguished. I pray that they forgive us for all the suffering that we have knowingly and unknowingly inflicted on their families. I pray that they can find forgiveness before their hate kills them. Christ, I surrender to you. I surrender. Teach me Lord not to hate. Teach me true forgiveness. I surrender. Amen."

Tears streamed down his cheeks as he looked up and gazed out the bedroom window into the early morning darkness. In that moment he had no judgment or fear. He felt total peace. It was that same feeling that overcame him inside the basilica at Notre Dame. The Holy Spirit in his mind saw only beauty, and rejoiced. The cross he'd carried dropped from his shoulders. Christ had risen within. The shackles fell from his hands, and the blinders disappeared from his eyes. It was the first time in years that he'd felt free. The forgiveness was real and complete, and it healed him. The Father, the Son, and the Holy Spirit communed in peace. Outside, a golden finch fluttered his wings, hovering in front of the window. "You are my beloved Son in whom I am well pleased." Keith's burden lifted from his shoulders.

James woke up Christmas morning, just after 9am, with the smell of coffee in the air. Karen was already up preparing breakfast. James raised his head to look out the window. It was snowing large flakes outside. His hands extended into the air and his legs, down to his toes, stretched under the covers. Then he relaxed his whole body as his head collapsed against the pillow. "There is nothing like Christmas morning." He thought out loud. James continued to lie in bed for a few minutes debating if he should get up. He looked around the room as daylight shined against the walls. He thought how much life has changed for him over the last year. He thought about his new job and how Michael and he can start to build a relationship. He punched the pillow and rolled over onto his side. He took a deep breath and exhaled with a sigh. James heard a sound of foot steps entering the bedroom. He rolled to look up. There was Karen walking towards his side of the bed wearing a blue silk robe that was partially open revealing yellow flannel pajama bottoms and a red tank top. He saw that she was carrying something in both of her hands. In her right hand, were the unwrapped Tiffany's box and the blue wrapping paper. The other hand was extended with her palm open, displaying the bracelet with the gold heart clasp in her hand.

"I found this laying under the Christmas tree and thought it was an ornament that the cat knocked off. I saw the pretty blue paper so I opened it. Sorry."

Karen shrugged her shoulders and crinkled her nose, hoping for approval. She sat on the bed next to him.

"I am glad you opened it. It is a nice way to start our day." James grabbed her hand to admire the piece. He forgot that he bought it last winter but found it in his drawer the month before. He stuck it in the tree a few days prior. He thought about telling her that he bought the bracelet months before in Chicago but decided not to take away from the moment.

Karen lifted both of their hands and gently kissed her husband's hand.

"Are you ready for coffee, babe?"

"I would love some" James stretched his arms out into the air.

Karen secured the silver bracelet around her wrist by clasping the gold heart. She stood up and kissed James one more time on the cheek before exiting. James watched his wife waltz across the room to the door.

"I am truly blessed. Thank you, God for Karen and Michael. Thank you for all of the great things in my life. I am truly blessed, not because of money, but because you have given me a good life and have shown me the way. I know God that miracles may not come in monetary value. Sometimes the miracle is more like a feeling. Maybe that is all we need. I am grateful for my life. Thank You for teaching me The Four Givings. Thanks for the miracles in my life. I hope someday you will reveal to me what the greatest miracle is. In Christ's name I pray. Amen."

James felt an overwhelming sensation of happiness. He felt his connection to God. He knew his life was good. James looked down at the crinkled, baby blue paper lying on the bed that Karen left behind. The radio was playing in the living room. The one hit wonder from the band "Men without Hats" came on.

We can go when we want to
The night is young and so am I
And we can dress real neat from our hats to our feet
And surprise 'em with the victory cry
Say, we can act if want to
If we don't nobody will
And you can act real rude and totally removed
And I can act like an imbecile

I say, we can dance, we can dance
Everything out of control
We can dance, we can dance
We're doing it from wall to wall
We can dance, we can dance
Everybody look at your hands
We can dance, we can dance
Everybody takin' the cha-a-a-ance

 James remembered when he told his brother Keith that Safety Dance is the greatest 80's dance tune. He remembered that day when he stuffed the wrapped gift in his coat pocket. He thought about his brother, Keith, and how hard it must be, coping with everything. James thought about that weekend in Chicago and the four keys that he learned. He realized that his pride has come between him and his brother. James picked up the telephone and pressed the speed dial button next to the name 'Keith'. As he held the telephone to his ear Karen returned, standing in the doorway, looking down at her bracelet. Her other hand was holding the bracelet clasped around her wrist.

 "Did you know that there is an inscription on the bracelet?" Karen queried.

 "No, what does it say?" James watched her fidget the new piece of jewelry.

 "It says, 'God's greatest miracle is YOU'."

 The bedroom was dark when he opened his eyes. All blinds were closed so that not even the glow of the moon could shine in. A ringing alarm had interrupted his sleep. Keith Kerrigan slammed his hand against the clock radio but the ringing continued as he lay there. The fog cleared and he realized it was the phone. He glanced at the clock — 6:29

a.m. Who would be calling this early? Maybe it was his wife, he thought. She was out of town, staying with her parents in Phoenix, Arizona, for an extended holiday. Desperate to stop the annoying sound, he groped for the handset. On the third attempt he found the cradle but the handset was missing. He shot up in bed as the ringing continued. The next ring identified the living room as its probable location. Darting out of the bedroom, he tripped over a basketful of clean clothes in the hallway. His body fell hard onto the carpet as the answering machine picked up from the base station on the nightstand. He ran to the coffee table. The handset was sitting on the newspaper. He quickly picked it up and hit the "Talk" button.

"Hello?"

The clock radio's alarm was triggered by the next digit of time. It was set to play music. Peter Gabriel.

Climbing up on Solsbury Hill
I could see the city light
Wind was blowing, time stood still
Eagle flew out of the night
He was something to observe
Came in close, I heard a voice
Standing stretching every nerve
Had to listen had no choice
I did not believe the information
just had to trust imagination
My heart going boom boom boom
"Son," he said "Grab your things,
I've come to take you home...

Bibliography

A Course In Miracles by The Foundation for Inner Peace, ISBN-10: 096063889X, ISBN-13: 978-0960638895

The Game of Life and How to Play It by Florence Scovel Shinn, Publisher: Hay House; ISBN-10: 1401907962, ISBN-13: 978-1401907969

Ask and Given: Learning to Manifest Your Desires (The Teachings of Abraham) by Esther and Jerry Hicks, Publisher: Hay House; ISBN-10: 1401904599, ISBN-13: 978-1401904593

The Power of Intention by Dr. Wayne Dyer, Publisher: Hay House; ISBN-10: 1401902162, ISBN-13: 978-1401902162

There's a Spiritual Solution to Every Problem by Dr. Wayne Dyer, Publisher: HarperCollins; ISBN-10: 0060192305, ISBN-13: 978-0060192303

You'll See It When You Believe It: The Way to Your Personal Transformation by Dr. Wayne Dyer, Publisher: Harper Paperbacks; ISBN-10: 0060937335, ISBN-13: 978-0060937331

The Science of Getting Rich by Wallace D. Wattles, Publisher: Tarcher; ISBN-10: 1585426016, ISBN-13: 978-1585426010

The Greatest Miracle in the World by Og Mandino, Publisher: Bantam; ISBN-10: 0553279726, ISBN-13: 978-0553279726